OF ECHOES BORN

What Reviewers Say About 'Nathan Burgoine

Advance Praise for *Of Echoes Born*

"The best short story collections are treasure chests that sparkle—not from the gems they contain, but with a light greater than the whole as the reader is left knowing more about life. In such work the mysteries aren't solved, but the questions get redefined. And so the tales in *Of Echoes Born* shimmer like gold, and not the kind you'll covet. This is one of those books that, when finished, you hurry to buy copies for friends."—Tom Cardamone, Lambda Literaray Award–winning author of *Green Thumb*, *Night Sweats: Tales of Homosexual Wonder and Woe*, and *The Lurid Sea*.

Light

"What's stunning about this debut is its assurance. In terms of character, plot, voice, and narrative skill, Burgoine knocks it out of the park as if this were his tenth book instead of his first. He, along with Tom Cardamone, has the considerable gift of being able to ground the extraordinary in the ordinary so that it becomes just an extension of everyday life."—*Out in Print*

"Burgoine's initial novel is a marvelously intricate story, stretching the boundaries of science and paranormal phenomena, with a cast of delightfully diverse characters, all fully nuanced and relatable to the reader. I honestly could not put the book down, and recommend it highly, as I look forward to his next novel."—Bob Lind, *Echo Magazine*

"*Light* manages to balance a playful sense of humor, hot sex scenes, and provocative thinking about the meanings of individuality, acceptance, pride, and love. Burgoine takes some known gay archetypes—the gay-pride junkie, the leather SM top—and unpacks them in knowing and nuanced ways that move beyond stereotypes or predictability. With such a dazzling novelistic debut, Burgoine's future looks bright."—*Chelsea Station Magazine*

"*Light* by 'Nathan Burgoine is part mystery, part romance, and part superhero novel. Which is not to say that *Light* emulates such 'edgy' angst-filled comic book heroes as the X-Men; if you'll pardon the pun, it is much lighter in tone."—*Lambda Literary*

Triad Blood

"'Nathan Burgoine is a talented writer who creates a fascinating world and complex characters...If you're a fan of demons, vampires, wizards, paranormal fiction, mysteries, thrillers, stories set in Canada, or a combination of the previously mentioned, do yourself a favor and check this book out!"—*The Novel Approach*

"*Triad Blood* was a fun book. If you're a fan of gay characters, urban fantasies, and (even better) both of them, you'll enjoy *Triad Blood.*"—*Pop Culture Beast*

Triad Soul

"'Nathan Burgoine's *Triad Blood*, the first book in this series, was one of my favourite books of last year and *Triad Soul* is, if anything, even better...what sets it apart, and makes me genuinely love this book (and series) is the depiction, both in fact and in allegory, of queer community. The prose is generally crisp and cleanly written, but there are also flourishes of creativity that elevate the writing above the prosaic. It has heart, imagination, and skill. Like *Triad Blood* before it, I suspect this is going to be one of my favourite books of its year."—*Binge on Books*

"'Nathan Burgoine really excels at creating a fascinating and unique supernatural world full of interesting politics. If you are a paranormal or a suspense fan, I think there is a lot here that will appeal to you, particularly if you are looking for a unique take on the various supernatural beings. Burgoine has really created something engaging here and I definitely recommend the series."—*Joyfully Jay*

By the Author

Light

Triad Blood

Triad Soul

Of Echoes Born

Visit us at www.boldstrokesbooks.com

OF ECHOES BORN

by

’Nathan Burgoine

2018

Acknowledgments

We don't inherit our stories.

That's an oversimplification, and especially in our current world, I know quite a few queer parents, but the reality is most of us queerlings aren't born to queer parents and queer grandparents and queer great-grandparents. I was not raised on stories of those like me—at least, not those who were queer like me. None of those stories came up across the dinner table or on the school bus.

In fact? The first version of a character like me I read was a short story taught in English class in high school. The character died and died cruelly and violently. And the whole class listened to the teacher explain why he had died (and died that way): he was gay.

That story was my first fictional me. It was terrifying.

The notion of a chosen family—a queer family—is not a new one. We find each other. When that works well, and we get past our own baggage, it can be a magical, lifesaving thing.

That's not hyperbole.

When I first came out, I was saved by drag queens and bears. Both communities took me by the hand and gave me a place—not just a place to be myself, but a literal place to sleep at one point—and they gave me their stories. I was so very lucky, I came out young enough to be blessed to speak with many people who are now gone.

No, not gone. Taken. Erased. Their families rewrote obituaries, rewrote the queerness from so many of their lives. Untold their stories. Took their words back and swallowed the sound of their voice.

Decades later, when I became a writer, I met another chosen family: queer writers. My first visit to the Saints and Sinners Literary Festival in New Orleans was a second dose of that same chosen family magic.

So many new voices. So many new stories. So much noise.

The title of this collection is *Of Echoes Born*, which is how I've always felt we queerlings come into the world. We have to work to find others who sound like us, to hear things that are for us and about us. We don't even know what we don't know, we don't know what stories were hidden, what voices were silenced. It's not taught.

It's not inherited.

These stories? I hope they add to the noise. I hope they echo loud enough that some queerling somewhere who hasn't yet seen themselves in fiction has even a slightest bit more chance of seeing a character live, and breathe, and be joyfully, unbeatably queer, even in the face of loss or pain or however many people who say they should not be.

And for that, I thank all my queer author family, and my queer editor family, and my queer publisher family. Jerry L. Wheeler, most especially, needs to be thanked for his wisdom and willingness to make this noise the best damn noise I think I've made yet.

I also need to thank Bold Strokes Books for bringing me into the family.

And, of course, above and beyond everyone else is my husband, who hears all my noise every single day but still lets me kiss his eyelids at night.

For all the editors of short fiction anthologies who gave me a shot
and polished my words to a shine, especially Becky and Tim,
who were first to get me started on this wild ride.

Contents

Love isn't red. That's probably the first thing to know.

Despite what the greeting card companies would have you believe, red has nothing to do with love. Love isn't pink, either. Or fuchsia, or violet, or lavender, or any other shade from the Valentine's Day rainbow.

Love is also more than just a color, which I hope isn't a surprise.

Start with the pale blue of a robin's egg. Add the texture of feathers of a newborn chick and the motion of a hunting bird in flight. Once you've got that soft, gentle blue soaring in wide circles, imagine all of it glowing from deep inside the chest and shining behind the eyes. Picture it reaching out from one person to another, being met with the same light.

Got it? That's love.

I have seen love in the elderly and the young. I have seen it in the weak and the brave. I have seen it in the last moments of a dying woman and within just hours of a baby's birth. I've even seen it in the eyes of a dog.

If it ever gets hard, look for the blue.

There & Then

The world shattered. People, the classrooms, even his own hands—no matter where Christian looked, he seemed to be staring through layer after layer of broken glass windows in a place without gravity. Triangles of the view shifted and rotated, coming in and out of focus, and the world didn't line up right behind them. It distorted everything along sharp lines, sometimes twisting, sometimes rotating, but always broken.

Maybe he was dying. Maybe he was going mental.

Either way, he was totally blowing off third period English.

He hadn't ever skipped a class before, but he hadn't lived under a rock. He knew where to go. Now, under the Art wing stairwell like a far more practiced malcontent, he tried to figure out what to do next.

Tucked up tight, out of view of any stray teachers, he sat and rested his forehead against his knees, trying to get past the pain and the way everything kept shattering when he opened his eyes long enough to think.

He'd had headaches before. Lots of them. They ran in the family, his mother had told him the first time he'd had weird blurry spots across his vision. She'd told him to lie down and take some painkillers before the headache hit. His mother's migraines would knock her off her feet at least once a month, so he'd taken her advice.

When he'd gotten his first headache at thirteen, it had made him weep with pain. That was right after he'd been skipped a grade and dropped into high school. They hadn't stopped since.

But three years later, this headache had come. It was worse than anything that had happened before and was so sudden and fierce, he nearly screamed out loud when it hit in the middle of biology class. Instead of blurry spots, he saw weird trails of color and light so bright he thought he was going blind.

Then everything had started shattering, and that was it. He'd had enough. He put his hand up, asked to go to the bathroom, and had been here ever since.

Dying or crazy? Dying or crazy? The two options danced along with the beat of his pulse.

"Breathe," he said. Sometimes when the headaches were really bad, he'd start yawning, which always made it worse. He took deep, even breaths, waiting for the extra-strength painkillers to kick in. He always carried them.

The pain receded a bit. He didn't know if it was from the cool quiet where he was sitting, or the pills, but he'd take it. He lifted his head and opened his eyes.

He could see the wide green field outside the school through the floor-to-ceiling windows running along the stairwell's east wall. Strange trails of light still swam around the edges of his vision, but it wasn't quite as bad as before, and at least nothing was cracking.

But then his view of the field shattered, pieces breaking off and spinning away, and behind them…the field…only…there was snow? He thought he saw some people walking around, too, covered from head to toe, complete with toques.

He rubbed his eyes with the palms of his hands.

"Stop it," he said. "Stop it."

When he opened his eyes again, the glimpse of snow was gone and the field was green again. There were no people. Colors still twisted in the corners of his vision, but at least he could see what was in front of him. That was better than nothing. And the pain was letting up. Finally.

Christian exhaled, relieved.

A cloud of bruised blacks and browns bled from above. He glanced up and waved a hand, thinking it was smoke until they seeped through the stairs, not reacting to his touch.

A moment later he heard footsteps on the stairs above, and Dawn Solati slid in beside him a few seconds later.

"I didn't think you skipped classes," she said.

The awful twists of black and brown, as well as dark purples, were coming from her. They sort of *pulsed* out of her.

Christian rubbed his eyes. "Headache."

"Figured there was a reason," she said. "Scoot over."

He moved. He was a little surprised himself. Dawn was solid B-crowd. Track athlete, decent grades, a bit standoffish, sure, but otherwise she blended in with the crowd. She had a lean, lanky grace that made Christian think of horses, and though boys teased her about being skinny, she tossed back insults with a sharp tongue and a wicked, aloof smile.

Those horrible colors didn't suit her, he thought. He couldn't help but look again.

The bloom of black and purple was a thundercloud around her. He could imagine the sound of thunder. But he still saw her despite the dark, roiling mass. He felt like he had two sets of eyes or two different lines of sight, both of them looking at the same person but seeing something different.

He saw other colors inside the bruised cloud, but it was almost impossible to see past the dark layers. The more he tried to focus on the cloud of dark colors, the more the pressure in his head seemed to pull back. He stared at her, trying to understand what was happening.

Dying or crazy? Dying or crazy?

Or…?

"Something on my face?" Dawn said.

"Sorry," Christian said. He'd been staring at her for far too long, but just before he looked away, he finally slipped past the roiling storm clouds surrounding her. Inside, he saw a tiny spark of something that burned with a golden light.

"Seriously, what are you looking at?" Dawn snapped.

"Are you pregnant?" Christian said.

Dawn gaped.

Christian's mother never touched him. He had only consciously realized it at his thirteenth birthday party, a week after his sister's sixteenth and two days after his first migraine, when he had quite suddenly and clearly remembered his mother hugging his sister and congratulating her on blowing out all the candles when he had only received a distant smile for the same feat. He was so hyperaware of it after the party, he had started keeping himself out of her reach.

It resulted in the same lack of touch, but he could pretend it was up to him.

Since he had started seeing colors, he couldn't ignore how she was different around him.

Like now.

"Are you coming home right after school?"

The words were said with all the right tones: interest, concern, even something that passed for love. But the soft lemon-yellow that had been swirling around her while she was putting the Dutch oven in the stove had blown away on an invisible wind the moment she'd noticed he'd come into the kitchen.

She was making bread. Something for the church. She and his father were presenting something or working on some project or fundraiser. She'd been humming to herself as she baked.

When she'd seen him, though, the humming stopped. When she asked the question, she'd walked to the counter, picked up a towel, and started wiping her hands as though they were dirty. The yellow cloud had blown away, replaced by a dull, oily sort of green. A stain, or a patch of mold, it grew between them.

That's what he always saw. A kind of rotten green that spread away from her, always between them.

Christian looked away. "I might stick around and wait for Bao. He's got track tonight."

"We'll be out at the church," she said. "Your lunch is in the fridge, and there are leftovers for dinner."

"Thank you," Christian said, but she'd already hung up the towel and was on her way out of the kitchen.

He inhaled a deep breath of baking bread, and by the time he exhaled, the green stain was gone from the room.

❖

Dawn didn't speak to him again for three days. Christian ate lunch with Bao and his track buddies most days, at a table tucked into the corner of the cafeteria. Since that day under the stairs, the colors hadn't stopped. The headaches weren't as bad, though. Sometimes he could almost ignore the colors entirely—look past them and pretend they weren't there.

Other times, though, they were like a Technicolor punch to the forehead.

Dawn's cloud of blacks and browns, for instance.

Bao had gone to get himself another drink, and Dawn had sat beside Christian, coming from behind him and dropping into Bao's empty seat. She reached out and took one of Christian's french fries.

"How did you know?" she said, glancing at the guys at the other end of the table. They weren't even looking Christian's way. He was pretty sure they didn't like him much and wondered why Bao still hung out with the smart kid who hadn't ever been cool. "I'm…not far."

He was surprised it took her this long to ask.

Christian stared at his tray. The blacks and browns swirling around Dawn were hard to look at.

"It's kind of strange," he said. "You'll think I'm insane." Just talking about it made him feel queasy.

Her black and brown cloud parted for a second, revealing a burst of light blue and green. He turned, unable to stop himself, and watched the swirl blur into a bright cyan. She smiled at him. "Whereas I'm the picture of sanity and grace?"

Christian raised an eyebrow. "Compared to me? I think so."

They'd probably never spoken face-to-face before the stairwell, and he'd kind of distracted by announcing her pregnancy. He was used to the way she was looking at him, and he waited for the inevitable.

"Your eyes are two different colors," she said.

"Yep."

She stole another fry. "Seriously. How?"

"Genetics. It's called heterochromia."

She shoved his shoulder. "Don't be an asshole."

Christian looked at her. Deep below the purples and blacks was a rich blue that made him feel warm.

"I see things," he said.

"You see things?"

"Colors. And other stuff. Sometimes. But mostly colors. It's like people have these clouds of color that follow them."

To Christian's surprise, she didn't laugh. In fact, she looked thoughtful.

"So, like an aura?"

He shrugged. It was as good a word as any.

She looked around the cafeteria with a gaze that reminded him of his father and his uncles when they went out hunting. He shivered.

"What about Rick? What do you see?"

Rick Barritt was the most popular guy in school. A big jock who wasn't a complete dickhead, he was sitting with his jock friends and nodding at whatever they were saying. He seemed like a nice enough guy most of the time. Christian looked at Rick and saw a fuzzy orange and brown around him. It wasn't a great color, sort of bland and maybe even sickly.

"Bruised orange. Kind of swirly, too, like cotton candy?" Christian said, trying to describe the motion and color as best he could.

"Okay," Dawn said. "What does that mean?"

Christian looked around, as if about to reveal a great secret. Dawn leaned forward.

"I have *no idea*," Christian whispered. "It's not like there's a manual."

Dawn threw a fry at him. Then she grinned. Another flash of cyan.

"So, let's write one."

"Pardon?" Christian said, but then Bao came back with his drink, and he looked very surprised to see Dawn sitting with Christian.

"Hi," he said.

"Hi," Dawn said. She turned to Christian. "I'll catch up with you later."

After she left, Bao sat down again.

"Dude. Dawn Solati?"

Christian saw greens gather around Bao, especially near his eyes. *Huh.*

❖

At church, Christian watched his mother and father interact with the rest of the congregation, holding himself back as usual. During the sermon, some of the people in the rows around him—including his mother—had begun to gather a bright gold around them, in a pretty pattern that made him think of the way frost formed on the inside of his bedroom window in winter. It seemed brittle, like a single warm breath could melt it away, and it faded shortly after the priest stopped speaking.

The congregation had mostly been buried in browner shades of orange that settled down around their shoulders in drifts, piling thicker as time went by.

Boredom, he'd decided, was the faded orange of autumn leaves and just as nearly dead.

His head started to ache again, and he rubbed his eyes. His parents were always the last to leave, so he wandered out of the church to stand in the cool breeze and turn his face to the sun. Sometimes that helped.

When he opened his eyes again, he saw barely visible spiderweb lines, and he swallowed. It was going to happen again. He got out of the way of the people who drifted to the parking lot, and he slipped around the corner of the building. In the church's graveyard, a long, wide field, he stopped trying to resist.

The view shattered and behind it, dancing among tombstones, was a little brown-skinned girl in a dress patterned with tiny hopping frogs. She stopped at one of the tombstones and looked behind her while she pointed to it. Christian glanced to see who the girl might be talking to, but it was all gone between blinks.

He swallowed and pushed off from the wall of the church, walking to where he'd seen the little girl dance. It had been brighter there. Summer, perhaps. When he turned where she had been, he recognized the plain stone in front of him.

His grandfather's grave. The dates on one side of the stone were filled in—Christian had been five and barely remembered his grandfather—and the second little square where his grandmother planned to join her husband someday was empty.

Nothing else on the stone would make a little girl point and smile, he thought. Just a cross. His grandfather's name was at the top and his grandmother's below, which he'd always thought just a little macabre, given she was still alive. She lived in Toronto, and they barely ever saw her.

Christian stood there until his father called to tell him it was time to go home.

❖

"You coming to my meet tomorrow?"

Christian turned. Dawn had a way of finding him no matter where he was in the school. Today he was sitting out on the bleachers. He couldn't decide if it was comforting or creepy, but either way, he closed his book and nodded. "And miss dinner with my family?" He raised an eyebrow. "Absolutely."

Dawn smirked. She was in her school shorts and T-shirt, runners laced. She wasn't the only member of the track team putting in some after-school practice time.

"How you doing?" she said, leaning into a stretch.

He knew she wasn't asking about his well-being. It was the other thing. Always the other thing.

"Okay. I've nailed boredom as that funny orange-brown. *Everyone* turned orange-brown in biology today, even me."

"You can see your own aura?" She swapped legs, still stretching. "That's new."

"Sort of," he said. "Out of the corner of my eye."

"What about the other stuff?"

The shattering thing. Christian shook his head. That, thankfully, hadn't been happening at all. Sometimes everything shimmered, like maybe it was about to happen, but it usually passed if he closed his eyes tight, counted to ten, and waited. He knew Dawn would be angry if she knew he'd been actively trying *not* to let it happen. She wanted to know what it was.

He was pretty sure he already knew, and it terrified him. But he wasn't going to tell her unless he had to. So far, so good.

She looked past his shoulder. Christian glanced over. Bao Nguyen was walking past them, and he smiled at Dawn. "Good luck tomorrow," he said. Like Dawn, he was ready for a run. The T-shirt was tight across his shoulders.

Christian ignored the wisps of color in the corners of his eyes.

"Thanks," Dawn said.

"Hey," Bao said to Christian. "If I begged, could I get some help with Bio? Maybe come by after dinner?"

Relief flooded through Christian's stomach. Bao had been weird with him all week, but it seemed to be getting better. He didn't know what he'd do if Bao finally realized Christian was dead weight and needed to be tossed overboard. He couldn't imagine his day without sharing art class with Bao and drawing or painting side by side. All this week he'd wondered if Bao would take an easel by someone else in the room, but he hadn't.

"Of course," Christian said. Bao left them, but Christian was glad they'd be meeting up later. He didn't have other friends. Not really. Well, except now there was Dawn.

Then again, Christian wasn't sure if Dawn was a friend or not. If they were friends, they'd talk about her being pregnant. But the one time Christian had tried to bring it up, the cloud of blacks that had filled his vision had made it perfectly clear the topic was off the table.

"What about him?" Dawn said once Bao was gone.

"What do you mean?" He knew what she meant.

"Bao. What did you see?"

It felt weird to look at Bao that way—intrusive, maybe—but he did. Bao was tall, handsome, and strong, and in so many ways everything Christian was not. He felt his face heating up, but then the colors distracted him.

"Um." Christian squinted. "Sort of a blue. And red."

"Like purple?" Her grin was wide. "Wasn't purple horny?"

Christian could feel his blush spreading down his neck. "I'm still not entirely sure that's right. But no, he's not purple. It's a mix of reds and blues. Like ribbons sort of twisting around him." Christian considered. "I think blue is…like, *friendship.* Or maybe a crush."

"With a dash of horny?"

"Red isn't horny. It's…angry. Or frustrated."

"Sounds like all the horny boys to me."

He laughed. "You're awful."

"Don't you forget it," she said. Then she was off at a sprint toward the track. He watched her run, letting the colors stay at the front of his attention. Blurs of oranges and yellows were around most of the runners on the track, Bao included. Happy colors.

He reached into his backpack and pulled out the small spiral-bound notebook Dawn had given him. He flipped it open to the page marked "yellow" and wrote "happy."

He ignored the colors he saw out of the corner of his eyes.

None of those were yellow.

❖

"Your grandmother is coming to stay with us," his mother said.

"Okay." Christian hated how he spoke around his mother now. Tentative. Careful. Every word was half a question, like he was asking permission to exist. The sickly green bloomed between them no matter what he did, but sometimes it was worse when they spoke. That made it too much like his own fault.

"She's not well," his mother said. To his surprise, for the briefest moment, a thread of orange-browns and strange shimmery pale green twisted around a soft blue pulse, suddenly gone as if they'd snuffed out the blue light. The dark browns, which he thought of as hopelessness or disappointment, weren't new to his mother, but he didn't know the pale green yet. He'd seen the blue enough to know it was a good thing. Blue was compassion. Friendship. Love, even.

The blue was for his grandmother, though. Not him. He knew that. He saw how it shifted depending on who his mother was talking to or who she was talking about.

"Not well?" he said, ignoring what he saw. It was becoming second nature.

His mother exhaled. "She's dying." The words came out with a rush of the hated green stain between them. He'd seen the same color a few other times, in a few other places. When his biology teacher called on one of the kids who never got a question right, that same color spread out from him, even before the student tried to answer.

Disgust, Christian thought. Or something like it.

"Oh," he said. He wanted to say something right. Something better. Something that would make the aura around his mother match the calm mask of her face and the soft voice she was using. But he had nothing.

His mother held his gaze for a few seconds, and then she turned and walked away, leaving him there with his toast.

Christian closed his eyes. His grandmother was dying. He should feel more about that, but they barely saw her. If he was honest with himself, he was surprised she was coming here.

Then another thought. A terrible, *selfish* thought.

What would *dying* look like?

Christian closed his eyes and breathed until he was sure he wouldn't cry.

❖

At the meet, Bao surprised him by joining him on the bleachers after his run.

"You were awesome," Christian said.

"Thanks." He wasn't even breathing heavy. You'd never know he'd just blasted his way down a five-hundred-meter run. He used his T-shirt to rub his face, and Christian glanced away, scanning the field for Dawn and hoping Bao didn't notice.

"What's wrong?" Bao said.

"Huh?"

"You skipped art class. And you've been weird."

Christian looked back at Bao, frowning. "Weird," he said.

Bao raised both hands. "Come on."

Christian sighed. "Okay. Sure. Weird." He swallowed. "It's nothing."

"You never skip art."

"I'm turning over a new leaf." Christian shrugged. "A slacker leaf, maybe."

"Dude."

Christian looked at him. Rich blues, little twists of green near his eyes, and flickers of red beneath. It was such a mess. He rubbed his eyes. Was that darker blue kindness or was it pity? He'd never figure it all out, and it was driving him crazy how much he just wanted to see those blues when someone was talking to him. Anyone.

Or not just anyone.

"I keep getting headaches. My parents are driving me mental. My mom, she's…" He stopped. His mother was surrounded by bands of dark brown that gathered tighter and tighter around her chest every day.

"Your mom?" Bao said.

She hates me. Christian opened his eyes but tilted his head back, staring at the sky. "Something's up. And my grandmother's coming to live with us. Because she's dying."

"Oh, man, I'm sorry. That sucks." Bao winced.

"I think my parents are fighting about it." He blew out a breath.

"My mother is…I don't know. Maybe she wants a divorce? I don't know."

"You think?"

Christian shrugged. "Like I said, I don't know. Maybe it's not that."

"Maybe."

He looked at Bao again. Blue and green and red and now a kind of yellow seeping in at the edges. Christian told him his grandmother was dying and now he was *happy*? He couldn't reconcile it all.

Christian went back to looking for Dawn in the crowd. She was at the blocks now, and he leaned forward.

"We're okay, right?" Bao said. "You'd tell me if I'd fucked up or something."

It was so far removed from anything Christian expected Bao to say, he laughed. "You're asking me? You're pretty much my only friend. Even if you do draw better than I do, I'm not gonna ditch you."

"I don't draw better than you do." Christian could hear the relief in Bao's voice, though. The palest yellow spread from him in a slow bloom. He'd never understand why Bao stuck around, but he was lucky he did.

"Yes, you do." Christian bumped Bao's shoulder with his own and looked away before he could see the flash of deep purple in the corner of his eyes. At the side of the track, Mr. Pike was lining everyone up now, and…

He saw little holes in the colors around the teacher.

Christian frowned.

"What's wrong?" Bao said.

"Nothing."

Mr. Pike counted down, hit his stopwatch, and the runners launched from the blocks.

When Dawn ran, the cloud fell behind her like the ending of a storm. Christian was pretty sure the roiling, bruise-colored mess would re-form once Dawn was done with the race, but as her long legs ate up the track, she briefly lit up in waves of yellow and a bright orange that made him warm inside. It was a little like the people in the church, and just as fragile.

Dawn left trails of light as she shot around the track. She took an early lead and managed to keep it.

"She's great," Bao said. "I'm sorry if…" He trailed off.

Christian glanced at him. "What?"

"Do you like her?" Bao asked.

Colors replayed themselves in Christian's memory as he remembered the few times Bao and Dawn had interacted over the last couple of weeks, and it finally clicked.

Bao liked her. Those twists of blue, and the way he got kind up upset…Bao was jealous.

Christian's chest grew tight. He forced himself to smile. "She's just a friend."

"Oh," Bao said. He turned back to watch her run. "Okay."

This time, the relief in Bao's voice twisted the knot in Christian's chest. Dawn was almost around the track.

"It makes her really happy," Christian said, just to say something.

"Winning?" Bao said. Dawn was in the lead, and it was looking good.

"Doesn't matter if she wins. She just loves running."

Dawn stumbled.

Christian rose first and Bao followed. She carried on a few more steps. People had noticed now. Even Mr. Pike was looking at her.

But only Christian saw how the golden orange inside Dawn flashed.

"No." Christian rushed down the bleachers.

"Christian?" Bao called after him.

She didn't quite make it off the track before she fell. As Christian ran, he saw Dawn curl up on her side, openly weeping now. There was blood.

By the time he got to her, the golden sun inside Dawn Solati had set.

❖

His grandmother had him put her large suitcase on the bed in the spare bedroom, and now she was slowly unpacking clothing into the small closet. Christian saw her aura was swimming with absences. They weren't dark, they were completely *gone*, in a way that almost hurt his eyes.

His sister was upstairs. She'd said she had just wanted to visit for the weekend, though Christian knew his mother had likely demanded she do so. His mother and father were in the kitchen.

Dark colors, mostly. He'd written a lot in the journal Dawn had given him, and the more connections he made, the more things made sense. He knew part of what he'd seen around his parents and his sister was sadness—muted mints, but he'd been surprised by the pinks—embarrassment—and, of all things, the reds of annoyance and anger. As though his grandmother's death was somehow *inconvenient*.

It was the same red, he thought now, as the Bible his grandmother had placed on the bedside table.

"Can I help?" he asked.

She looked at him strangely for a moment, then she shook her head. "No dear, I'm fine."

He wished that were true. He left her in the room with an awkward smile, heading up to his bedroom.

He wondered if everyone had whole pieces of their auras missing when they were dying, or if it was specifically cancer.

He opened the journal, but he didn't write anything down for a long time.

When he did, it was just two words.

Mr. Pike.

❖

After Dawn was taken to hospital and the story began to spread, the whole school began staring at him. Everyone had seen them together, everyone had seen them talking and hanging out, and while it hadn't been worth much discussion before, now it was the perfect speculation.

Was it possible? Dawn Solati and *Christian Simon*?

Whispers died when he entered a class. Even his art teacher, Ms. Blanchard, who sounded no different than before, stared at him, surrounded by deep reds when she spoke to him.

Anger. She was angry at him. She hid it well, but she couldn't hide it from his other eyes.

The worst, though, was Bao. When Bao took up an easel at the other side of the class, he knew it was over. He'd *maybe* had two friends. One was now a scandal.

The other was done with him.

They were supposed to be working on analogous colors, a tiny slice of the color wheel. Christian found painting much more difficult, though he thought he might have a knack for it if he really worked. Still, he'd always preferred drawing. He looked at the simple figure he'd outlined and picked up his paint brush. Pausing only to glance at Bao, he painted the riot of colors he saw.

A dark, rich purple, almost black? Hurt. Deep, rich red? Anger. Pale, minty blue-green? Sadness. And two, thin lines of a rich, vibrant green that seemed to slice through the middle of Bao's face, burning from his eyes.

Well. That one was already folklore. Jealousy.

Ms. Blanchard paused as she circled the room.

"Christian…" she started, her voice still pleasant and professional. Red pulsed as she gathered her thoughts.

He couldn't bear to listen to her tell him he was doing the assignment wrong. He didn't care.

"Sorry," he said, before she could speak. "I…I need to go."

She frowned at him, but he didn't wait for permission. He hadn't even asked, really.

He walked out of the classroom. He stopped in the hallway, leaning against one of the walls with his eyes closed, trying to force the memory of the colors out of his mind. He was still there when the bell rang, and he didn't move as the noise of the period change went on around him. It would pass, and he'd be alone again.

He didn't even care if he got in trouble. He didn't go hide under the stairs. He just wanted everyone to go away.

Except when the noise died down, and he finally opened his eyes, he wasn't alone.

Bao looked down at him.

"Is she okay?"

Christian exhaled, on the edge of tears.

"I don't know. I'm going to the hospital tomorrow."

Bao nodded. "I have your stuff." He lifted Christian's books. "Are you going to class?" His voice was brittle, tight.

Christian blinked, hard. The tiny fragile lines were appearing again. Before he could turn away, Bao shattered, and a taller man in a dark suit or uniform stood in front of him.

The pieces spun away, and Christian stared through them.

It was a police officer. And it *was* Bao. But it wasn't. He was too tall, and bigger, and…

Older.

"You two have class?"

Christian and Bao both turned. Mr. Pike was frowning at them, leaning out from his classroom into the hall. The shattered world put itself back together.

"Sorry, Coach," Bao said. "We're late."

Mr. Pike nodded at them once. Christian wondered if they'd get in trouble, or if Mr. Pike would cut his track athlete some slack. The decision seemed to swirl around Mr. Pike, annoyance warring with a deeper shade of blue Christian didn't quite understand yet. Maybe it was like kindness.

And again, he noticed some small absences in the cloud of colors around Mr. Pike.

"Well, hurry up, then," Mr. Pike said, and went back into the room.

"Come on," Bao said. He pushed Christian's books into his hands, and Christian took them with nerveless fingers. "Let's go." All the colors from before, the hurt and anger and jealousy were still there, but they were buried under a compassionate blue. That was Bao. He might be seething, thinking Christian—*Christian, of all people!*—had fucked up Dawn's life, but he'd still get him to class on time.

Maybe he'd still even be his friend, eventually.

"You're gonna make a great cop," Christian said absently, still thinking of the tiny holes in Mr. Pike's aura. They were gathered near his waist, in a cluster on one side.

"What?"

"Sorry. Nothing." They started walking.

During biology, Christian pulled out a piece of paper and started writing. After class, he took the letter and slid it under the door to Mr. Pike's coach's office.

His heart pounded, and he hoped no one saw him leave it. If they did?

Well, that would be interesting.

❖

Dear Mr. Pike;
You have no reason to believe me, but please go to the doctor. You have cancer. I swear this isn't a prank, or a joke, or some mean trick. I know you're ill. I'm hoping you feel something or you've been ignoring something. Please don't.
Please go to the doctor. Especially your stomach. I think it's close to your stomach.
Make them do tests.
Please.
I swear I'm not lying.
Your Student

❖

Dawn looked up from her pillow and smiled wanly.

"Hey," Christian said.

"Hi," she said.

"I'm sorry I couldn't get here sooner," he said. She nodded. The colors shifted around her so quickly he couldn't keep track.

"Please don't *look*…Okay, Christian?"

Christian glanced away. "Okay."

They fell into a silence for a long moment.

"Hello?" came a cold voice.

Christian turned. Dawn's mother and stepfather, he assumed.

"Mom," Dawn said, "this is Christian."

Dawn's mother said nothing. Anger and outrage surrounded her in a crimson and magenta halo. Like everyone else, she probably thought the worst of him.

"Hello," Christian said, rising. Dawn's mother's gaze didn't falter, and he looked away, guilty without reason.

To his surprise, Dawn's stepfather was much calmer. Bored, if the brownish-orange was to be believed. It seemed a little bit callous to be bored. But it wasn't just that. Bands of odd sickly greens—the disgust he was used to seeing from his mother—twisted and writhed through the man's aura.

He offered Christian a hand.

Christian couldn't think of a reason not to shake his hand. He took it, and the world shattered.

It wasn't like with Bao, or the church, or any of the other times. Nothing stayed still. Images *violated* Christian. Bile rose in his throat, and he gagged. He saw the man in front of him in a horrifying montage—not now, and not someday, but a string of moments he knew on some instinctual level were *thens*. Things that *had been* were echoing in front of him, showing him, and he had no choice in the matter.

Christian saw the things this man had done to Dawn.

"Stop," he said, the word barely a breath. He couldn't make his hand let go, and he felt Dawn's stepfather trying to twist free of Christian's iron grip. Christian clenched his eyes, willing it to stop, but even with his eyes closed, he could still see the things this man had done. He tried to push it all away with a mental muscle he hadn't known he possessed, but instead of release, the world spun and shattered over and over again.

Back farther. Before Dawn.

Others.

Christian's eyes felt like flame. With a desperate cry, he pushed himself away from the man, shoving hard, his hand finally letting go.

Christian knew rage for the first time in his life.

"Get the hell out of here," Christian told Dawn's stepfather. His eyes ached with pain, but his voice went flat and cold. "If you ever touch her again, I'll kill you."

❖

His parents came to get him once the police were done. They didn't speak in the car ride home, and it took everything Christian had not to yell at them.

Don't you know I can see how much you hate being around me?

Instead, he tried to ignore the dark colors filling the car, and the way his mother wouldn't look at him, and the way his father frowned whenever their eyes met in the rearview mirror.

His eyes still ached. After the police, there had been time for a doctor. She told him not to worry.

"Is she okay? Is Dawn okay?" he'd asked. He'd been pulled away once the yelling had started, and it had taken him some time to realize he'd been the one yelling the loudest. Telling everyone who'd listen what that man had done to her.

The doctor had regarded him with a long, careful silence. "Thanks to you, I think she will be."

The car stopped. Christian realized they were home. His parents got out of the car, and he counted to three before he followed them, closing the door behind him.

"I'm going to go lie down," he said.

Neither of them argued. Relief was a pale-yellow bloom.

The door to his grandmother's room was open. She called out to him as he passed. "Christian? Is that you?" Her voice was reedy.

"Yes," he said, coming through the doorway. She was in the bed under the blankets. A glass of water and many little bottles of pills covered the table beside her. Her well-worn red-covered Bible lay open on the bed beside her thin hand.

"Oh my word," she said when she saw him.

"I'm okay. The doctor said it's just a burst blood vessel." His eye whites were red with blood since the…*thing*…with Dawn's stepfather.

But his grandmother shook her head. "I'm a fool."

"What?"

"How bad is it?" she asked. "Is it just colors, or…Well, no. Of course not. Your eyes."

Christian froze.

His grandmother raised her hand. "Come in."

He stepped into the room and sat in the single chair right beside her bed. She looked exhausted, and her skin had an ashen, grey tone to it. The gaps in her aura outweighed the few colors Christian could still see.

There isn't much time, those gaps said. *There isn't much time at all*.

"I knew it had skipped your sister," she said. "I thought that was for the best. You mother…Well. She refused it, in a way. But I didn't think…" She sighed. "You're a *boy*."

"I'm a boy," Christian repeated. He was shaking his head slowly. "Do you…" He swallowed. "Can you…*see*?"

"I can," she said. "I'm so sorry. I never expected…" She closed her eyes, like she was drawing on uncertain reserves. He supposed she was. "I'm so sorry."

"There were *horrible* things." His voice broke on the words, and he barely fought off a sob. "I just saw it."

Her hand, dry-skinned and paper-light, found his.

"And what will you do about that?"

❖

Bao found him at lunch, sitting by himself at the top of the bleachers. It wasn't warm enough to be outside, but it was better than all the staring and the whispers.

"I'm sorry," Bao said.

Christian looked at him. Blues and browns and faint yellows.

He scowled, angry. "For what?"

"I didn't mean to…" Bao started, but that was all he said.

Christian waited a beat longer, but Bao just sat there. "Were you mad because you like her, and you couldn't imagine that she'd want to be with someone like me when there's someone like you around?"

Bao shook his head. "No. No, I—"

"You have no idea, do you?" Christian said. "I'm not a sidekick. I'm not a pet project. I can't live off crumbs. God!" He took a deep, shuddering breath. "My grandmother is dying, my parents don't want me around, one of our friends is going through, like, the worst thing ever—which, bonus, *partly my fault*—and my best friend? My *only* friend? He took off." His eyes filled with tears, and the humiliation of that was more than he could handle. He stood up.

"Christian," Bao said. "I'm sorry. I thought you and Dawn—"

"You *took off*," Christian said. "I don't…" He swallowed. "I don't even like her that way, Bao. I don't like *girls* that way. Okay? Do you get it now?"

Bao's eyes widened, and that was it. Christian was done. Just done.

"Leave me alone. Stick with your jock friends and leave me alone." He left, one foot in front of the other, all the way down the bleachers and then back to the school. His chest ached, and all around him he saw faint lines in the air, fractures ready to give way.

He blinked until the threat of the future—or the past—went away. He'd seen enough of both.

The present was more than enough to deal with.

❖

She'd let him in without a word, and then walked up to her bedroom.

Dawn climbed onto her bed and lay down, looking up at the ceiling. Christian knew her mother was at work. Her stepfather was gone. There had been police, he'd heard. And other girls. He stopped just inside her room, not sure if he should go farther, and then he sat on the floor, leaning against the closed door.

They sat in silence as the minutes ticked past.

Finally, Dawn turned her head to look at him. "You been drinking?" she said. "Your eyes are all bloodshot."

"Ha," Christian said. "And ha again."

She smiled. It didn't reach her eyes.

More silence.

"I'm sorry," Christian said, when he couldn't stand it any longer.

"For what?" Dawn sighed. She curled up on the bed and shrugged one shoulder. "Let's face it. I'm one of those after-school specials, aren't I?"

"You redefine special," Christian said. "If it helps, I've been cast as the gay best friend."

"It helps," she said. Finally, she sat up and patted the bed.

He got up and joined her. They sat staring at the wall, side by side.

"Homo, huh?" she said.

"Yep."

"Am I allowed to say I'm not surprised?"

"Oh, this is fun."

"Sorry."

He looked at her. "Don't be. I mean, I'm pretty sure my parents are going to explode, so maybe I won't be coming out any time soon, but honestly, I don't think I can handle us all pretending much longer. Anyway. You get to know."

"Thanks." She bit her lip. "How…how did *you* know?"

He frowned. "That I like boys? Ever see Bao without his shirt on?"

She laughed and shook her head. "Not what I meant, but fair point."

"Oh," he said, cluing in.

"Right."

"That shattering thing." He took a deep breath. "So, it turns out it's more than the colors. I can see other stuff."

"Stuff."

He met her gaze and nodded. "The past, I guess."

"So, you just…saw it."

He nodded. "My grandmother says I need to be careful with people. The first time I touch someone, especially. I might see things."

"Your grandmother?"

"Apparently this runs in the family. Or, y'know, it ran into me. Full speed. Head-on. She's the same, but I guess it's not as strong with her. And, here's the kicker. My mom might be able to do it, too, but somehow, she refuses. Which, maybe, explains why she doesn't like me. I think she can tell I'm…" He shrugged. "Well. Y'know. Homo. So, that probably doesn't work well with her whole churchy-thing."

"That's…" She blew out a breath.

"Right?"

They sat a while longer. This time, the silence didn't feel uncomfortable.

"I am leaving this town," Christian said. "I am so leaving this town."

"Me too. You gonna graduate first?" Dawn said. "Only a few weeks left, right?"

"I'm fifty-fifty on it. Not seeing many reasons to stay, present company excepted."

She leaned on him, putting her head on his shoulder. "Hey, Christian?"

"Yeah?"

"Wanna be my prom date?"

He turned his head. "You *want* to go to prom?" It was the last thing he expected.

"Yeah," she said. "More than anything."

The blacks and browns parted, and beneath them, the golden and yellow fire spread, fragile and tentative.

Christian got it then. It was hope.

"Okay," he said. "It's a date."

❖

Only two days of school were left when Christian wrote the second letter. He waited until after classes were out to head down to the coach's office. Once he was there, he knelt down to slide it under the door, a slight sense of déja vu making it all surreal.

"Christian?"

He jumped. Mr. Pike looked pale, but he was still working. Awful timing. Christian looked at Mr. Pike's aura again and saw what he'd seen earlier in the week.

They stood there, facing each other.

Mr. Pike reached out and took the note from Christian's hand.

Christian swallowed, hard. He waited, frozen to the spot, while Mr. Pike unfolded the note and looked at it for far longer a time than it would take to read.

They regarded each other. Even pale and drawn, Mr. Pike was an imposing figure. A tall man who'd obviously been an athlete at Christian's age and beyond. The track coach. Popular.

The whole school had rallied around his news.

Christian felt small and thin and *unimportant* beside him.

Mr. Pike cleared his throat, opened his mouth to speak, then closed it. Finally, he just flicked his fingers. A dismissal.

Christian turned and left, working hard not to flee as fast as he could. He was almost to the stairs when Mr. Pike spoke.

"Christian?"

Christian paused and turned.

"You're welcome," Mr. Pike said, going into his office.

They both pretended there weren't tears in their eyes.

❖

After his grandmother's funeral, once everyone had gone, Christian went to his room. He hadn't cried yet, and he didn't know what that said about him. He changed out of his black shirt and dress pants, hanging it all carefully, and pulled on a pair of jeans and a T-shirt.

He thought about the priest's eulogy for his grandmother, whom the man hadn't known at all. There'd been a lot of stuff about the sanctity of family and truth, and none of it had really sunk in. There would be dates carved on the tombstone now. Someday, Christian thought, a little brown-skinned girl might even point at them.

Christian crossed the room to his mirror, regarding himself. So much was a mess. Dawn. Bao. His parents.

And what will you do about that?

Good question. Maybe it was cowardice, but he'd been accepted into university in Ottawa, and he'd wait until he got there to finally tell his family. And then...?

What'll happen after that?

A web of fine, shimmering lines spread across his reflection. Christian winced and was about to fight off the intrusion, but his vision shattered so quickly he didn't have time.

Mismatched eyes regarded him with surprise. One green, one blue.

Christian's heart hammered in his chest, and he stared, unable to look away. The grown man looked back at him. He had a trim goatee. Choppy hair.

And Christian's face.

Older, more angular, with little lines by his eyes.

The reflection smiled at him. It was a kind smile, and it warmed the man's whole face. He looked like someone with a lot of love to give, actually.

He realized then. The reflection could *see* him, too.

Christian raised a hand, touching the cool glass.

The man pointed at him, then held up his hand, circling his thumb and index finger, the rest of his fingers spread.

Christian shook his head.

The man repeated the gestures. He pointed at Christian.

You.

He circled his thumb and index finger, and spread the rest of his fingers again.

Okay.

Christian felt the ache starting behind his eyes. He'd have to let go of this soon, let the pieces of the world come back together in front of his eyes.

The man raised his eyebrow. It was so very *him* to do that.

Did he understand?

You. Okay.

Christian swallowed.

You are going to be okay.

Christian nodded at the older version of himself.

The older him smiled and was gone. He was staring at his own face, which seemed rounder and softer and certainly had more acne. At least he knew that would clear up. And he'd eventually be able to grow a beard. He took a shaky breath.

Okay. If he thought about it too much, he'd go mental, so he decided there and then to just accept something as truth.

Someday, he'd be okay.

He just had to get there.

❖

Dear Mr. Pike:

Me again.

I know you are still worried, but I hope you'll believe me—again—when I tell you: your cancer is gone. You're going to be fine.

I figure the doctors will tell you soon or maybe make you do more chemo just to be sure, but I figured now is better.

I'm sure it was horrible for you, and I don't know if this will make it better or not, but you believed my note, went to the hospital, and you got better.

You showed me I could do more than know these horrible things.

I can try to help.

You can't know what that means to me.

Thank you,

Your Student

There are other blues.

Rich, deep blue is the color of kindness. It reaches out much the same as love but moves with a steadier pulse. It gathers behind the eyes. Pools there. Grows there. Flows steadily between people.

Good humor flickers in cyan blue-greens, teasing the same in return. A wave of that color is laughter in motion, and watching it rush over a crowd is a pleasure every time.

The darkest blues settle deepest into lives lived in charity and compassion. People who have made giving and loving a way of life. People who have waited and given time and thought to others at least as often as themselves.

Those kinds of blues are rare and important, and they leave a mark on everyone they meet.

TIME AND TIDE

Death had made us leave Fuca, and now death was bringing me back. When I stepped off the bus, the scent of the ocean was the only thing about my childhood town that seemed the same. The bus station had been completely rebuilt and looked nothing like the run-down building I remembered. The glimpse of the town I'd had coming around the final curve of the road and down into the valley had been quick, but the mix of the familiar and the new added to the sense that none of this was real.

My father was dead. Holding my backpack and duffel, I stared without seeing and just breathed. You couldn't see the strait from here, but like always, the streets seemed to deliver the scent to every corner of Fuca.

"Dylan?"

Even after a dozen years, I knew that voice. I turned and saw Laurie, arms crossed, leaning against a shiny green cab. Her spill of curls was tucked under a beret, and her curves were on display in a tight turtleneck and faded jeans. She smiled, her expression still somehow sad.

"Laurie." I hugged her and dropped my bags. She squeezed me once, and then I stepped back.

Face-to-face with her, I couldn't find words.

"Where are you staying?" she asked.

"The Cabins," I said, frowning. "I'm not exactly sure where that is, but apparently the hotel closed?"

Laurie nodded. "They knocked it down. There are a bunch of cabins down on the strait now. Part of the new Green Fuca." She waved a hand at the cab, and I saw the strip of text beneath the Fuca Cab Company logo explaining the cab was electric.

"Green Fuca?" I said.

"Get in," Laurie said, opening the trunk and taking my duffel. "I'll give you the dime tour on the way. Meter's off." She tucked my bags in and closed the trunk. Then she met my gaze. "I'm sorry about your dad."

My cabin was small but comfortable. It was built with an open concept. The kitchenette opened up on the living room and faced the water through large sliding glass doors, with a two-seater breakfast nook built to enjoy the view. I put my bags on the counter and shivered. The cabin was so new I still smelled a trace of sawdust, but the strait looked exactly the same.

I could see the waves breaking on the beach down below. I unlocked the glass door and slid it open.

The sound—and the ocean's voice—washed over me. I closed my eyes, aware I was shaking.

Shhhh... Shhhh...

A mother's voice soothing a fussy baby.

Shhhh... Shhhh...

Finally, I cried.

"It's good to have you back, though I wish... Well."

I grew up thinking of Ikuko Webster as my homeroom teacher. I had a hard time reconciling the image of a kind and wonderful woman in lavender blouses with the woman in the chic navy suit and steel-grey hair in front of me. Mayor Webster, as she was now known, had been at the funeral home when I'd arrived and had been reintroducing people to me all afternoon, helping me reconnect faces with names and supporting me above and beyond the call of a former teacher.

I turned my attention back to her instead of watching the door. Cary Kelby wasn't coming. I shouldn't have expected otherwise.

"Thank you," I said. "The town looks amazing."

She visibly brightened. "Greenest town in the province."

"Laurie was telling me." I nodded to Laurie, who was standing across the room speaking with the pastor. She winked. "And the city funded the change to the electric cabs?"

The mayor nodded. "There's so much still going on. The cabins opened up last month, and they're booked solid for September and October already. The diner has a new hundred-mile menu, the local farmers and fishermen are filling the open market, City Hall has solar panels, and the influx of tourism has been palpable." She blushed, catching herself. "I'm sorry. Not the time or place."

I shrugged. "He would have approved."

She touched my arm. "He did. One of the voting voices." She paused, then pushed ahead. "Could I ask you…That is, the city…" She bit her lip, once again the nervous teacher with a student she was trying to mentor.

"Go ahead," I said.

She smiled. "We'd like to commission a piece from you. Local celebrity and all that. It seems so wrong Fuca doesn't have an original Dylan Hurley of its own."

My fingers itched. It would be a very welcome distraction.

"Absolutely," I said.

"Wonderful! I'll have my assistant call you with the details. We'd like something for the center of the roundabout. The intersection got a makeover, but it needs a centerpiece." She held up a finger. "But! Local materials only."

I laughed. "Of course."

She touched my shoulder again and then introduced another one of my father's friends, whom I didn't remember and didn't know. I couldn't reconcile this grim event with my father, who had worked so hard to make me laugh and smile all my life. I surreptitiously checked my watch. Another hour and I'd be free.

My eyes returned to the door, watching for Cary.

He didn't come.

❖

Back at the cabin, I started sketching.

My ideas have always been of two sorts. The first hide and bury themselves in the deepest places of my head, where I have to flush them out and capture them and wrestle them into submission. The other sort are tenacious beasts that demand all my attention. I was pretty sure this idea was going to be one of the latter.

Before long, I had a rough sketch and an idea fleshed out enough to send to the mayor's assistant. I snapped a picture with my phone, thumbed an email, and sent it off. Before I'd managed to unpack my duffel and backpack, my phone pinged with the reply.

Mayor Webster loved it, and we had a deal.

I did research on my phone's tiny screen until my eyes burned, and I decided to call it a day when my stomach informed me it was almost two hours past dinner. I tucked my wallet into my pocket and locked the cabin behind me, walking into town.

The future site of my piece was on the way to the diner. The mayor was right. The roundabout was lovely now, a small park in itself where the roads met, full of hostas but somehow not quite finished. I pictured it with my piece installed and nodded to myself. It would work. And they didn't mind the extra construction on the curbs and sidewalks surrounding it.

My stomach rumbled again.

I turned my back on the roundabout and walked down to Market Street. I considered the diner but decided I wasn't in the mood for a crowd, so I kept walking. Two blocks past was the open market where a few stalls were still occupied even as the hour grew late.

I bought some local bread, local butter, and local milk, along with some local tomatoes and local cheese. One thing was missing. I asked where I could score some coffee while the guy in the stall wrapped up my purchases. I found a bottle of instant at the corner store. I felt like a smuggler trying to procure something illegal, and the cashier laughed when I said so.

I was walking back through the market with my purchases in hand when the ocean's voice started talking again.

Shhhh... Shhhh...

It was getting clearer. I hesitated, shifting the bag to my other arm.

"Already shopping like a local, eh?"

His voice rolled me over, lost me in the wash, and removed my sense of up and down. I turned.

"I'm sorry about your dad," Cary said.

I nodded, not willing to trust my voice.

He was wearing jeans and a faded Fuca High Athletics T-shirt. He hadn't shaved today. His hair was long enough to stir in the wind, and his eyes were still the most impossible deep blue.

"Where are you staying?" he asked.

"The Cabins." My voice only cracked a little. I cleared my throat.

He nodded. "Great idea, those were." I noticed he was carrying a package of his own. Fish wrapped in paper and some greens I didn't immediately recognize. The rest of it was buried underneath in the reusable bag.

"So I hear," I said. I wanted to touch him. I wanted to run away.

Why did you agree to build a piece for Fuca? I thought. *You can't leave until it's done!*

He seemed to read my mind. "How long are you staying?"

"I was just going to stay for three nights," I admitted. "Deal with the lawyer and everything. But…" *But?* "Ms. Webster commissioned a piece." I sounded pathetic. I felt pathetic.

"About time we had a piece of you," he said. He smiled, and the gap between his front teeth was like a punch to my stomach. "What are you making?"

"You'll see when everyone else sees," I said, intending to sound playful but coming off sharp.

He nodded. "Right."

"I miss you." It was out before I could stop it. As always, Cary pulled things from me. He had his own gravity, even after all this time. Everything in me wanted to touch him.

"I missed you, too." Past tense, I noticed.

He looked at what I was carrying.

"Are you making your sliced tomato sandwiches?"

"Yeah." The tension broke and I smiled.

"How about some salmon to go with it?"

The ocean whispered, clearer still. *Yessss… Yessss…*

"That sounds great," I said.

He used the small grill on the deck, wrapping the fish in the greens and tinfoil and butter while I sliced the tomatoes and cut the bread. I couldn't help but smile. Local bread. Local butter. Local sea salt. We had a sandwich each while we waited on the fish.

"I'm sorry I couldn't come to the funeral," Cary said. He looked at me. "How are you doing?"

"It's strange to be back. I remember everything, but I'd forgotten it all, too. Everything is different, but all the same things are tucked between. Does that make sense?"

"Yeah."

"He never let me visit," I said, though it was embarrassing to admit I'd let my father dictate this to me. "When he moved back here, after I graduated, I mean. He visited me. Every Christmas, and his birthday. And mine, a few times. I'd call and say I wanted to see him and he'd say, 'No, you stay put. I'm the retired one.'" I sighed. "I let him have that, I guess. I think he was afraid…" I trailed off. I've never quite been sure just what my father felt he had to fear about me being in Fuca.

"Memories of your mother," Cary said.

He was right. Time to change the subject. "How's your family?"

Cary smiled. "The same. My brothers are still around. They got married, and I've got multiple nieces and nephews I get to spoil rotten. I took over the business when Dad retired, but Mom still comes in every day at lunch to thank the guys."

"How many you got now?"

"We downsized, actually. Just three ships, twelve men. But now we take people on tours, and we have our own fish farm." He met my gaze. "Mom's a watchdog, makes sure everyone is respectful and kind to the fish." He blushed. His mother had not been a fan of my father.

"Sounds wonderful," I said.

He looked out the window. "Gets me out on the water."

"Do you…" I almost asked him if he remembered, but I backed out. "Do you think the fish is ready?"

He went to check. It was. We ate. Then we opened up a bottle of wine and ate the cheese. We leaned closer to each other and talked. The ocean whispered through the open glass doors.

Hushhh…Hushhh…

We stopped talking. I kissed him.

He spent the night.

❖

While he used the shower, I made toast with the last of the bread, along with some illicit coffee not from the same continent. He came out in a towel, smelled the coffee, and grinned at me.

"Coffee isn't on the approved list of local beverages," he said.

"Here. Be an accomplice in my illicit coffee smuggling ring." I handed him a cup and kissed him again. He tasted like spring water, clean and fresh.

He swallowed some of the coffee, then regarded me over his cup.

"When do you go?" he asked. There it was. The question. He might as well have asked me when I planned to hurt him again.

"I'm not sure," I said. "I have to find somewhere to stay. I need to rent a work space, too." It was an unfair answer.

"We've got an empty boathouse," Cary suggested. He drank some more. "And you can stay with me."

His hair was completely dry. That hadn't changed. *God*, I thought. *Nothing has changed.*

"I'd like that," I said.

He nodded.

"I'd better get dressed. Have to be at work soon."

We looked at each other a moment longer. I was the one who broke.

"Thank you," I said, not sure exactly what I was thanking him for.

He took my hand and squeezed. Then he got up, got dressed, and left. His coffee cup was still half full. The liquid inside was spinning as though it had just been stirred. I picked it up and held it until it began to spin in the opposite direction.

Nothing had changed.

❖

A day. Three days. Two weeks. I worked in the rented boathouse despite Cary's protests that I could have it for free, adding it to Fuca's bill. At night, we walked from the docks together to his small house. We had breakfast and dinner together. Most days I made us sandwich lunches. He claimed not to be tired of my sliced tomatoes.

The old things hadn't gone away. When Cary showered, or swam, or got caught in the rain, he dried off in moments. When I held a glass of water, the ice cubes spun in the glass. Salt arranged itself into patterns across the counter if I spilled it. Gulls fell quiet as I walked by. And the whispers from the ocean grew louder and gained harsher consonants among the sibilants.

My third week, I woke in the middle of the night to find the bed empty. Through the open window I could hear water. I tugged on my shirt and jeans and padded barefoot down the slope behind Cary's house to one of the many creeks that fed into the river. There he was, sitting beside the water.

He looked at me, and even in the night I could tell he was blushing.

"Sorry," he said. It lay between us, a non-discussion. His bare feet were in the water.

"It's fine," I said.

He looked at me.

"Do you still…Does it still…?" He sighed, frustrated. Not talking about it for the past three weeks had become a bad habit.

"Yes," I said. "It got less…It was less in the city, but it still happened."

He relaxed. *We're going to talk about it*, I thought. I was afraid.

Saaaay… The ocean again. *Saaaay…*

"How's the piece coming?" Cary asked. He meant, *When are you leaving?*

"Pretty well," I say. I meant, *Soon.*

"Good. Do I get to know what it is?" *You're breaking my heart.*

"You'll see it when everyone else does." *I know.*

We fell silent. The ocean whispered. *Saaaay…*

"Dylan?"

"Yes?"

"Take my hand?" He held it out. I looked at his feet in the water.

I took his hand. I wasn't calm enough, and in moments, the creek began to roll. Waves formed, gentle at first but growing larger.

He dropped my hand, and the creek stilled.

"Well," he said. "There's still that."

I meant to laugh, but I cried instead. He led me back inside and wrapped himself around me until I fell asleep.

His feet, of course, were already dry.

❖

My mother was leaning on the railing beside Cary's parents, her hair tied back under a white cotton scarf. My father was at the wheel, laughing about something and making her smile, chasing away that lonely look she wore on her face so often. Cary's brothers were chasing him around the boat until their mother raised a hand, and they gave him one last shove before settling in at the back.

Cary looked so frustrated and sad. I pushed off from the railing and sat beside him. When I was sure no one was looking, I took his hand and squeezed.

The boat lurched. My mother turned her head and frowned, looking down to see our hands.

"Dylan," she said, but the boat lurched again, and water sprayed onto the deck.

"Choppy," my father called out. "Everybody take a seat. I think—"

The boat dropped and rose with a sickening lurch. I tumbled from the bench, landing hard on one knee. My head spun. There was a roar in my ears. I couldn't get past it to even think. The boat jumped again, twisting and rolling now. Cary took my hands. He was scared, eyes wide, and I saw his mouth move, but the noise in my head was too loud. My vision blurred. The boat dropped away from beneath us again, and I went sliding down the deck. Cary scrambled after me, and I saw his brothers grab out for him, catching him by the shoulder and halting him. Our eyes met. I saw him say my name, though I couldn't hear him.

The boat rolled, and I was in the ocean.

It pulled me under and tore me away. The roar in my head didn't abate, and I curled up into a ball. I was going to die. I opened my eyes—the salt water didn't sting at all—and felt my body relax. The ocean continued to pull at me, tugging me even deeper. I realized I wasn't scared. I wasn't even cold. I wasn't struggling. In fact, I felt calm and peaceful.

I was welcome here.

The water tugged and twisted around me, drawing me farther and farther down. I opened my mouth and felt the bubbles of my last breath rise past my face.

A hand took mine. I turned my head and saw my mother's smile.

She shook her head once, kissed my forehead, and then she just came apart. One moment she was there, the next blurred as though the water were full of sediment that held the shape of her body, and then just gone. The water around me seemed to let go, and I felt myself jetting upward to the surface.

The world returned, and I sucked in a breath as sunlight hit my eyes. I heard my father's voice and Cary weeping. Then everything went black.

I came awake with a strangled cry and reached out into empty air. Once again, Cary was gone, but this time sunlight streamed in from the window. He'd let me sleep in. I stretched, the images in my head fading as I mentally prepared for the work I'd be doing on the piece today. It was very nearly done, and I tried not to dwell on that as I took a shower and then had breakfast. My coffee circled in the cup, and I closed my eyes for a moment, feeling the echo of its movement in my chest, calming myself until the motion ceased. When I opened my eyes, the coffee was once again still.

On the front door, there was a note. It said: *We're out of tomatoes.*

I smiled and went back for one of Cary's shopping bags.

Laurie was at the market, and I bumped shoulders with her. She turned and smiled.

"How are you?" she asked. "You look great."

I shrugged. "I feel good."

"I'm sure that has nothing to do with your accommodations, eh?" She twisted her lip in a smirk.

"You're very funny."

"I'm also right."

I picked up some tomatoes. "You're also right."

She grinned. "It's so good to see him happy again."

My chest tightened. "He hasn't been happy?"

"Cary?" Laurie raised an eyebrow. "Not since you left. You must have known that."

I bit my lip. "I guess I figured he would have moved on or something." I grimaced. It sounded pathetic. I started eyeing local cheeses like choosing one would be the most important decision I'd ever make.

"Dylan," Laurie said.

I looked at her.

"Are you staying?"

I breathed. "Good question," I said.

"It's the only question," another voice added. We both turned. Cary's mother regarded me frankly. "Laurie dear, may I have Dylan for a while?"

Laurie nodded and left us.

❖

We didn't speak while she led me to one of the benches around the outside of the open market, away from the crowd and any ears. Seated, we regarded each other. Jennifer Kelby had the same deep blue eyes as Cary, though none of her other sons had inherited them. Cary's gaze made me feel protected. Jennifer's made me feel accused.

"I'm sorry about your father," she said.

"Thank you," I said. "I know you two didn't get along."

That surprised her. "You knew?"

I smiled. "Cary told me you argued. When I was staying with you. After my mother…After we lost my mother."

Jennifer pursed her lips. "Ah." Then, as though steeling herself for bad news, she said, "Do you love my son?"

"Yes." The word came out of my mouth before I could even consider it. I felt a weight I hadn't known was there lift off my chest.

She nodded. "And are you leaving or staying?"

I rubbed my eyes. "I don't know. It's…" I swallowed. "It's hard to be here." As if cued, a large wave crashed against the pier on the other side of the market, audible even from where we were sitting. We both flinched.

Jennifer took my hand. Immediately I felt the rush inside me, and our eyes met. She squeezed and let go. "You are a wonderful young man," she said. "And doubly so because you make my son happy."

"He's the wonderful one."

"I won't argue that, but I'm biased." She sighed. "I promised your father something, and I'm regretting it."

"It's okay," I said. "Cary and I talked about it before I left. I know about the old families in Fuca. I know my mother was from one of them."

She stared at me, open-mouthed. I couldn't help it. I laughed.

"But…" She shook her head. "I told him your father didn't want you to know."

I smiled. "My father wanted to leave. When you told Cary what was happening to him, he knew I was the same. We'd spent enough time together. Cary wanted me to stay, so he told me. I think my father was afraid I'd feel responsible if I knew I was…" I looked at her. "Naiad, is it?"

"Myself, yes. And Cary. Or at least half for me, and a quarter in his case. But you're not a naiad."

"I know. Cary and I figured that out before I left. I stay wet. I'm different from the two of you. Different things react to me, and I can hear voices in the ocean."

"Salt water," she said. "Understand, your mother and I were very close, and we knew to watch the two of you, but we had no idea the gifts would be so strong in either of you."

"Gifts," I repeated, scornful.

She heard the anger in my voice. "Yes. Gifts. The river for me, but the ocean for her—and you. Did you know not a single sailor was lost or drowned while your mother was here?"

I hadn't known that. I shook my head.

"The ocean is very strong, Dylan. I'm sure you feel its pull, don't you?"

I nodded. "Sometimes. Mostly I just hear its voice."

She thought about that. "I imagine it gives good advice."

I didn't know what to say.

"She felt it every day, Dylan. Every time she went on the water, it wanted her to stay, and every time she resisted. She could keep the ocean calm. You were so young. When you went under…" Her eyes filled with tears. "You have to understand, what she did, she did for you." She sighed. "She wanted you to have time to decide for yourself where you wanted to be, who you wanted to be."

I swallowed. "Is it the same for you?"

Jennifer shook her head. "Rivers flow. They don't have tides. I like the streams and rivers and they like me back, but they don't demand my attention. Though they occasionally flood." She smiled at her own joke, wiping at her eyes. "Rivers find their course and stick to it. But mostly they're content to be."

I smiled. "Sounds lovely."

"It is."

We sat a moment longer.

"I'd best be going," she said. "And I hear you're almost done with your sculpture."

"Yes."

She rose and turned to me. "I should have told you back then, your father be damned."

I shook my head. "I still felt responsible, either way."

"You weren't," she said, and then she walked away.

I sat for a while longer, then I picked up my tomatoes and started for Cary's work. I had something to show him.

❖

"What do you think?" I asked.

Cary regarded the sculpture with his incredible blue eyes. "I think it's beautiful."

The sculpture itself was a simple steep triangle, but I'd spent hours working on the surface, carving waves and ocean creatures both fantastical and real along both sides. Local rock had given me only the barest shades of different colors to choose from, but the subtle patterns of the various pieces, now completed into the one large shape, made an overall effect I liked. I was proud of the piece.

Cary walked around it, reaching out to touch some of the waves and smiling when he saw a merman.

"Usually those are women," he said.

"Artistic license."

He smiled. "Is it supposed to be like a dolphin's fin? The whole thing, I mean."

I shook my head. "It's a sundial."

He looked at it again. "Oh wow."

"They're going to rebuild parts of the sidewalk and curb around it to mark off the hours, with and without daylight saving time." I watched his eyes take in the sculpture all over again. "It's called *Time and Tide*."

"It's wonderful." He looked at me. "Thanks for showing it to me before anyone else got to see it."

I smiled.

He looked back at the sculpture. "When will it be installed?" The casualness of his question didn't fool me. I felt my chest ache, and the sound of the ocean on the beach seemed to double.

Saaay… Saaay…

"Next week," I said. "The mayor wants to make a big ceremony around it."

Cary nodded. "So, then you'll be off?"

I thought about what Cary's mother had said. I thought about my father, sending me away where the ocean couldn't call to me. I thought about my mother, giving me time to choose with her own life. I closed my eyes, and heard the ocean.

Saaay… Saaay…

"No," I said. "I'm not going anywhere."

Cary was silent for so long I opened my eyes. He was still looking at the sculpture, tears spilling from his eyes. He made no move to wipe them.

I stepped up to him and took his hand. "I'm so sorry," I said.

He looked at me. I raised my free hand and touched his cheek. His tears glistened once, then vanished under my fingers. *Salt water*, I thought.

"I love you," I said. "But we have to buy coffee. I don't care how far away we have to import it. I need coffee."

"Okay." He laughed, chest still shaking. "I love you, too."

He tilted his head forward, and I put my forehead against his. We stood together, letting the shadow of the sculpture fall over us, and I held him until he stopped crying.

The ocean whispered.

Staaay…Staaay…

I listened.

Orange belongs to the mind.

If it fades and corrodes into something browner and brittle, it's boredom, but when it softens and ripples like someone has skipped a stone along its surface, it's a kind of curiosity.

A new thought, a new take, or a new opportunity.

People expand—or close—with oranges. The palest shades of peach, often looking just as soft, are indecisions, and when they spread, they can wash away every other shade in view.

Everything can rise or fall to moments like that. Wait too long, and the opportunity has passed.

But brighten the orange, and you have freedom. The undertaking of a risk, the willingness to court success at the potential price of failure.

The orange is the same whether it is a sunrise or a sunset, but where one brings a darkness, the other turns into a new chance, a new start.

A new day.

Of course, it's not always easy to recognize the difference.

Pentimento

Jill met him on the sidewalk after the reading of the will.

"How did it go?"

"He left me his studio and all his paintings." Michel was keenly aware of the others gathered on the sidewalk in front of the lawyer's office. He kept his voice low, aimed for Jill alone.

"How did that go over?" She put a hand on his arm.

"About as well as you could expect," he said. "I have instructions, too." He touched his coat pocket, feeling the stiff envelope.

"Of course you do." Her smile pushed off some of the chill in the air. "It wouldn't have been Hans without instructions."

He nodded. Without intending to, he caught the gaze of Hans's niece. She stared him down, cold and unmoving. Her husband took her arm and said something low into her ear. He caught the word "sue."

"Let's go," he said to Jill. "Before they decide to take a hit out on me."

Jill looped her arm in his and led him away. He felt them looking at him until he and Jill turned a corner.

"Coffee?" she asked.

"I'd like that. And then I'll head over to the studio."

"Did you want company for that?"

"Would you believe he instructed me to go there alone?"

"I would. He was my teacher, too." She lowered her voice, going for Hans Köhler's deep timbre. "Miss Binder, if you continue to not *listen*, you will continue to not *improve*. I do not instruct lightly."

"He really was a font of joy, wasn't he?"

"He could be," Jill said. She squeezed his arm. "When he wanted to be."

That was true.

"Bittersweets?" he suggested.

"Yes please. They have the best macaroons there."

"Those are from a candy shop in the Village, you know. It just reopened."

"You gays have all the best things."

"It's true. We do."

The key was in the envelope the lawyer had given him. It seemed practically antique and weighed heavily in his palm. The lock itself clicked easily, surprising him, and he stepped into a sacred space to which he'd never before been invited.

Hans's studio was a remodeled house tucked among other small homes in the Glebe, and when Michel crossed the threshold, the scent of oil and paint thinner seemed to take him gently by the hand.

This was not a space Hans had ever shared with him. As far as he knew, it wasn't a space Hans had shared with anyone, but it was instantly familiar to Michel. Comfortable. The sort of place he could imagine having created for himself. And he had permission to be here.

And instructions.

He flicked on the light. The ground floor was a simple layout. From the entrance, a small hall was split by stairs to the right and a kitchen behind. What must have been a living room/dining room to the left was instead bare, though shelving had been installed along the walls between the small windows. Paint, canvases, wood, resins…The windows themselves were covered with heavy curtains. And stored in a set of racks opposite, finished paintings were carefully covered and stacked in columns and rows. He wondered how many pieces there were, but instead of pausing to check, Michel took a brief glance, then walked through to the kitchen.

Here there was some function. A small table and single chair. A plate, bowl, and exactly one setting of utensils were drying in a small rack beside the sink, and a bright red mug waited beside a small coffeemaker.

Coffee, not Paint was written on the mug. Michel smiled.

Nice to know even the greats had made *that* mistake. His own mug was yellow and had his name on it.

He checked the fridge to clean out any leftovers, but it was all but empty except for some condiments and a jug of water. The cupboards held some canned goods, some dried. Nothing that would spoil. This space obviously wasn't lived in so much as it was used on occasion. It could have been the small kitchen he had behind FunkArt, his own little gallery, though he was pretty sure he could find a couple of things in his own fridge he should have tossed out yesterday.

Michel sat at the small table and pulled out the envelope. The instructions were taped closed, and he ran his finger to undo them.

To his surprise, there was very little text. He'd expected a detailed list of paintings and instructions for each, but instead he got only seven brief lines of script in Hans's impeccable, almost anachronistic, cursive with only the slightest tremor in the strokes crossing every T. He'd had ample time to plan, ample time to know. From what Michel had experienced at the reading of the will, Hans had taken every second of it and used it to the fullest. Every detail planned.

Michel,

You can do with the pieces as you wish, though I am tasking you specifically as there is one thing I need from you to do most of all.

Paint over the triptych. You will know the one.

If you think it might require one, I offer my sincerest apology. It was a different time, and then it was too late. I trust in your discretion.

Hans

Michel looked at the note for a long time, frowning.

Triptych?

He didn't imagine it would be among the paintings in the former living room. He tapped the empty envelope against the table, then got up, annoyed at his own inertia. He filled and turned on the coffeemaker, and after finding no other cups, he rinsed out Hans's red mug and found the sugar. Two teaspoons later, and he turned his back to the machine and eyed the stairs.

He'd come back down for the coffee when it was ready.

❖

Upstairs, Michel found Hans's studio. What had likely been the master bedroom had been redone with skylights as well as a large bay window that ran the length of the wall. The closet had been removed and storage put in its place, the room's floor stripped to bare wood to collect drips and stains and spills. Also here, on one of two large tables, was an empty green mug with the same font. This time, it said, *Paint, not Coffee*.

Michel smiled again.

The three easels were all bare. He wasn't surprised, though some small part of him had wondered if there might be an unfinished piece.

But no. Hans would have included instructions.

The bathroom was tidy and serviceable, a bath/shower combination, a single sink. In another home, it would have been too little for even most couples, but this had been an old building even when Hans had bought it, and always used as a work space.

Hans had used the smaller of the upstairs rooms as a bedroom, and it was the first sign of comfort in the whole studio. The blankets and pillows looked well-worn, and the bedside table held a few battered paperbacks and a sketchpad and pencils. Michel smiled, stepping into the small room, and when he turned, he saw it.

The triptych.

The three separate panels were placed equally along the wall across from the bed, where anyone sleeping would see them upon waking in the morning. The technique was entirely Hans, with realism blending into suggestion, leaving the viewer to swear they were looking at something half photograph, half dream.

Michel allowed the triptych to capture him and lead him as it would. The first panel was outdoors, an early winter in front of a large building Michel only half recognized. It was night, and the suggestion of figures of men seemed to be arriving from the streetlights, more shadow than not, all with a singular purpose. Footsteps and the swirl of snow led his gaze onward.

The middle panel was indoors, a bar of some kind, and though the crowd as a whole was indistinct, two men, tucked together on one side of the image, were clear. The first of the two men moved among the suggested figures, head high, smiling, and was just passing the other, who sat at the bar and watched the passing man. Michel could feel the longing in the moment, the desire for this second man who sat at the bar with his drink, hands on the bar top, frozen in a paralysis Michel could so easily understand. Glancing around the scene, Michel caught more details, letters on glasses and above the bar, and then he realized why the building looked so familiar. It was in the city, downtown. The Lord Elgin.

The final panel of the triptych was the other half of the first, the same suggestion of traffic and motion, but this time in egress. The painting saw people leaving, only the hotel remaining. And just at the outside edge of the panel, barely visible, the hint of a coat or jacket. A single pair of footsteps in the light dusting of snow.

It was Hans, of course. At the bar. He didn't know the other man. Didn't need to. The story in three images was as frank and clear as all of Hans's paintings.

He'd had no idea.

If you think it might require one, I offer my sincerest apology. It was a different time, and then it was too late. I trust in your discretion.

Grief tightened Michel's chest so immediately he had to sit on the bed, and he pressed his fist against the sensation beneath his skin.

Was this why, of all of Hans's students, he'd chosen Michel? Was it as simple as this? An old, closeted gay man asking his former student—his former *queer* student—to make sure no one would ever know?

I trust in your discretion.

He looked at the painting through a welling of tears. He remembered the press of Hans's hands on his shoulders, the guiding strokes of his brush, his constant litany of "every stroke must count," and the backhanded compliments of the direction in which Michel's talents seemed to lie.

You are a powerful mimic, Michel. I don't think I've ever seen anyone who can paint as others paint struggle so hard to find a style of his own.

"I'm the mimic?" Michel said. "You sure had me fooled."

His phone pinged. The sound felt out of place in the room, and he fumbled the phone out of his pocket. It was a text from Jill.

Did you want to meet up before the wake?

Michel eyed the triptych again.

He'd never felt so alone.

Yes, he typed his reply.

❖

Just in front of the building, his foot skidded.

"Whoa, Michel," Jill caught his arm. "Are you all right?"

"I don't know," Michel said. He felt dizzy and disconnected. Was that laughter? Music? He blinked away an afterimage of balloons he'd never seen in the first place. "I think…"

It passed. He took a few long breaths, watching his exhalations swirl in the air between them. "Wow," he said. "That was…That was something."

"Are you sure you want to do this?" Jill said.

"I arranged it," Michel said. "I should really make a showing."

The wake for Hans Köhler wouldn't have fit in his own small gallery, so he'd rented a larger venue where he often threw launches for artists with a sizeable catalog. Happily, that meant the owners were handling the coats and greeting and keeping the drinks flowing. He'd almost waited until he could collect art from Hans's studio.

Now he was glad he hadn't. As it was, the pieces on display— some borrowed from private collections, others gathered from galleries around the city and beyond—would fill the venue.

And he hadn't had the images of the triptych in his head when he'd made his selections for the evening.

They went up the steps together, and entered, some of the first to arrive.

The quiet gathering was mostly artists, and at a glance Michel had his suspicions confirmed: none of Hans's family had shown.

He wondered if any of them had known.

"Are you sure you're up to this?" Jill asked.

"I am," Michel said. "And I've decided. I'm going to donate his paintings to the school gallery. They can sell to fund-raise or place them among the collection as they'd like."

Jill's smile was beatific. "That's amazing. Are you sure?"

"He'd have liked that, I think. Or at least, he'd like still being among the school and the students in some way." Michel nodded, looking around the room at the somber, well-dressed crowd. "His family aren't even here. He left the paintings and his studio to me. I don't see why else he'd do that unless he wanted them to be seen." He paused. "Most of them."

Jill tilted her head. "Most of them?"

"Never mind," he said. "It's nothing important." The words felt like ice on his tongue. He shivered into his coat, even as they moved to the coat check.

It was going to be a long evening, and after…

After he'd head back to Hans's studio.

No. That wasn't right.

After he'd head back to *his* studio. It was his now.

He remembered Hans's niece and her husband. He remembered the word he was sure the man had whispered into her ear.

Sue.

Yes. He'd go back to his studio tonight.

He faced each of the paintings in turn, waiting. They stood on the three easels, oiled down and waiting for what he would do. He'd filled the red coffee mug up. He'd left FunkArt in Justin's capable hands, and he'd reread the note so many times he knew it by heart.

Paint over the triptych.

Four words, in the imperative.

His hands shook. Oiling down the canvases to make sure they wouldn't flake had been the first step, but it hadn't *covered* them. It hadn't *broken* their image. That would come once the clear coat had dried, and he picked up a brush and…

And did what?

Michel swallowed, grateful when his phone rang. He glanced at the screen. Justin, calling from the store.

"There was a lawyer just here to see you," Justin said. "You were right."

Michel exhaled. It hadn't taken the niece long, not even one full business day. "Did you tell them where I was?"

"No."

"Thank you."

"Hey, you've sold more of my abstracts than any other gallery. My loyalty can be bought."

Michel laughed. "Well, thank you anyway."

"What are you going to do?"

"Until they serve me, I don't have to do anything. Best guess is they want Hans's paintings he had stored. I'll hide out here until I'm ready. I brought my computer and my phone and my camera. I don't have to answer the door. So I can catalog the collection and work with Jill's people to get the donation documents organized and signed. If they want to sue me after, hopefully that will make things too late, or too complicated. At least, that's what my lawyer said. Hans's will was very well written. I doubt they've got a real shot."

"Do you have everything you need? You think they'll be watching for you there?"

"I'm sure they'll check. I filled the fridge. I'll be fine. This is one time flying solo works to my advantage." Michel laughed. "I don't have to answer the door. I even brought my noise-cancelling headphones."

"Smart man. I can cover the gallery until you're ready."

"It shouldn't take more than a couple of days. There's really only one thing that's going to be a problem." He eyed the triptych.

"Is it something I can help with?"

I trust in your discretion.

"Unfortunately, no. Thanks, Justin. You're going above and beyond here."

"Good luck. I'll let you get to it."

Michel put the phone down on the small table and took a sip of coffee.

Okay. He'd work on cataloging, and when the oil down was dry…

Maybe by then he'd have some idea what to do.

I don't think I've ever seen anyone who can paint as others paint struggle so hard to find a style of his own.

"You're kind of an ass, Hans," Michel said to the room.

❖

It had been a day in his own company, and as he pulled himself into Hans's bed, he wondered how many of Hans's days had been just the same. He'd felt a little paranoid, and the doorbell had indeed rung a few times throughout the day, but so far, so good. His own lawyer kept him up to date with the donation process, he'd heard from Jill, and thanks to the wonders of digital signatures, the paperwork was all under way.

Michel told himself it was the lack of light that made him put off the triptych until the morning. He'd been working hard to give no sign outside the house that he was even present, and luckily Hans's setup had lent itself to that lie. Heavy blinds covered the windows, and if he didn't bother with lights, no one would see him from outside. The bedroom looked over the backyard, but even if some light was getting around the blinds, no one would see from the street.

But as he pulled the covers over himself, he knew it wasn't entirely true. Yes, he wanted good light for working on the three canvases. Of course he did. But what he really needed was some sort of inspiration.

He ran a gallery for a reason. FunkArt was a daily joy. He could connect art with people, and he did that very well. His own painting had lessened after opening the gallery. It was partly time, but only partly.

How had Hans put it? Michel was a *mimic*. He could paint in many styles, and his family had delighted in some of the pieces he'd made for them. The family forger, they'd joked, when he'd recreated a Monet for his mother or a Van Gogh for his uncle.

But creating his own work had never quite reached the same level. People liked his paintings, but that was it. That was all they ever seemed to say.

"I like it."

Damned by faint praise.

His teachers had praised his technical skills and glossed over the lack of emotional impact of his own work, but Hans had never glossed over anything.

There's nothing here. No heart. You paint beautiful, empty things.

Maybe that was what he should do with the triptych. Or at least, he could mirror a style if not a specific piece. Three beautiful, empty things.

He shifted onto his back, staring up into the darkness. The bed was too comfortable. This whole day had been comfortable in a way that unnerved him. This could easily be his life.

He sighed. No. He wasn't Hans. He wasn't closeted, for one. Single, yes, but he didn't hide his queerness from anyone. He wasn't closed off, he was shy. There was a world of difference between the two. If it came down to it, Michel believed he would take a chance.

Maybe that was all he had to give, really. Maybe that would do. He could paint something beautiful, something technically gorgeous. Hell, he could even do it in Hans's own style.

He closed his eyes and willed himself to sleep.

Michel painted.

He moved from one easel to the next, spending time with each panel of the triptych and working carefully to both obscure what had been and to build from what was already there. He grew more sure of the balance with every step, something directly in his own lane.

A talent for mimicry.

Hans had painted his suggested imagery with a cadence Michel found easy to echo. He borrowed the technique but took the pieces in another direction.

In *his* direction.

Under Michel's brush, spring had come to the Lord Elgin Hotel. Instead of the dusting of snow, petals of pink and soft yellow littered the sidewalk. Daylight spilled instead of lamplight, and the cold hues of the stonework were replaced with warm sunshine. Inside, what had been a dimly lit bar full of half-seen figures now burst with light.

Instead of peering through shadows, the triptych became an image of squinting into brightness.

Paint over the triptych.

Michel did, though he refused to destroy it.

You will know the one.

And he did know the one. He lived the same one, after a fashion, and in his own way. Decades later, perhaps, but trapped. By his own tongue and his own thoughts, rather than laws and justified fears.

If you think it might require one, I offer my sincerest apology.

It didn't. The more he painted, the more sure Michel was of that beyond all else. It didn't require apology. Not at all. If anything, he should have been apologizing to Hans.

I'm sorry this was the world for you.

I'm sorry I never noticed, never reached out.

I'm sorry the best I can do is oil on canvas, in your own strokes, in your own style.

He transformed the hotel, piece by piece. The realism and suggestion both tinted instead of shaded, the tone of the piece Michel created over top of Hans's was, step by step, changing to something brighter.

It was a different time, and then it was too late.

Well, now it's not. Look at you now.

This took longest of all. The passing figure in the bar tilted his head just so, his eyes aimed just a little farther to the right. His left hand, raised in a small wave to the people suggested all around him, no longer seemed like an invitation so much as a simple acknowledgement. Yes, friends, that wave says, I see you. But just a moment.

At the bar, Hans's shoulders are higher, his gaze up. He reaches out to the man passing through the bar, and that man's right hand is reaching back.

It's spring. And that man? That man sees you looking.

I trust in your discretion.

I hope you can.

On the edge of the final panel, two shirts are barely visible among the breeze of petals.

Michel took a step back. Tears came, and he let them. The red cup was long empty. He was thirsty. But he stood still a long time, regarding the triptych, allowing it to lead his eye on the same path, only different.

He filled the mug with water from the bathroom and crawled into the small bed. He needed to shave, but he didn't care. He'd never felt so free as he did in that moment, trapped in that house by lawyers and families and the request of his teacher.

❖

In the morning, he felt fuzzy and off. He stumbled into the side of the bed walking out of the little bedroom, misjudging the space, and made it across the hall to the studio. The paint was dry enough to treat, and Michel got to work before he even thought of breakfast. Once it was coated, though, his hunger returned. He went back to the bedroom for the single red mug, then stopped. He kept blinking. He was looking at the world through a haze that wouldn't clear no matter how often he wiped at his eyes. He gripped the mug.

The texture was off.

An unease that raised the hair on the back of his neck washed over him, and he turned. The room itself, the two bedside tables, the lamps, the little shelf of books…

The bed. He wiped his eyes. It didn't help. Was it the bed?

He frowned at it, not quite sure what was upsetting him.

It was, after all, just a queen-sized bed.

He bit his bottom lip and shook his head. He stopped at the bathroom to splash water on his face, but it didn't help the cottony feeling determined to wrap itself around him. Though he peered into the reflection, he could see nothing wrong with his eyes, and the blurriness seemed to be fading. It should have made him feel better. It didn't. He wiped his face with one of the green towels, and the feeling of *wrongness* returned.

He eyed everything in the room. The shower curtain, the towels—a set in green and another in white—even the little mat. It was all mundane, all…

Between breaths, he *felt* a shift. Like something he heard behind him, only there was no actual sound, just the pressure of *change*.

He turned. It took him long minutes to see what bothered him.

Toothbrushes. His own, which he had brought. Hans's.

Another.

Had someone broken in? Had the niece hired someone to come into this place? He took the stairs as fast as he dared, but at the bottom, the door was locked.

There were bookcases in the living room. Tall ones. The room itself had been divided and was more full than it had been because of it. The front half held so many books, the back half the paintings, still in the racks in the order he'd returned them after taking photos, cataloging them for Jill and…

It was harder and harder to think. Like the barrier between him and the world was growing more solid around him, and he wasn't keeping pace. The bed. It was bigger. Two sets of towels. Toothbrushes. Books.

The blurriness was almost gone, the clear sheen fading like…

Oh God.

Like paint. Like a painting. Like a painting almost dry.

Michel turned for the stairs again.

Too late.

❖

Just in front of the building, his foot skidded.

"Whoa, Michel." Jill caught his arm. "Are you all right?"

"I don't know," Michel said. He felt dizzy and disconnected. It grew too quiet and too dim. He blinked away an afterimage of dark-suited men he'd never seen in the first place. "I think…"

It passed. He took a few long breaths, watching his exhalations swirl in the air between them. "Wow," he said. "That was…That was something."

"Are you sure you want to do this?" Jill said.

"Danya is expecting us," Michel said. "We should really make a showing."

The wake for Hans Köhler couldn't have fit in his own small gallery, so Michel had suggested a larger venue where he often threw launches for artists with a sizeable catalog. In Danya's hands, the space had been transformed into a dizzyingly bright party, with balloons and music and more people from the Village than Michel had realized knew Hans and Danya.

They went up the steps together, and entered. He shared a glance with Jill. He'd honestly thought they'd be some of the first to arrive.

Danya greeted them a moment later, waving to a group of laughing men in his wake.

It looked familiar.

"Ma Belle. You made it," he said. Michel shook off the déjà vu and smiled at the nickname.

"How are you?"

"I am having a grand time," Danya said, then glanced to Jill. "Jillybean, darling. You look beautiful."

"I wore red, like you said I should."

"I refuse to throw a dismal wake. I know Hans would probably go traditional, but if he'd wanted dibs on designing a funeral, he should have let me die first."

They all pretended not to hear the hitch in the man's voice.

"Drop off your coats," he said, after recovering. "I need to check on the wine, but then we'll catch up. The place is full of old queens, and we are going to celebrate in style."

They moved to the coat check. It was a raucous mix of artists and queers of varying ages, many of whom had been mentored by Hans like he and Jill had. At a glance, Michel had his suspicions confirmed: none of Hans's family had shown.

Their loss.

He smiled, then frowned. A coolness ran up the back of his neck.

"Are you sure you're up to this?" Jill asked.

"I am," Michel said. "Sorry. I'm a little out of it. It's just *this*."

"This?"

"There's not enough of this."

Jill turned to him. "I don't follow?"

"This…" Michel gestured to the room at large. "All of us together, telling stories, sharing our history. There's not enough of it." As full as the room was, he knew from Hans's and Danya's stories how *empty* it was as well. How many people *weren't* here.

"You can't fix history." Danya's voice was warm, and he turned to see the little grey-haired man had reappeared behind him, arms wide. "Come here, Michel Ma Belle." He sang the words.

They hugged.

"So," Danya said, letting go. "You will notice we borrowed the staff from local bars, and there is a bartender in particular working across the room."

"Danya." Michel colored.

"Who's this?" Jill grinned.

"*Clive*," Danya said, drawing the word out into a long breath. "The last time we took Michel here to lunch, he barely strung two words together, he was so busy watching Clive work the bar."

"Clive is handsome," Jill said, rising on her tiptoes to look past the crowd.

"Both of you, stop it," Michel said.

"Sweetie," Danya said. "It's Hans's wake. I'm the bereaved party. I get my way tonight."

"Oh Jesus," Michel said, but he laughed.

"I meant what I said, Ma Belle."

"Sorry?"

"You can't fix history, Michel, but you can repeat it." Danya patted his shoulder and eyed Clive with a knowing look before turning back to him. "And let me tell you, there's nothing more attractive than a shy man reaching out. Now. If you'll excuse me, I'm going to do my duty to capitalize on the moment and hit some of these rich queens up for a donation to the Village Legacy Project while they're weepy and half in their cups. Marion would simply whip me if I didn't take the opportunity."

"You're unstoppable."

"I am," Danya said. "I'm also a role model."

He left with purpose, and Michel watched him enter a small group of men in their fifties or so. All wore well-tailored suits. He shook his head, amused, then took a breath.

Jill drifted off to speak to someone she knew, and he took a moment to look around the room—and not at a certain bartender. Hans's paintings were hung all over, many on loan from local galleries he'd worked with. It had been a labor of love helping Danya choose the pieces, and there'd been one series he'd never seen before, something they'd hung in their home.

There it was.

Three panels. He'd heard Danya tell salacious stories about the so-called Lord Organ Hotel, and how it had been quite the gay meeting place back in the day. He'd known him long enough to know when he was embellishing the truth a bit, though, and he knew just how limited they'd been at the time. Illegal. Persecuted. Moving through shadows, ducking past notice.

The triptych told a different story. Two men meeting and starting an amazing life together, all thanks to a single moment of courage from a shy man. They'd outlived so many, lived through so much, and the Village Legacy Project owed a great deal to their donations and time and memories. He'd been damn lucky the day Hans Köhler had accepted him into his class. If it wasn't for him, he might never have opened FunkArt.

He'd miss that man. He wished he had something more to give.

You can't fix history, Michel.

Something about that bothered Michel, but as he looked at the warm spring colors of the triptych, he couldn't quite put his finger on it.

But you can repeat it.

He gave the triptych one last glance, took a deep breath, raised his shoulders in a gesture he hoped would at least pass for courage, and went to order a drink.

Red isn't love, but it's not only anger, either.

It is anger, of course. Bright, vibrant red will roil like a storm, anger gathering above and around someone with the same promise of ruin and fury. The brighter the red, the more emotion is at play, and the tighter the clouds, the more compact and controlled, the larger the fury will be when it breaks.

But red can be more. Pale reds are anger turned inward: embarrassment, or shame, often made by their own hand. Be gentle with those paler reds and pinks, as it's not hard to deepen them with the wrong word and give birth to an anger instead.

The deeper reds, the richer reds, the ones reaching within and spreading out like wings? Those reds change the world. People march with those reds, they defend with those reds, and they fight tooth and nail with those reds.

Determination is a kind of anger, aimed at the unjust.

Every time I've seen someone facing down the unfair, I have hoped to see the reds darken and spread out behind them. I've hoped to see them ready to fight.

Ready to try.

A Little Village Magic

"Hold this."

Gabe turned, sighed, and held out his hand. Behind him, Bailey Haliburton held something in her hand over his open palm.

"Did you just sigh at your boss?" she asked.

"Maybe a little," Gabe said.

"Gabe, love, that's what we call a 'career limiting move.'" Bailey smiled as she said it, though. She dropped a small clear purple crystal into his hand.

Gabe looked at it. "Amethyst?" he said.

"Yes." She peered at him. "Anything?"

Gabe regarded her with a patient smile. He loved Bailey, who was the best boss he could hope for. Working at Third Eye was perfect for him. Bailey scheduled him around his university classes, letting him work mostly evenings and occasional weekends to give herself a break. He didn't want to insult her. She was very much like the cool aunt he'd never had.

"It's pretty?" he said.

Bailey took the crystal back. "I don't understand." She peered at it like it was broken, and then she tucked it into her pocket.

"It's possible I'm just not…uh, mystically inclined." Despite the many courses he was taking on philosophy, comparative religions, and mythology, he wasn't a big believer in much of anything. He'd learned pretty early having faith in anything but yourself left you open to getting knocked on your ass.

"Nope," Bailey said, waving her hand. "The first time you walked in, I felt your potential. You're humming with it, Gabe. I'm just having a hard time undoing the locks."

Gabe couldn't help but grin. The idea that Bailey, self-professed Fairy Godmother of the Village, felt some sort of potential in him was charming, if silly. She didn't have wings, or a wand, or a glittery tiara. Instead, she wore an orange blouse cut low enough to show off her curves and a long black skirt that hugged her hips.

She always wore handmade jewelry she got through FunkArt, the art gallery across the street and a couple of doors down. Today it was understated: simple silver bands on her fingers, a black leather and silver wire bracelet, a carnelian teardrop in the hollow of her throat, and matching earrings. Bailey wasn't particularly tall, so the heels on her black pumps were pretty impressive. They could look eye-to-eye when she wore those shoes, which reminded Gabe of just how not-tall he was himself. She was pretty, too, with an oval face, kind hazel eyes, and dark brown hair she usually wore in a French twist.

No, she didn't look like a Fairy Godmother, or even a witch with a gift for crystals, as she claimed. If anything, given all the orange and black, she looked like Hallowe'en.

He kept that thought to himself.

"How's the day been?" Gabe asked, changing the subject.

Bailey let out a breath. "Slow." He'd heard that far too often and was starting to dread it. Sure, it was only May, it would pick up during Pride, but post-Christmas hadn't really been hopping, and from the conversations Gabe had overheard Bailey having with some of the other business owners in the Village, Third Eye wasn't the only place having a slow year.

"I'll try and sell one of the geodes," Gabe said. People often exclaimed upon seeing them, but their exclamations generally ended when they looked at the price tag.

Bailey laughed. "Please do. Oh, and we got more books. I left them for you."

Gabe perked up. "Thank you." Third Eye had a great little spirituality, self-help, new-age, and religion selection, and it was Gabe's favorite part of the store. He did like the crystals and the candles and the rest of the paraphernalia that was Third Eye's stock-in-trade, even if he thought Bailey's belief in the properties of stones was far-fetched. But he loved the books the most. Some were kind of hokey spell books to attract lovers, that sort of thing, but many had a decent depth of research to them. He'd learned more about Druids, Buddhism, and Kabbalah here than he had in some of his university classes.

Bailey nodded back toward the checkout counter, and Gabe wandered over. She started wiping down the glass cases of crystals, and he found the order tucked neatly behind the counter. He lifted the first box onto the countertop and carefully cut the box open.

"Yes!" he said, opening the box. The first book he could see was *The Sternglantz Encyclopedia of Symbology*. He'd had Bailey order two copies so he could pick one up for himself as soon as they arrived. It came highly recommended. Sternglantz was a genius of research and knew her stuff cold. This book was going to make his academic life so much easier. He flipped open the book and felt the excitement tingle through his fingertips. The Futhark runes, the talismans, the angelic script—it all struck him as so darn pretty.

"Officer Hotbody," Bailey said, breaking his reverie.

Gabe looked up. Sure enough, the sinfully delicious police officer who often walked the Village was strolling by.

"I've done wrong," Gabe said. "I should be arrested."

"Get in line, kid," Bailey said.

Tall and buff, Officer Hotbody didn't glance their way. He generally looked straight ahead as he walked. He wore his dark hair buzzed almost to the scalp, and the one time Gabe had actually made eye contact with him outside the store, Gabe had been tongue-tied at how dark Officer Hotbody's eyes had been. When Bailey had asked him what the police officer's name was, Gabe had had to admit he'd been so thunderstruck he hadn't thought to look at his name tag.

He hadn't had another opportunity since, either.

"I think his arms are bigger than last time," Gabe said. He was pretty sure Officer Hotbody's thick biceps were bigger than Gabe's thighs.

"All the better for resisting arrest," Bailey said.

"Aren't you married?"

"My husband likes 'em big and strong, too."

They shamelessly walked the full length of the front windows, craning their necks to watch as the man left their field of vision. As the cop reached the intersection, Gabe noticed the side of FunkArt for the first time.

"Hey, what happened to the memorial?"

Bailey exhaled. "Someone defaced it."

A thick heat pooled in the pit of Gabe's stomach. The memorial had been on the side of FunkArt since before Gabe had come to university and discovered the little gay village strip. A simple list of names beneath a single rainbow stripe, the small plaque that was attached indicated they were all local lesbian, gay, bisexual, and trans people who'd been in some way important to the movement in the city or who had fallen at the hands of hate crimes. Or both. Standing in front of those names had been a life-changing moment. Even though they were people he never knew, could never know, he'd felt for the first time a sense of history to his own queerness. His family hadn't wanted him, but looking at those names, Gabe had caught a glimmer of a whole other family waiting to meet him.

Learning someone had ruined the mural felt like the very memory of that sense of belonging had been damaged. Seeing the whole thing muted with a thin cover of white paint that blurred all the names and left most of it unreadable was startling. Erased like it had never been. He clenched his fists and realized he was angry.

"What's Michel going to do?" Michel owned FunkArt.

"He's hiring someone to do something new there. I don't know what he has planned," Bailey said. She looked up at the small clock that hung over the cash register. "Okay. I'm going home. If Mother Marion drops by, let her know I haven't forgotten the shelter drive, I just haven't had time to go through my closets yet. But I am knitting up a storm of socks."

"Will do," Gabe said. "Have a good night."

Bailey got her purse from the back room, and Gabe took a few more seconds to look out the window at the smudged white wall that had once held so many names. It had been such a key part of the Village. He sighed and went back to the cash desk to pull out the rest of the books.

❖

Gabe was tracing his fingers across a Lu symbol in *The Sternglantz Encyclopedia of Symbology*, admiring the symmetry of various Chinese prosperity symbols, when movement outside the window made him glance up. It had been another quiet evening. They hadn't gotten much traffic even though the May weather was nice.

A guy was carrying a ladder and buckets down the street. He seemed to have everything balanced just so, but he wasn't struggling. Gabe got up from behind the cash and wandered over to the front window to watch.

The guy was fair haired and lean. When he crossed the intersection, he turned carefully, swinging the ladder around, before he lowered it to the ground with both buckets. He was right in front of where the memorial had once been. He straightened and stretched, rolling his shoulders, and then he took a couple of steps back, looking up at the space.

He stayed like that for a few minutes, just looking at the hastily covered mural. Gabe noticed how tight the T-shirt was across his shoulders and had no difficulty imagining how nice it would be to rest his head on a shoulder like that. After a while, with a small nod to himself, the man pulled a cloth from one of the buckets and spread it along the bottom of the gallery wall. From the same bucket, he pulled out a can of paint and then a roller and handle and also a brush. He set the ladder up at one corner of the space and then opened the can. When the man started to climb the ladder, Gabe couldn't help but notice his calves, which were roped with muscle.

At the top of the ladder, the man stopped, put the paint can on the top step, and began to cover what had been the memorial with a coat of bright white paint.

"Bye," Gabe said, watching as the last remnants of the memorial were covered. He was sad, though certainly the painter would be fun to watch over the next few days. Those legs alone were worth study.

Gabe turned away from the window and walked back to the cash. A glance at the clock told him he only had a half hour left before he closed the shop. He grabbed the broom and started sweeping. As he swept, he wondered what new mural was in store for the side of FunkArt.

He took another look when he'd finished sweeping and had stacked the receipts for Bailey, but the guy and his ladders were gone. The memorial was now completely covered with a fresh coat of white, and a rope had been put up between two pylons letting everyone know it was wet paint.

Gabe sighed. Maybe they'd just restore it. Repaint the rainbow stripe and put all the names back. Surely someone had a picture or a list of who had been on the wall before? He didn't think he'd ever taken a photo of the memorial himself, but surely it had happened.

He cycled the debit machine through the end-of-day process and printed out the day's sales results through the computer. It wasn't a large total, though at least he'd had some people come in and pick up some crystals, and he'd rung through his own copy of the Sternglantz.

He took a deep breath and exhaled. He had a paper to finish tonight for one of the two summer classes he was taking at the university. It was going to be a late night.

He locked up the shop, his book tucked under his arm, and waited for the bus. More than once, his eyes were drawn back to the large white space where the memorial had been.

❖

"It'd be easier to ask him out if you introduced yourself to him."

Gabe jumped and turned away from the window. He could feel his face turning crimson but feigned nonchalance. "Pardon?"

Bailey just laughed at him. "Aw, sweetie. You've got a bit of a crush, huh?"

Gabe exhaled. "It shows?"

Bailey didn't laugh at him a second time, which he appreciated. Sometimes Gabe wondered if the name of her shop, Third Eye, was sort of autobiographical. She certainly seemed a little bit psychic sometimes.

Or maybe I'm transparent.

She'd come in this morning sporting high-heeled boots, a series of silver bracelets, and a low-cut top designed to, in her words, "show off the ladies."

"Well," Bailey said, looking out the window and across the street where Gabe had been staring a few moments earlier. "He certainly has nice shoulders."

"Yep," Gabe said, joining her. "Do you have one of your nonsense spells that makes guys with nice arms notice guys with..." Gabe faltered. "Uh..."

"Good souls?" Bailey offered.

"Thanks. The best I had was 'a good GPA.'"

Bailey shoved his shoulder. "You are far more than your GPA."

"Tell that to the scholarship people," Gabe said. Then they turned back to watch the tall guy with the nice arms, tilting their heads to get the right viewing angle. He'd been there two days in a row, and as far as Gabe could tell, he was cleaning the mural site. He'd coated the wall twice with white paint, and as the day had grown to be one of the first really warm days of the year, he'd shucked his shirt. At that point, Gabe had lost all will to resist watching the painter as he went up and down the ladder.

Which had apparently been obvious.

"First," Bailey said, "it's not nonsense." Gabe gave her a rueful smile. "And second, the best spell in the world is to say hello."

"If you say so."

The little bell over the door rang, and they both turned.

"What are we looking at?"

The woman who'd just arrived was older and had obvious taste. She wore a peach-colored blouse and classy touches of understated gold jewelry, including a lovely pendant that looked like a small leaf dipped in gold. She used a hand-carved wooden cane and walked with the confidence of someone who was not going to slow down.

"Gabe's crushing on the painter," Bailey said.

"Hello, Marion," Gabe said, blushing. It still felt a little weird to him to call the older woman by her first name, but she insisted after the first time they'd met. She was a regular up and down the Village and was one of his favorite people. Bailey had introduced them, surprising Gabe by telling Marion that Gabe was "a fellow castoff." He hadn't known what that meant at first, but Marion had cleared it up for him with her usual blunt honesty.

"Ah, my parents were like that, too. Fuck 'em. Welcome to your new family."

He'd fallen in love with her on the spot. Most of the people in the village called her Mother Marion.

"Too much penis for me," Marion said, peering through the window at the painter. "I heard about the mural." She frowned. "Assholes."

"Do they know who did it?" Gabe said.

Marion shook her head. "No one saw. It got vandalized overnight."

"I didn't hear anything," Bailey said. Like many of the businesses in the Village, Third Eye had two apartments overhead. Bailey and her husband lived in one.

"Are they going to put the names back?" Gabe asked.

Marion smiled at him. "I hope so."

It occurred to Gabe that for Marion, many of those names were people who'd lived and breathed in her lifetime.

"Why don't you go ask him?" Bailey said. "Then you could introduce yourself."

"Yeah, right," Gabe said.

"Would you?" Marion said.

Gabe froze, looking at her. Oh no. "Uh," he said.

"It would be a load off my mind," Marion said. She leaned heavily on her cane and looked over her glasses at him. "My dear Chantal was on that wall."

Well, shit. Chantal was Marion's late wife. What was he supposed to say to that?

Gabe squirmed. "Okay," he said, voice cracking. He coughed and looked at Bailey. "I'll be right back." He tried not to glare at her.

"Wait," Bailey said. "You need some bling."

Gabe gritted his teeth while Bailey went to the jewelry case. He was wearing a white T-shirt and a pair of comfortable jeans. No bling was going to make him look anything other than a boring lanky nerd with kind of poofy black hair. She came back with a thin silver necklace with a square of dark grey metallic stone on it, polished to a high shine. She undid the clasp and put it around his neck, leaning over him.

"There," she said. "You look great."

It took all his willpower not to stick his tongue out at her.

"I'll wait right here," Marion said. Was it just Gabe, or was her voice wavering? "I could use a rest."

Gabe nodded, smiled tightly at them both, and left the store.

Marion snickered. "That boy looks like he's going to pass out."

"You were a little over-the-top there," Bailey said. "'I could use a rest'? Really?"

Marion shrugged. "Over-the-top was that necklace."

"Pardon?" Bailey's eyes widened, the picture of innocence.

"Dear, when you first opened this place, you gave me something just like it when I told you I felt foolish going on a first date at my age. You said it created confidence and opportunity." The grand dame of the

Village leaned forward. "I started bumping into her so often I felt like a stalker. That lady and I were together for ten wonderful years, and I have been thanking you ever since. So don't tell me you didn't give that boy the same shiny rock."

"Hematite," Bailey said. "Don't say anything to him. He's not a believer."

"If I didn't know better," Marion said, narrowing her eyes, "I'd say you were meddling in love lives again."

"You want to watch through the window?"

"Who do you take me for?" Marion rolled her eyes. "Of course I do."

❖

Gabe was grateful the guy had come back down the ladder and put his shirt back on. In fact, it looked like he was packing up. He just hung the Wet Paint sign on the rope as Gabe arrived. No one else was on the corner, thankfully. If things went south, at least there'd be no witnesses. Gabe shivered despite the warmth of the sun and the clear skies.

He could do this. He could ask a complete stranger about a wall. He was a smart man. Conversation was something smart people could do. He was standing right behind the guy, and this was insane.

Speak.

"Are you going to repaint the memorial?" Gabe forced himself to say the words.

"Jesus!" The guy jumped, nearly knocking over one of his buckets, and turned, pressing a hand against the center of his chest.

Gabe took a step back. "Sorry." His face was burning.

The guy laughed. "No, it's fine. I didn't notice you were there."

Story of my life. "Didn't mean to scare you," Gabe said. "Really."

The guy nodded, dropping his hand. Up close, his hair wasn't just fair, it was the kind of blond with patterns of lighter and darker strands in it, an effect people spent a lot of money on in salons, but his looked natural. He was definitely handsome, too. Great eyebrows. Little dent in his chin. When he smiled at Gabe, obviously embarrassed at having been surprised, Gabe saw a small gap between his front teeth and decided it was the most adorable thing that had happened to a smile ever.

"Yes," the guy said.

Gabe blinked. "What?"

"Yes, I'm repainting the memorial. Redesigning it, actually, once I figure out what I want to do." He shrugged. "Michel gets the final vote, but I've been working on some ideas." He looked at the fresh coat of white paint. The wall looked very much like a blank canvas now. "I can't believe someone ruined it."

"I can," Gabe said. "But I don't have much faith in humanity." He groaned inwardly. *Yes. Definitely lead by mentioning you're a misanthrope who thinks everyone sucks. Now he'll be sure to want to get to know you.*

The guy nodded. He was a bit older than Gabe, maybe. It was hard to tell. He was lean and fit, and he had the softest green eyes.

Gabe remembered why he'd come in the first place. "Will you put the names back on?"

"I think so," the guy said. "But I want to splash it up a bit." He paused. "Here, let me show you." He reached down into one of the buckets and pulled out a battered sketchbook. He opened it and flipped a few pages, stopping at one in particular. He showed it to Gabe.

Gabe leaned forward, eager to see what the painter had come up with. He was impressed. It was done in colored pencil, and made with simple, light strokes, but the idea was obvious. What began as a typical pride rainbow broke apart and crisscrossed in a series of interwoven X's. Where the stripes crossed there were silhouettes of figures. Some were dancing, some were kissing, some were holding hands. It was stylized and modern and really cool, and more celebratory than the old memorial.

"I like it," Gabe said. "Very eye-catching."

"I'm not sure about the repeating pattern," the guy said. "I'm wondering if it might seem too negative? Like a big ol' sign of X's."

"In Futhark, an X would be Gifu. That means partnership."

The guy tilted his head. "Futhark?"

"Runes," Gabe said. "It's an old language." He felt his face burning again. *Hi. I'm a misanthrope who likes to talk about dead symbology. Isn't it amazing I'm still single?*

"Cool," the guy said. Then, to Gabe's surprise, he stuck out a hand. "I'm Justin."

"Gabriel," Gabe said, shaking. "Everyone calls me Gabe, though."

They stood there a moment. Justin cleared his throat.

"Well, I need to tidy up and get going," he said.

"Of course," Gabe said. "Thanks for showing me the sketch. I'll see you around. I work over there." He pointed at Third Eye. "I've been watching you through the window."

You did not just say that.

"Ah," Justin said.

"Okay. Bye," Gabe said, and fled.

❖

"His name is Justin, he's redesigning the memorial, and yes, he's going to put the names back," Gabe said, stepping back into the store. The bell rang again as the door closed. "Also, I told him I watch him through the window."

Marion leaned over to Bailey. "Maybe a bit too much confidence?"

"Hush," Bailey said. "I'm sure he was flattered."

"Oh yeah, totally," Gabe said. "I'll just make sure to use the back door from now on so he doesn't take out a restraining order." He reached up to undo the necklace Bailey had put around his neck. The clasp refused to open. "Also, this won't come off."

"Keep it." Bailey waved a hand. "It suits you."

"I should go. Thank you for the socks," Marion said. Gabe saw she had a paper bag with her now, and remembered Bailey had been knitting socks. Marion helped the local shelters keep themselves stocked in clothing. Socks were high need.

"Any time," Bailey said.

Marion waved to them both, walking out with the bag in one hand and her cane in the other. The bell jingled again.

"So," Bailey said. "Tell me all about it."

Gabe shook his head. "Too mortifying. Doesn't matter. He's way out of my league. He's really hot."

"Don't do that. You're cute."

Gabe sighed. On a good day, he might have agreed with Bailey, but today was not that day. He felt too skinny, and his black hair was doing that puffy thing it did when he really needed to get it trimmed. Back when his father still spoke to him, he'd told Gabe their family was a Heinz 57 special sauce. His grandparents were, geographically speaking, somewhat mixed. His mother's mother was Lebanese, and his mother's father Greek. On his father's side, his grandmother was Métis, and his grandfather was French Canadian. He'd grown up speaking four languages poorly—though he was working on his Michif—and answering the question "Where are you from?" every time he met someone who realized he wasn't just sporting a tan. Tall blond guys with wide shoulders didn't generally realize Gabe existed at all.

He looked at Bailey. She meant well. "It's fine. Really. I'm sure he already has a boyfriend. Assuming he's into guys."

Bailey just shook her head. "Don't sell yourself short, Gabe. I mean it. You're short enough already."

"Ba-dum-bum," Gabe said, but he smiled. "You're here all week."

"Don't forget to tip your waiter."

"Isn't it time for you to go home?" Gabe asked.

Bailey nodded. "You're okay if I go?"

"I've got a paper to work on, and I'll sell as much as I can." He certainly hoped for a better night than the last couple.

Bailey gathered her purse, and Gabe took his bag from the cash desk. Once she left, Gabe pulled out his notebook and uncapped his pen, and looked across the shelves of stock. Third Eye was like a second home to him; he wanted it to do well. He tapped his pen against the page a few times, then got to work.

He didn't look out the front window again.

❖

"Save me from myself," Gabe begged the next morning. Like the rest of the short line of customers, he'd waited his turn to get to the front of the queue at NiceTeas, where it was finally his turn to order a drink.

"Rough day at summer school?" Ivan asked. Ivan owned NiceTeas. Other than Third Eye, NiceTeas was Gabe's favorite spot in the Village. The tea shop wasn't frenetic, like Bittersweets, the coffee shop, and he often came here when he needed to power through some chapters. Even when the place was packed, NiceTeas stayed quiet. Gabe liked to think the customers had some unspoken agreement that tea was more civilized and calm than coffee.

Gabe had been coming here for over a year, and he trusted Ivan to whip up something that suited his needs. The man had a knack for blending teas. He'd even found a matcha that Gabe could stand, which Gabe had figured impossible.

Gabe considered telling Ivan about the awkward verbal vomit he'd dumped on Justin, but decided against it. Instead he said, "I'm having trouble focusing on things that are good for me," which was a white lie and a misrepresentation but close enough to truth. He was focusing on Justin. That wasn't good for him. Hot guys never liked him back.

Ivan nodded. Not for the first time, Gabe wondered why he couldn't just crush out on someone like Ivan. Ivan exuded calm charm and was good looking in a mysterious-stranger way. Even if he had a few more tattoos than Gabe thought strictly sexy, he was still a great guy and a fantastic listener.

But Gabe's sex drive didn't ping for Ivan. He knew this because he could speak to Ivan without saying something stupid within the first few seconds.

"Got just the thing," Ivan was saying. "White tea, hibiscus and blueberry."

"Perfect," Gabe said. He handed Ivan three toonies and waved off the change. He felt better already. Maybe he'd stop obsessing over telling Justin he was staring at him like some sort of pervert.

"That sounds good," a voice said. "I'll try that, too, if I can?"

Of course, Gabe thought.

"Sure," Ivan said. He stepped back to the many metal tins that lined the wall behind the brewing area. "It'll be about four minutes." He set to work.

Gabe took a deep breath and turned. "Hi," he managed.

"Working today?" Justin said. That little gap between his front teeth mocked Gabe. Gabe was sure that little gap wanted him to suffer. "It's Gabriel, right?"

"No," Gabe said, then shook his head. "I mean yes. Yes, I'm Gabriel. Gabe. But no, I'm not working." If there was any justice, he'd just have a massive coronary right now. "I've got a ton of reading to do for a class. I like the quiet here."

"What are you reading?" Justin asked.

"I'm rereading the Narnia series," Gabe said. "I'm writing a paper on religious allegory in children's literature."

"Oh." Justin nodded politely.

"I'm not religious," Gabe said. "I just study it."

Justin revealed the little gap again. "Now, that's interesting. You think you needed to tell me you weren't religious."

"Is this the part where you tell me you're a devout Mormon?"

Justin frowned and crossed his arms. "Is that a problem?"

Gabe blinked. "Oh, wow. I'm so sorry. No, I mean, of course not…uh…"

Justin laughed. "I'm not a devout anything."

Gabe let his breath out in a whoosh. "I am not good at talking around you," he said. Then he closed his mouth and clenched his jaw before more words escaped. What was it about the guy that turned him into an idiot? Y'know, other than the shoulders that didn't quit, and the eyes that swallowed you whole, and the lips that looked like they'd be pretty damn soft to kiss…

Even Justin's laugh was sexy. "You're kind of adorkable."

"Like a chia pet." *What? Oh my God, what's wrong with you?*

"Two teas," Ivan said, and Gabe all but threw himself at the counter to get his tea. That was the longest four minutes of his life. He picked up his cup.

"For you," Ivan said, nodding at Gabe, "add some honey." Then he looked at Justin. "I think you'll like it better without."

"Thanks." Gabe walked off to the small counter where the milks, creams, and sweeteners were kept. He squeezed a little honey into his tea, which smelled wonderful.

"I have a question," Justin said.

Gabe jumped. He hadn't realized Justin had followed him.

"Now we're even," Justin said. There was that little gap again.

"Fair enough. What's the question?"

"You said the X's were like a rune. For partnership?"

"Yeah, Gifu. From the Futhark alphabet." Gabe stirred his tea, watching the honey melt away from the bottom of his cup. He brought it up to his lips and took a small sip. It tasted wonderful, and despite the hot guy who was talking to him—actually talking to him!—he felt a calm warmth spread through his stomach.

Forget Bailey's crystals. The real magic in the world was tea.

"Right. Futhark." Justin said the word awkwardly. "Well, I showed my first idea to Michel, and he wasn't sold." He paused, and tasted his own tea. "Wow. This is good." He looked across the shop. "Do you mind if I sit with you for a little bit? Maybe pick your brain about something?" He smiled. Gabe swore little motes of light gathered in the corners of his eyes. "I promise I won't keep you long."

"Sure." Gabe closed his mouth so he couldn't say anything else to ruin the perfectly functional conversation they were having. They moved to one of the couches near the back. Gabe caught himself touching the silvery-black rock around his neck and chided himself. This had nothing to do with Bailey's necklace, which still wouldn't come off.

They sat.

"Michel wants something with more history to it," Justin said. He put his tea down on the low table in front of them. "I think he thinks my idea was a bit too much in the present. Like, everyone's dancing and partying and celebrating." He shrugged, conceding the point. "He's right. I didn't want something maudlin, but I guess I went too far in the other direction."

"Maudlin is a great word." Gabe snapped his mouth shut again. Apparently, his brain was still set to "moron." He cleared his throat. "Sorry. Go on."

"Well, I thought about your rune thing, and then I thought about maybe going with triangles instead. You know, like the pink and black triangles?"

Gabe did know. The symbols queer people were forced to wear in Nazi camps.

"But," Justin said. "That's maybe too…" He paused, hunting for the right word. "On the nose? I don't know. I want something that's not too depressing. Those names are meant to be a celebration and a memory of people. And I don't want to shortchange it." He sighed. "This is why I usually paint abstracts."

"You paint abstracts?"

Justin nodded. "Yeah." He opened his sketchbook. "Anyway, this is the idea I'm floating right now…" He showed Gabe the page, and Gabe could see the merit right off. It was still the pride rainbow coming undone, but instead of repeating in an "X" weave, it broke off in asymmetrical lines, forming a random pattern. And where lines crossed—often forming triangles—the silhouettes of people were present again, but some were marching and holding signs and some stood, fists raised. Some were dancing and obviously having a good time, but Gabe could see Justin had made an effort to represent earlier times and hard-fought battles.

"You've made an Othel here. And a Kenaz here," he said.

Justin raised an eyebrow. "What?"

Gabe traced the patterns over the sketch: the diamond-with-feet of Othel, and the sideways-V of Kenaz. "More runes," he said. "If you use straight lines, you're going to make runes." He shrugged. "Sorry. I was studying them recently, so I can't help but see them everywhere."

"What do Othel and Kenaz mean?"

Gabe thought about it. "Othel means wealth, but not monetary. Things of value, like friendship, or what a family is supposed to be. Kenaz can mean a torch, or it can mean illumination in a symbolic way, like learning. But they're touching, which makes a bind rune. That turns them less into strict symbols and more into a metaphor, in the realm of luck charms and stuff. If I saw them drawn like that, I'd wonder if maybe it was meant to represent a cherished memory." He smiled. "Like, say, a memorial."

"You really know your runes," Justin said. It didn't feel like teasing.

"I like symbology," Gabe said. "I like finding the commonalities in different cultures and beliefs. It reminds me we're not all so different. There have been places and times for all kinds of people, even if they don't feel it now."

Justin put down the sketchbook. "Maybe that's my problem."

"Sorry?"

"I feel like the least qualified person to paint this mural." He ran a hand through his hair. Gabe watched what it did to the guy's lean biceps. It took a second for his brain to catch up.

"Why?"

"Being gay? I haven't had any trouble. Like, ever." Justin shrugged. "My mother is a university professor. My stepdad, too. When I came out, my high school already had a GSA. It was an art school, so it was already pretty open. My parents joined PFLAG and never so much as blinked. I look at Michel's list of names, and I feel like an impostor."

"But that's the whole point," Gabe said.

Justin looked at him. "Pardon?"

Gabe took a swallow of tea and warmth moved through him again. "I didn't have that. At all. I grew up in a town of eight hundred people.

I didn't come out until I came here. My folks took it badly, to say the very least, and cut me off. If I hadn't had my scholarship…" He shook his head. "Well. I was on my own. And when I found this place—the Village, not NiceTeas—I got a home again. Bailey, my boss at Third Eye? She's great. She got me through some rough weeks. And Ivan over there? He was one of the first people who ever listened to me when I was really feeling alone. Have you met Mother Marion?"

Justin shook his head. "No."

"You have to meet her. She's amazing. She was here when the Village began. She marched the first marches. When she talks about her relationships, it's incredible. She and her first girlfriend were arrested just for being together. It was them against the world. She's like the grandmother of the whole Village." He grinned. "Y'know, if your grandmother would talk to you about dental dams and quoted dyke beat poetry."

Justin laughed. "Okay."

"But that's what that memorial always meant to me," Gabe said. "It's like those common symbols I was talking about. Those names? They're a family I didn't know I had until I got here. They're the people who made it possible for your school to even have a GSA."

"And that's the point," Justin said.

"Exactly," Gabe said. "We all want a place where no one has to worry they'll lose their family or their friends." He took another sip of his tea. "Or their life. That's the Village."

Justin looked at him, meeting his gaze in a way that made Gabe feel exposed. Why had he said all that stuff?

"You know what?" Justin said.

"What?" Gabe was blushing. He could feel it.

"I think you're talking around me just fine."

"Ah," Gabe said, because he couldn't think of a single other thing to say.

"Symbols," Justin said.

"Yep."

"You're right. That's what those names are, and…" Justin picked up his sketchbook, flipping to a new page, and pulled a pencil out from the spiral of wire that bound the book. With only a few confident strokes, he had a shape like the wall on the side of the gallery, and a few more for the now familiar fractured rainbow effect he wanted to work with. He looked at Gabe again, and the smile he offered made Gabe's stomach flutter.

"I need a crash course in symbology. How would you feel about consulting on a community art project?"

❖

"And then basically we sat there for an hour talking about some of my favorite symbols," Gabe said. "I barely made a fool of myself."

Bailey reached out and tapped the necklace he wore. "Imagine that."

Gabe shook his head. "It's not magic to talk about something I've studied for years." He wandered away from the cash desk and headed to the bookshelves. He stroked the spine of a book at random. "Anyway, he wants to show me his sketches when he's done. He borrowed my Sternglantz."

"Oh." Bailey's grin was self-satisfied.

"What?"

"You loaned him a book?" She tapped her lip with one fingertip. "Flirty minx."

"It's just a book." His face was heating up.

"Right," Bailey said. "I've known you long enough to know you don't loan your books to anyone."

"Just doing my part for the Village."

"Is that what kids call it these days?" Her eyes glinted with amusement.

"Right," Gabe said, pulling a book someone had laid sideways on top of the others and putting it back where it belonged. "It was so sexy. He was there with his tea and I was there with my tea, and we just couldn't hold back." He leaned around the edge of the bookcase and wagged his eyebrows. "We opened that book and we looked at every. Single. Page." His voice dropped. "We didn't even care people were watching."

Bailey fanned herself with her hand. "See? Books are sexy."

Gabe rolled his eyes, but he had to admit showing Justin the various diagrams in *The Sternglantz Encyclopedia of Symbology* had been kind of the best thing ever. Justin got a little line between his eyebrows when he was concentrating, and sometimes when he sketched he bit his bottom lip, which revealed the world's sexiest tooth gap.

"Hmm," Gabe said, noncommittal. "I'm sure he'll give it back, and then I'll never see him again. I don't even know what he does for a living. He's done school. I think he's older than me. He might be thirty."

"Truly, he's ancient," Bailey said, voice flat.

"That's not what I meant, and you know it." Gabe frowned at the second bookcase. Someone had done a number on the alphabet, again. He started reorganizing, even though he wasn't strictly supposed to start work for another half hour. "Though I'm not sure what we have in common. He had those rainbow unicorn parents I've heard so much about. Y'know, the ones who throw you a party when you come out?"

"Lucky him," Bailey said, without malice. Gabe aimed for that level of grace, but often fell short. He knew Bailey's father had not been a positive force in her life. One of the many things they'd bonded over.

"Anyway," Gabe said, kneeling down. It would be easier just to pull all the Wicca books and start over. The little bell rang over the door, and he lowered his voice, not wanting to yell across the store while there was a customer. "It's pretty much pointless. I can barely string two words together around him, he's so damned pretty. Every time he smiles I stare at the gap between his front teeth, and I'm struck dumb. Who knew dental imperfection could be sexy?"

"Did you just make fun of my teeth?"

Gabe froze. Maybe if he didn't move, he could blend into the floor.

"Gabe, your friend is here," Bailey said. She sounded positively giggly.

Gabe exhaled, rose, and turned. Sure enough, Justin was standing by the cash desk with Bailey. He had his sketchbook, Gabe's copy of Sternglantz, and a sly smile that revealed the sexy tooth gap.

"Hi," Gabe said. He looked to Bailey, imploring.

"Well," Bailey said. "I need to run. Thanks for coming in early, Gabe. I'll catch up with you tomorrow. The mister and I are going out on an actual date." She grabbed her bag, slung it over one shoulder, and was out the door before Gabe could have said "traitor."

The bell rang in the awkward silence.

"I brought your book back," Justin said.

"I hope it was useful."

"Let me show you."

"Okay." He left the Wicca books where they lay on the floor and walked over to the cash desk. So what if he'd just declared the guy had sexy teeth. They could be adults.

Justin flipped open the book, turning it around to face Gabe.

"Oh, wow," Gabe said. Justin hadn't just used a couple of symbols, he'd incorporated dozens of them into the design. The fractured rainbow was still there, but instead of splitting into six crisscrossing rays, the Pride Flag seemed to burst into shards. Some of it was fairly obvious. Gabe could see the peace symbol, a fleur-de-lis, and a maple leaf—but there were also runes, a hieroglyph…

Justin had used the symbols themselves like frames, putting the silhouettes inside them. They weren't only dancing. Some marched. Some held fists raised in the air. Some were getting married. And around them, the various symbols Justin had taken from *The Sternglantz Encyclopedia of Symbology* made sense, Gabe realized. Gifu was over the marriage ceremony. And Lu, one of his favorite symbols, and one he'd specifically pointed out to Justin while they'd talked, was there, front and center, within a silhouette of the Village itself. Prosperity. Love. Family. Protection. Knowledge. The symbology was everywhere.

"It's beautiful," Gabe said. When he looked at Justin, he saw Justin was biting his bottom lip, staring at the drawing beside him.

"You think? I figured I needed to make notes on the history—like, where I put stuff about strength and family I put the people marching. Probably doesn't matter if people get it all, though I could explain it across the bottom or something. I can match the names that way, too. I'm sure Michel knows why each person was on the memorial." He looked at Gabe and bit his lip again. "You don't think it's too abstract?"

"I think it's perfect." He meant it.

Justin exhaled. "Good. I'll show it to Michel, and if he okays it, I'll project it, outline it, and then get going." Justin paused. "Wanna help?"

"What?"

"Don't worry. It'll just be painting inside the lines. I'll show you."

"I'm not much of an artist," Gabe said.

"Gabriel," Justin said, and, wow did Gabe like the way Justin said his name. "Relax. It'll be fun. Besides. You owe me."

Gabe frowned.

"Dental imperfection?"

"See," Gabe said. "I was hoping we could pretend that whole thing didn't happen."

"Thanks for the book," Justin said, putting the Sternglantz on the counter. He picked up his sketchbook and headed for the door. The little bell jingled as he opened it, but he paused to look at Gabe.

"You know, most guys just ask why I didn't get braces."

Gabe knew he was turning red. "I'm glad you didn't."

Justin smiled, and let the door close behind him.

❖

As much as he tried not to stare through the windows when he worked in the evenings, he couldn't help but notice the white space on the side of FunkArt was being transformed. To his surprise, Justin had put on yet another coat of white paint. After that, Justin began drawing on the side of the building with a pencil, tracing lines he'd projected onto the white paint with what looked like an ancient overhead machine.

"I might not need you next weekend," Bailey said. She'd gathered her purse and was ready to turn the store over to him for the evening.

"Okay." Gabe kept his voice even. He could use the money, but sales hadn't been so great the last few weekends.

"My man is speaking at a conference, and frankly I don't want to go with him. Since I'm flying solo…" She shrugged. She looked uncomfortable.

"Of course," he said. "It's fine."

She looked out the window. Justin was close to the wall, carefully tracing a line on the new mural. "Maybe you could ask him out."

"Maybe," Gabe said. "Or, y'know, I could throw myself under a bus. That could also be fun."

Bailey shook her head. "He seemed pretty charmed to me."

Gabe looked out the window. "He's very charming."

Bailey put her hand on his shoulder. She didn't touch him often. In fact, people rarely touched Gabe. He figured he put out some sort of don't-touch-me vibe that people picked up on. "What's the worst thing that could happen if you ask him out?"

"I could throw up on him halfway through asking, and he could have me arrested for assault."

She stared at him.

"I think about these things," he said.

"He could say no," she said. "And that's it. How is that different from what's happening now? You're not going out with him now, either."

Gabe didn't know what to say. She was right. "But right now I can pretend it's possible," he said. Admitting it made him feel dumb and not just a little bit pathetic.

Bailey squeezed his shoulder. "Have a little faith."

"Remember who you're talking to?"

She nodded. "I know exactly who I'm talking to." She let go of his shoulder. "When you've been let down by the very people who were supposed to love you no matter what, you understand what an amazing thing faith is." She tugged open the door, making the little bells jingle. "We're the ones who know it's worth the risk."

She left him mulling that over. He watched Justin work. He couldn't see much from across the road, but he could tell how carefully Justin was marking the painted brick.

When Justin stopped and turned to do something with the overhead machine, Gabe saw him look for him in the window. Gabe raised a hand and waved.

Justin waved back, then gave him a thumbs-up and got back to work.

Gabe took a long, deep breath.

Worth the risk, eh?

❖

"Today's the day?"

Justin didn't jump this time. He gestured to the paint cans around him. "It'll probably take a couple of days. I hope to be done by Monday."

Gabe looked at the sketch Justin had taped up beside the wall. The colors were bright and vibrant. It seemed amazing to Gabe that you could use six colors and create something that stylish.

"I can't wait to see it," Gabe said.

"You have a front row seat."

"Actually, I'm not working this weekend. That's why I wanted to talk," Gabe said.

"Oh. What's up?"

"Okay," Gabe said. That little gap derailed Gabe's thoughts for a second. He tried not to hyperventilate. He could do this. Bailey was right. "Since I'm not working," he said. "I thought maybe…"

He froze. It dawned on Gabe that after painting all day, Justin wouldn't want to go out after. He'd probably be sore and dirty and tired. Actually, the more he thought about it, the more selfish the request seemed. *Hey, I'll be all rested and bored. You wanna hang out, even though you'll have stood in the sun all day and be high on paint fumes?*

"Maybe?" Justin said.

"Uh," Gabe said. Crap. "I know you'll be really busy and tired, so…" *Think, Gabe. Think.* "Maybe I could bring you lunches?"

Was it Gabe's imagination or did Justin's smile falter for a second? It was back in a blink. "That's really sweet. Join me and eat with me? That way I'll stop for a half hour or so." Justin knelt and opened the first can of paint. It was a bright red.

"Great," Gabe said. He clenched his fists at his side. Okay, so that wasn't asking him out, exactly, but at least it was spending time together. Y'know. A half hour. Twice. To eat.

Ugh.

"What time do you eat lunch?"

"Anytime after noon." Justin dipped a thin stick into the paint can and stirred up the paint.

"Okay. I'll be back." Gabe tried not to cringe.

"Did you want to give it a shot?"

"Pardon?"

Justin offered him a paintbrush.

"Oh," Gabe said. "I'm not very artistic."

"So you said. Relax. Anyone can paint inside lines."

"Are you sure?" Gabe's voice cracked.

"It's just paint. I promise anything you screw up, I can fix." Justin handed him the brush. Gabe stared at it like it might bite him.

"What should I do?" he asked finally.

"I was going to start with the red because it usually needs extra coats. So, pick a red spot, and paint. I'll outline in black when I've done all the color. There's a map." Justin pointed to the sketch that was taped up.

Gabe looked at the sketch, and right away he saw the red Lu symbol. Prosperity. It was near a silhouette of the Village, with FunkArt's taller building front and center.

"I'll do this part," he said, looking on the white wall for the symbol, which was outlined in pencil. "If that's okay?"

"Absolutely." Justin was already starting on the opposite end, where the red beam of the fractured pride rainbow went off the edge of the mural. While Gabe had decided, Justin had already poured some of the paint into a tray and gotten to work. He'd also poured some more into a second tray, which was obviously for him.

Gabe picked up the tray and dipped the brush into the bright paint.

The moment the paintbrush touched the wall, something changed. The street noise grew muffled, and all the color drained out of the world except for the red. He almost dropped the brush, but the weight of the hematite Bailey had given him seemed to hold him together. It grew cold against the hollow of his throat. Gabe shook.

Paint. A fierce instinct seemed to speak to him. *Just paint.*

As Gabe moved the brush, he felt resistance. A heaviness fought every move he made. He painted the first red arc along the inside of the line. The resistance grew, the pressure building all the more as he reached the bottom of the circle.

Coming back up from the other side of the symbol made his arm ache, pushing against the invisible weight.

What's happening to me?

Even getting more paint on his brush was daunting, as though the air itself was thick. He filled in the circle, and then set to work on the lines within, each stroke more difficult than the last.

Dip the brush, follow the lines, fight the weight. His own voice again, but stronger. Lu, he thought, remembering the symbol's name. *Dip the brush, follow the lines, fight the weight.* It became a mantra.

His hand was shaking on the final stroke, gripping the brush so tight his fingertips whitened. He held his breath and gritted his teeth as he filled the last small space outlined by Justin.

The Lu was done.

The moment he finished, the pressure released. He gasped and fell back from the mural wall. He hadn't realized he'd been leaning against the weight.

"Gabe?" Justin was looking at him, a small line between his eyebrows. "You okay?"

"Yeah." Gabe found his voice. His heart was pounding, and his palms were wet with sweat.

What just happened?

"That looks great," Justin said.

Gabe stared at the Lu he'd just painted. The red shone brighter than the rest of the world. He blinked a few times, but the sense that it was *more* didn't go away.

"Thanks." He couldn't look away.

"If you want to do more, you're welcome to."

Gabriel managed to break his gaze away. His heart was settling back into a regular beat. It took everything he had to smile naturally at Justin.

"Thank you," he said. He needed to get the hell out of here. "I gotta go. Now. Because…" Because? "Because I forgot working. At work. Forgot to go to work. For a thing. I'm not working today, like I said. But I need that thing. Okay. Bye."

He all but dropped the paintbrush in the tray and bolted. He dashed across the crosswalk and started for Third Eye.

He needed Bailey. He needed to ask her what it felt like when she drew magic out of crystals. He had a sick feeling he knew exactly what she was going to say.

Gabriel was pretty sure he'd just become a believer.

❖

He didn't even get a word out. Bailey took one look at Gabe and ran across the store to hug him. She squeezed him so tight he grunted, and then she stepped back and stared, a huge smile on her face.

"Look at you!" She started to clap her hands together, like she was applauding a third-grade play that turned out not to suck completely. "You're totally unblocked!"

He gaped at her, fish-mouthing.

"It's crystals, isn't it? I figured that's why I could tell so easily."

"Bailey."

"Wait, no. The necklace is still answering to me. Hmm." She tapped one manicured fingernail against her lips, staring at the necklace.

"Bailey." His voice was rising, on the edge of hysterical. He reached for the necklace. It needed to come off, now. What had she done to him?

"Oh, sweetie, this is so exciting!" She started clapping her hands again.

That was officially too much. Gabe shook his head, still struggling with the silver chain. The clasp refused to open. "Bailey." The word was more of a strangled noise than anything else.

She stopped clapping. "Gabe?"

He fought back tears. "Please tell me you're kidding. Please." He let go of the necklace, hands shaking.

"Oh, honey," Bailey gathered him back into a hug. "It's going to be fine." She gave him a little squeeze, then leaned back. "It isn't crystals, is it?"

Mute, Gabe shook his head.

"So, what happened?"

"I was helping Justin with the mural. I showed him some symbols I know, from a bunch of different faiths or mythologies or cultures…" Gabe shook his head. She already knew that. "He let me paint one, and suddenly it was like I couldn't move or breathe, like I weighed twice as much as I should. I thought I was going to pass out, but I kept painting the symbol, and when I was done…" He trailed off, looking at Bailey.

"Poof?" she asked, raising one eyebrow.

"Poof," he said. "I guess. Yeah. Poof." A small giggle escaped him. "Poof. Why not?"

"So what was the spell?" Bailey asked.

"Beg your pardon?" Gabe said. His voice was rising again.

"What spell were you aiming for?"

"I wasn't." Gabe's voice shook. "Because I don't believe in magic. I was just trying to ask out a cute guy, which I totally screwed up, by the way."

Bailey nodded. "Okay." She seemed to take that in. "But you definitely unblocked. That hematite is singing. What did you paint?"

"Lu." When he saw Bailey's blank expression, he said, "It's a symbol of prosperity."

"Well," Bailey said. "That's sounds promising."

"I nearly passed out in the middle of the street, and Justin stared at me like I was a drooling idiot, and I ran away, and did I mention *I don't believe in magic*?" His voice rose with every word. Gabe swallowed, then took a long, measured breath.

"Sweetie," Bailey said, "that doesn't matter. That hematite says different."

Gabe gripped the rock in question and the clasp came undone with a tug. He held it out in one hand.

"Hematite doesn't say anything. It's just a freaking rock," he said.

Something lurched inside him. The world dimmed, and he thought he was going to pass out, but a crunching sound brought him back to reality. He blinked.

Bailey cleared her throat. He frowned, not sure what she wanted. She looked meaningfully at his open hand. He looked down.

The hematite was nothing more than fine powder in his palm, the silver chain empty.

Gabe stared at it for a long moment. He'd done that. Somehow. Impossible. He wiggled his fingers, and the fine silver dust that had been the hematite charm drifted to the floor.

"Gabe? Sweetie?"

"I'm gonna throw up."

"I'll get a bucket."

❖

By the time he'd calmed down, and the remnants of the two almost-blackouts had faded completely, Gabe almost convinced himself he'd suffered from mild heatstroke.

Then he looked out the window.

The Lu glowed, even from here. The red circle was brighter than it should be, and it shimmered like air over hot concrete.

Once there'd been no threat of imminent vomit, Bailey had dashed out, saying she'd be right back. He'd stood, numb, eyes drawn over and over to the mural.

Justin had done most of the first red stripe. The difference between it and the glowing, shimmery Lu made Gabe's stomach threaten to revolt again. He turned his back to the window.

"Oh my God…"

The cases where Bailey kept the crystals for sale blazed like the sky on a cloudless night in the middle of the country. At least a dozen of the crystals that Bailey had worn recently or showed to customers radiated light. Like the Lu, but not as overwhelming.

He rubbed his eyes.

The little bell rang, and Gabe turned. Bailey had returned with two stoneware cups, and the scent of a minty tea of some type followed her into the store. She handed him a cup, and he wrapped his fingers around it, feeling the warmth seep into his fingers. He looked down at the tea, trying to stay calm, and…

The tea was glowing. Softer still than even the crystals, but… He peered closer. Yep. There was a pale radiance there all right.

Gabe groaned. "The tea, too?"

Bailey looked surprised. "Really? Huh. Ivan's keeping secrets."

Gabe shook his head. "This is insane. I've gone insane."

Bailey rubbed his shoulder. "Drink some tea."

Gabe drank some glowing tea. It tasted normal, at least. It was minty, but not oversweet. He liked it. He gestured behind him with his free hand, not wanting to look. "Your rocks are glowing."

Bailey's smile was gentle. "I bet it's pretty."

He frowned. "You don't see it? What about the Lu? Can you see the Lu? It's all shimmery and red. Aren't you the expert here?"

"I hear," Bailey said. "You see. Different people, different gifts. I'm sure if I went over to the gallery, I could hear it."

Gabe gripped his cup in both hands. "What am I going to do?"

Bailey took a swallow of her tea. "Well, that's up to you. You don't have to do anything. I quite like what I do. But you'll figure it out." She looked out the window. "You didn't ask him out, eh?"

Gabe snorted. "Wussed out. Offered to bring him lunch instead. Which I still guess I need to do. Then I nearly passed out, and ran away."

"The first time I got a crystal humming I fainted. It gets easier."

"Oh goodie," Gabe said, voice leaden.

"You're scribing," Bailey said thoughtfully. "Which makes sense. You love everything about iconography, don't you?"

Despite the absolute surety that this was all hallucinatory and at any moment he was going to wake up in an asylum, Gabe nodded.

He loved symbology and how the patterns showed up across so many different faiths around the world. How different cultures all seemed to have a connection to the moon and the sun, or things collected into threes. For every holy trinity in one faith, there was a maiden, mother, and crone in another.

"Well." Bailey raised her cup to him. "Now it loves you back."

It might have been the tea, or the pleased look on Bailey's face, but a warmth spread through Gabe then.

What the hell. Poof, as it were.

He raised his cup, and they clinked.

❖

"Delivery," Gabe said.

Justin turned. "I wasn't sure if you were going to make it," he said. Then he stretched, raising his arms high over his head and grunting with the effort. Justin's T-shirt rode up to reveal a thin stripe of his stomach, and Gabe decided arm stretching was second only to tooth gaps.

"Yeah," Gabe said. "Sorry about the abrupt exit. I'm..." He paused. "Sort of an idiot, I guess?" He held up the two white paper bags in one hand. "But I do come bearing the finest of ham and cheese sandwiches from NiceTeas, and Ivan promises me that the iced tea will chase away both the thirst from working in the sun all morning and the bad memories of my aforementioned idiot thing." He carried the teas in his other hand, held tight in a to-go tray.

Justin shook his head. "You're not an idiot."

"Thanks," Gabe said. "Did you need help tidying anything before we take a break?"

Gabe helped Justin put the lids on the open paint cans and cover them up with the drop cloth. They moved two pylons into place, with a Wet Paint sign strung between them.

"Where do you want to go?" Gabe said, picking the bags and teas back up. "The benches on the other side of the street are in the shade, if you'd like." It had turned into a pretty hot day for May.

"That sounds wonderful," Justin said. They crossed the street and Justin sat in front of the Second Page, the bookstore next door to Third Eye. Gabe handed Justin one of the bags and sat down. Justin had already taken a big bite of his sandwich by the time Gabe had opened his own. Gabe watched the handsome man eat and noticed Justin had a smudge of red paint near his right temple. Gabe could imagine him wiping sweat off his forehead and not realizing he'd marked himself.

"What?" Justin asked, after swallowing.

"You've got some paint," Gabe said, tapping his own temple. "Right here."

Justin nodded. "I'm sure I'll be covered in it by the time I'm done."

They ate quietly. Justin was definitely hungry, and when he finished his sandwich, he drank half the tea in one long go. He leaned back on the bench, exhaling. "That was perfect."

"I'll pass along your compliments to Ivan." Gabe hadn't even finished his first half of his sandwich yet.

Justin took a smaller drink of his iced tea. "Thank you for this. It's nice to have a lunch date."

Gabe knew his face was turning red. "You're welcome."

"Did you find what you were looking for?"

"Sorry?"

"At the store? When you left this morning, you said you'd forgotten something."

"Oh," Gabe said. "That. No." He'd gone racing back to the store hoping Bailey could fix what had just happened to him. "No, there's no getting that back."

Justin frowned. "It seemed important."

Gabe looked over at the memorial. The Lu was as vibrant and shimmery as ever.

"I guess I'll find out," Gabe said. He shook his head. "Sorry. I'm a bit maudlin."

"Maudlin is a great word. Does that mean I get more help?" Justin said. "Because you nailed that red circle thing."

"Lu." Gabe took a sip of his iced tea. Ivan was right. It was really refreshing. It also had that odd glow to it, which meant more than Gabe wanted to think about right now.

"Right. The red circle thing." Justin was showing off that little gap between his teeth again, and Gabe wasn't entirely unsure he wasn't doing it on purpose.

"I like you," Gabe said. It just came out. But for once, he found he didn't want to take the words back. Still, he took a big bite of ham and cheese to have something to do other than stare at Justin.

Justin blinked. "I like you, too," he said. It sounded a bit more fragile, though.

"I guess you probably knew that," Gabe said. "And I don't even know if you're single, come to think of it."

"Yes, I'm single," Justin said. His face was faintly flushed, and it suited him. Though, Gabe thought, if he was honest with himself, he was hard-pressed to think of something that wouldn't suit Justin.

"I know we don't know each other very well," Gabe said, "and like I said, I get that I can be an idiot around hotties, but if you'd like to hang out some time, I'd like that. I mean, after today. And tomorrow, if you want more help tomorrow. I'll still bring you lunch tomorrow, so don't worry about turning me down. You still get lunch."

"Hotties?"

"That's not exactly the most perfect compliment. I can probably do better."

"I dunno. I've heard imperfection can be sexy," Justin said. He leaned over and bumped Gabe's shoulder.

Gabe didn't die on the spot, which was really all he could hope for.

"Honestly?" Justin said, and Gabe braced for the worst. "I thought maybe I'd spooked you or something. You ran off. A few times. But I'd enjoy hanging out." Justin took another long swig of his iced tea. "After we get this mural done."

Gabe fought hard not to do something heroically uncool like punching his fist in the air in victory.

"Of course," he said.

If Justin noticed the sudden vim in Gabe's voice, he didn't comment. "You finished your sandwich?" He rolled up his empty bag and stretched again.

Gabe took a last big bite.

"You want to paint the symbols or the stripes?" Justin said.

Gabe looked into Justin's soft green eyes and grinned. He chewed quickly, and swallowed.

"I want to paint the symbols."

❖

The names took the longest, and as far as Gabe was concerned, that was exactly as it should be. Justin had created stencils for the men and women who would be memorialized, but certain letters—lowercase E's, O's, and A's—needed one last stroke of paint to finish them off. They went past their original quitting time on Sunday night, and Gabe finished the last vowels on Julian Mitchell, Hans Köhler, and Chantal Roy's names just as the light was starting to fade. He'd saved Chantal until last. The names formed a border around the top half of the memorial, and they'd left room for twice as many names again, he thought.

Future family.

He climbed off the stepladder and pulled it back from the wall. Justin was crouched at the bottom corner, and Gabe allowed himself a few moments of admiration for the way the man's T-shirt stretched across his shoulders. Even tired and aching from the weird pressure that descended on him with every symbol he'd painted, Gabe felt energized. Bailey was right. It was getting easier.

Justin let out a puff of breath and rocked back on his heels, crossing his legs underneath him and looking up at the memorial as a whole.

"And we're done," he said. He nodded to the bottom corner, where he'd been working. "And there you are."

At the bottom, stenciled in like all the others the wall memorialized, were two more names:

Justin Cochrane and Gabriel Riche.

Gabe's eyes brimmed with tears.

"I'm not sure I deserve the credit." His voice was husky. He was barely holding it together.

"You helped me come up with the idea, and you helped me paint it. You get some of the credit. That's how it works." Justin looked up at him, and his eyes widened in alarm. "Gabriel?"

Gabe shook his head. A tear escaped. He closed his eyes.

He heard Justin scramble to his feet, and a second later Justin had wrapped his strong arms around him. That did it. He choked out a laugh, knowing full well his eyes were leaking like crazy.

"I'm sorry," Justin said, obviously shaken. "I didn't mean to upset you. I didn't think you'd mind…"

"No, no," Gabe said. He laughed again. After one more squeeze from Justin, he pulled back. Justin let go. "I'm not upset, I'm…" Gabe wiped his face. Wow, he really was a colossal dork sometimes. Having his own name join all the others there on that mural, even in a small way? It was…incredible. It made him proud, and sad, all at the same time.

"Gabriel?"

Gabe took a deep breath. "You know, only my family ever called me Gabriel. My friends always called me Gabe. I don't know why. My father wasn't big on nicknames, I guess."

Justin winced. "I can stop if you want."

"No," Gabe said. "I like that you call me Gabriel. And I love being on the memorial. I guess it just struck me how much this meant to me." He nodded at the memorial. "I've been kind of preoccupied, I guess. And seeing it finished, seeing my name on it reminded me. Family. The ones you choose."

Justin took a couple of steps back, right to the edge of the sidewalk, and looked up at the memorial. The sunlight was starting to fade, but they could still see well enough.

"I guess that's your thorn," Justin said. "But what about the rose and the bud?"

Gabe frowned. "Pardon?"

"That's one of my family traditions." Justin shrugged. "When I was upset, my mom used to ask me to look at the whole plant. She said life is like a rose bush: there's the wonderful parts, the roses themselves, the not-so-great stuff, which are the thorns, and the buds, which are the parts you can look forward to. She'd ask me and my stepdad every day when we got home what was our rose, our thorn, and our bud."

"That's sort of wonderful."

"She's a great lady. My stepdad's awesome, too."

"This is the rose," Gabe said, pointing at the mural as a whole. "That whole thing. It's beautiful." He smiled slyly. "And the artist isn't half-bad, either."

Justin looped one arm over his shoulder. "We just need to set up the pylons and the Wet Paint sign, and then we can go. Oh and, Gabriel?"

"Yeah?" Gabe said, and turned.

Justin kissed him.

He pulled Gabe in with one arm, letting the kiss linger. His lips were definitely as kissable as they looked, and when Gabe traced Justin's bottom lip with his tongue, Justin opened his mouth and their kiss deepened. Gabe held on, sliding one hand behind Justin's back and pressing up against him.

Warmth flushed from his chest. He never wanted this to end, ever.

Someone whistled.

The two broke apart, and Gabe remembered they were standing in the middle of the street, Village or nay. He stepped away from Justin and turned his head, bracing, cursing himself for allowing that moment to stop him from thinking about how unsafe that kiss was—

—and saw Marion. She stood there, cane in hand, eyes full of mischief.

"Don't stop on my account," she said. "I just came to look at the wall."

Gabe's heart was racing. He looked up at Justin, who looked a little embarrassed himself.

"Justin," Gabe said. "This is Marion." He turned and pointed. "Chantal was her wife, and..." He found the image of the silhouettes holding up signs. "The photo you based this on? This is Marion and Chantal, right there, front and center."

"Best first wife a woman could have." Marion stared at the wall, looking over her glasses at the painted figures. After a moment, she turned. "It's perfect. Thank you, Justin."

"You're welcome, ma'am."

She raised an eyebrow. "You're new here, so I'll forgive you that, just this once. It's Marion. Some of the young ones even call me Mother Marion. I'll also accept Dame. Or even 'Hey, lady.' But never ma'am."

"Yes, m...Marion." Justin recovered just in time.

"Good boy. Now you two get back to..." She winked. "Whatever you were doing. I've got to get to my poker night." She left them, cane striking the ground with purpose as she strode off.

"Poker?" Justin said.

"I bet her bluff is incredible."

Justin looked at him. "So," he said.

"So," Gabe said. He noticed a smear of black paint just above Justin's lip. "You have some paint..." He waved a hand in front of his face.

"So do you. I wonder how that could have happened."

Gabe raised a finger to his lips. They still tingled.

"I kissed you," Justin said.

"Yep." Gabe's stomach flipped. "I was there. For the…kissing."

"You okay, there?" Justin was grinning at him. It was a confident grin. Confidence was sexy. Justin was sexy.

"Having trouble making words goodly," Gabe said.

"You're adorkable."

"So you keep saying." Gabe raised his eyebrows. "Is adorkable good?"

"Adorkable is good. How about we get the Wet Paint sign in place?"

Gabe nodded, and they sealed and gathered up the last of the paint cans, put all the brushes in the bucket Justin had brought for that purpose, and piled it all neatly to the side. They set up the two pylons and the rope and hung the sign.

"About the bud?" Gabe said.

Justin raised one eyebrow.

"That kiss," Gabe said. "That kiss was definitely the bud."

"You know what?" Justin said. "You're a closet romantic. You have way more faith in humanity than you let on."

Gabe shrugged and gave the memorial one last glance. Even in the gathering dark, he could see the glowing symbols he'd painted. Family. Prosperity. Partnership. Truth. Knowledge.

Love.

Not just symbols, *magic*.

"I'm working on it," Gabe said.

Be careful with your touch, but don't deny yourself either.

Touch makes things brighter, especially the first time you touch someone.

A kiss, a hug, or even a simple handshake will draw whole new layers beneath those already seen. The complexity of a blue both loving and kind might have soft green roots. The most inspired of gold crowns might redden behind the temples.

Love can grow from want; anger can be fuel.

Even the colors that seem the most obvious, the most solid and simple shapes and movements might be more than they seem.

If something doesn't line up or seems too simple, it might be worth risking reaching out with more than your eyes.

Use your hands.

It is easier to understand the things we touch.

The Psychometry of Snow

Almost everything has a voice.

It's not what you think. I've done my research as much as anyone can. The theories are all partially right and mostly wrong. There are exceptions, but the joys of life settle far more often than the pain. I've touched real history in my travels, and I haven't heard as many tales of blood and tears as I'd expected.

I have made a life from these voices. It's an odd one that has forced me to adopt many names to disguise its levels, but it's mine. I can and do help others understand what those voices say under one of my names, but mostly I use a second name to be a man who digs through random pasts. I have no real specializations, which rankles the academics. They cry I have no way to prove the stories I tell.

"He's doing pop star history," the grey bearded men protest. "It's entertainment, not archaeology."

Happily, so many lovers of stories enjoy being entertained and don't care about proof.

My duffel is from World War II, and it's mostly quiet these days, though the first time I lifted it to my shoulder, I felt the joy of putting it down and spreading my arms to hug a child I'd never even met but who could now walk. I set it down just inside the door of my rented cabin and turn around to glance at the falling snow. Unable to help myself, I close the door and step back out into the flurries. I hold out a hand, and small white flecks land on my palm, melting just a second later.

Nothing. I love winter.

I smile and take a deep breath. I haven't been here in nearly five years, but I love this mountain. It isn't tall or sloped enough for skiing, but it has two dozen cabins for rental and a beautiful view. People rent the cabins and commute to the ski slopes a half hour away to cut their costs, which means for most of the day I can tell myself the mountain is mine. I rarely venture down to the main buildings, happy enough with the single room, kitchen, small bathroom, and large fireplace.

It's calm. It's quiet. No doubt there'll be voices here, but they won't be loud and won't run deep.

I'm about to turn back to head inside when I hear someone come around the path, crunching through the snow.

"You're not going skiing?"

I turn to the voice. "No, I—"

We break off and stare at each other. He is carrying a tied bundle of firewood in both hands. He wasn't at the desk when I signed in. If I am honest with myself, I know I would never have missed his eyes, so dark brown his pupils are hard to spot, nor the neatly trimmed red beard he sports, or the way his neck widens into the collar of his coat. Barrel-chested, taller than me, and thick shouldered, the bearded man is a lug, which is entirely my type. He's handsome and masculine.

And familiar.

"I know you," he says, and I'm a little off balance. No one knows me. I've got three names, and even if someone knows two of them, they never know the one I was born with. But this time his voice triggers a memory, and I fight off a wave of fear.

"You went to Oneida High, right?" I ask. It has been over a dozen years, and I can't quite find his name in the gap, especially with the memories so blurred by chemistry.

"F…" He bites off the sound just in time and reddens. I know the name he almost says, and I flinch. How could I have forgotten my fourth name?

He tries again. "Luke, right?"

I feel a little sick. "Yes."

"I'm Rick Barritt. You lived on the street behind me, I think."

"You were on the wrestling team," I say, remembering now. "And football with my brother, Alex?"

He nods, and a smile cuts through his short, neat beard. Despite the sickness in my stomach, I smile back. Another time, another place, and I would be happy to see him smile at me like that. But he knows me as someone I'd rather not have been.

Still, he's definitely grown into his height.

"What brings you way out here?" he asks.

"Vacation. I came here once for work, and I kind of fell in love with the place." It's not entirely a lie, though I'm not sure I can really call it "work" since I didn't ask for money. I never do when what I find is a body instead of a reunion. I pause. "You?"

"My aunt and uncle own the cabins. I've been working with them for two or three years now." He puts down the load of firewood just beside the front door of my small rented cabin in a wedged-off area obviously designed to hold the logs. "I'm just bringing you wood."

I try to fight off a snicker, and fail. He frowns. He has great eyebrows, thick and masculine, just like the rest of him, and I see the moment he realizes what he's said. He smiles and shakes his head, rubbing his gloves along his jeans.

When he straightens, he doesn't leave. "It's been a long time. How is Alex?"

"He's good," I say. "Married, three kids, all girls. He's a good dad."

"And you? You're doing well?"

I know what he's really asking. I force a smile. "Don't worry. I'm not crazy anymore."

He winces. "I didn't mean…"

I shake my head. "It's okay. Really. I remember, believe me."

Rick Barritt regards me for a couple of seconds, like he wants to say more, then apparently decides against it. "Well. If you need anything else, you can call the front desk. If you're not going to ski, there's some great snowshoeing on the tree line."

"I know," I say. "Maybe I'll try that tomorrow. It was a long flight."

Rick nods again, then starts down the shoveled path back to the main buildings. I reopen my cabin door and am about to head inside when he speaks again.

"Luke?"

I look up.

"You weren't crazy." It's nice of him to say.

I nod once, then go inside.

❖

It doesn't take much to bring back thoughts of the time before I had a grip on what was happening. Words and memories chase themselves around in my head for hours before I go to sleep, and even in my dreams I am uncomfortable. Synaesthesia. Hallucinations. Schizophrenia. MRI. Algolia. Perphenazine. Clopamine. Institutionalization.

I'm walking through a street in a hometown I haven't seen in years, and I've already lost my jacket and my shirt. I'm leading myself toward the stone of the statue in front of the courthouse. Words and voices and memories drill into my thoughts when I think about that statue, and it makes some of the other noises in my skull back off for a while. I close my eyes and consider kissing the statue when I get there, but it's taller than I am.

Instead, I decide to take off my pants.

I wake up with my hands closed tight and pressed to my chest, fingers aching from the effort of holding them closed. The sun isn't up, but I know better than to try and get to sleep. I am three hours ahead of the day now and will be chasing the real hours for a day or two until my body catches up.

It's chill enough that I spend some time resuscitating the fire from the night before and then fill the kettle with water and put it on the small stove to boil. I make a whole pot of tea and enjoy my first cup just watching the fire. There's a striped hand-knitted blanket on the back of the small couch, and I smile when I tug it over my shoulders. Rick's aunt made it, a way to use up old stashes of wool and add a homey touch to the cabin. Knitting it reminded her of her grandmother, I think, but I don't press any further, and the blanket falls silent again.

The tea, the cabin, the fire. It's exactly what I want. I take a deep breath and relax in a way I normally can't. I'll make breakfast in a bit, from the bits I brought with me and stuffed into the fridge yesterday without sorting. And I decide that when the sun does come up, I'll head down to the main building and see about some snowshoes.

❖

The older man at the counter comes out to meet me as I approach.

"You must be Luke," he says, offering his hand.

I flinch. "Yes." I'm not used to being recognized. Recognition has never been good.

"I'm Hal. Rick told us about you," the man says, and I force myself to remain smiling as I shake his hand. I'm pretty sure Rick hasn't told him much, given that the man isn't treating me like I might explode or strip at any moment. Looking at him now, I can see a family resemblance in their stature, though I'm fairly sure that this man has never had ginger hair like his nephew, even before it turned white. He has the same dark eyes, however.

"Ah," I say, out of my depth. I have to clear my throat. "All good, I hope?"

Hal laughs and nods. "He had a good childhood in Oneida. Before his parents." The man nods at me like I know something I am pretty sure I don't know. "Well. Years ago. What can I do for you?"

"I was hoping for some snowshoes," I say. The snow is still falling lazily outside, and my short trek down provided me with a gorgeous view of the mountain covered with the pristine whiteness. I am all the more excited about the thought of following the trail now that I've seen the snow in the daylight.

Hal agrees. "Perfect morning for it. Go ahead around back, right through there." He gestures at a door at the far end of the large sitting room through an alcove from where we stand at the front desk. "Rick's out there now. He'll get you set up."

"Thanks," I say.

I find Rick outside, his wide back to me, looking out over the mountain. He holds a mug of coffee still steaming in the cold morning air. I clear my throat, and he turns. Again, he smiles, and again it feels uncomfortable. Why would he smile at me?

"Good morning," he says. He isn't wearing a hat now, and I can see the deep red hair that he'd always worn shaved short is even shorter now and greying a bit at his temples. "How'd you sleep?"

"It's always hard with the time change," I say, dodging the truth a bit. I am rusty at conversation. I spend most of my time alone.

"You're still in Ontario?"

I nod. "I live there."

"That's right. You said you came here on work. What do you do?"

I hesitate, and he catches it.

"Sorry," he says. "If you don't want to…" He doesn't finish the sentence.

If I don't want to what? Small talk? Discuss my job?

Remember?

"It's fine," I say. "Mostly these days I write. I sort of freelance." This is such a wild misrepresentation that I can feel my face burning.

But Rick smiles. "That sounds good." He has the darkest eyes, and the years have drawn their first few lines beside their corners. Smile lines.

"I thought I'd give the snowshoe trail a try this morning," I say, because this former friend of my brother is looking at me, and I'm enjoying looking at him far too much.

Rick puts down his cup. "That's a great idea. Do you know the trail?"

I don't. "Uh," I say.

Rick smiles. "I'll show you."

❖

I'm worried about more discussion, but instead Rick lets me set the pace and keeps the silence I obviously prefer. He walks with me, and we follow the tree line for a good twenty minutes. The slope is just pitched enough in places to make it a bit of a workout, but the view is worth it. Higher up the mountain, the valley suddenly appears around a short curve. I step out of the trees and see a beautiful white world below me, edged in rows of green trees and deep below the palest whites of ice and reflected sky in the river.

"Wow," I say.

"It's pretty amazing."

I nod, not turning when I feel Rick move up beside me. He stretches his back, then points off to the left. "See those falls?"

I squint and raise my hand, trying to see where he is pointing, but I don't find it. After a few seconds, he moves closer behind me and puts one hand on my shoulder, then points again, turning me slightly. The pressure of his hand, even with my coat and his gloves, is palpable. So is his strength.

I shiver.

"Cold?" he asks me.

"No, I'm okay," I manage. I catch sight of what he was trying to show me. "Oh! There. You can see some steam or something."

"It's a natural spring," Rick says. "Sometimes the falls freeze solid in the middle of winter, but right now they're just iced over." He pulls away, and I shiver again, though I don't think he notices.

It really is like going back in time. At least out here, surrounded by snow, there are no voices.

"Ready to head back?"

I nod. "Sure."

He pauses just a second, and the weight of it makes me look at him.

"What's wrong?"

"Would you like to have dinner tonight?" he asks.

I stare.

He laughs, a little scornfully. "Wow. I guess that's a no."

"No," I say, then realize what that sounds like. "I don't mean no, I mean…" I close my eyes. "Sorry." I feel sick and a little dizzy. Thank God we're alone out here, and thank God there is nothing out here with a voice I can't ignore. I take a deep breath and look at the big man again. "I'm just not sure why."

It is his turn to stare. "Why what?"

"Why you'd like to have dinner."

"I thought we could catch up."

Now I am even more confused. "Rick, you were friends with my brother." We both know I mean more than what I am saying.

"Fluke…" he says, and then as fast as he can, he says, "Luke. I'm sorry. *Luke*." He bites his lip, and his wide shoulders drop.

There it is: my fourth name. Fluke. An entire missed childhood and young adulthood all in one epithet. One insult. I am surprised to find it doesn't sting nearly as much as it should.

"I'm ready to head back," I say.

He leads the way.

❖

If I press against the stone of the statue, I can feel the musculature of the horse being carved from solid rock. If I close my eyes, I can see a woman chipping away in a large empty room. When I rub my lips across the stone, I can even smell the smoke from a cigarette that dangles from the lips of this woman. These noises and feelings and smells are so fucking real, and there is a part of me that is desperately trying to tell me they are not. But pressed skin to stone, my eyes closed, reality is hard to understand.

Tiny pinpricks of cold are landing on my back and shoulders. It's snowing.

I smile. Snow is always real. Then the smile fades, because real isn't what I'd like. Real is pills and doctors and time in small closed rooms where I seem to get better just long enough to come back to the world and get worse again.

I hear a car, and I wonder if it's a real car or not right up until I can see the headlights through my eyelids. I open my eyes, but I don't turn my head.

Snow falls into my exhalations and melts in midair.

I'm not sure how long I've been out on the little porch, but the mug of tea I brought with me isn't steaming anymore. I've been catching snowflakes on my fingertips all morning.

"Luke?"

I didn't hear him approach. I jump and turn.

"Sorry!" He raises his hand almost comically. "I didn't mean to scare you."

"It's fine," I manage. He has something under his other arm, and when he pulls it forward, I blink in astonishment.

"I wondered if you'd sign this for me."

I can't breathe. I step back and bump against the railing.

"Luke," he says again.

"How...?" I shake my head.

"I read it," Rick said. He's still holding out the book.

I catch my breath. "Come on in."

Inside, I pour out my cold tea and refill the kettle while Rick hangs up his coat and tugs off his boots. When I come back into the room with the teapot and two mugs, he's sitting on the small couch, and the book is lying on the little table.

"I really hate that cover," I say.

"It's a little pink," Rick says, and I can tell he's trying to be neutral.

Pink cover, a pile of random stuff that barely had anything to do with the content, red letters in a terrible font. A false name. One word.

Psychometry.

"It's ugly," I said. "The second printing was much nicer."

"Luke."

I cross my arms and look up. He's sitting almost primly, his large hands clasped on his knees. His expression makes me laugh.

"You look so contrite."

He blushes. It suits him. I try not to look at the dark red hairs that are visible where the top button of his shirt is undone, or the way the shirt is straining across his chest. I fail. I sit down beside him. God, he looks good, thick and strong and so comfortable in his skin.

"So you read it," I say, and to stop myself staring, I nod at the offensively pink book.

He nods. "A few times."

"And you figured out it was me?"

"Class ring, missing student. You changed the name, the province, a bunch of stuff. But you kept the mascot." He looks up at me, and I can tell he's actually a little proud of figuring it out. He's talking about one of the first chapters. It was the first time I realized what was actually going on with me, between two cycles of medication and one of the few times my mother had put her foot down and overruled my father's desire to use every chemical option under the sun to make me "better." I'd almost had my wits about me. Then Bailey Haliburton had packed a bag and gone missing, and her mother had come to our home to talk to my mother because they were friends. Bailey had left behind her class ring. They hadn't even noticed me walk up while they were talking. I'd picked up the ring, and that ring had spoken to me.

"She swapped it for the ring he gave her."

Both women had turned to stare at me. Mrs. Haliburton had looked uncomfortable, but my mother's face was a practiced mask of gentle concern.

"Honey, do you need to lie down?"

"She's in love with him. He's tall. He's native. They like the same plays." I saw it all unfolding in my head, and even saw the very moment she put the ring on her bed to trade it for the plain band he offered her. It wasn't as fancy as half the other jewelry in her room, but it made her heart so full. I heard her say "Yes."

"Oh my God," Mrs. Haliburton said. "Oh my God."

They'd caught up with them both after that. Bailey Haliburton's father had been furious about his daughter running off and marrying someone he felt was "inappropriate." In the book, I'd avoided using the word "racist" on the advice of my lawyer and editor, and I'd changed all the names and places and every other detail they figured could possibly matter.

None of us had caught my inclusion of a teenager in a giant bird costume.

"Tommo the hawk," I say. "Who'd've thought a stupid bird would out me?"

Rick smiles. "I'm sorry."

"What?"

"You talked about what it was like. In high school. When they were putting you on drugs, when everyone called you names…"

"Fluke," I said. It hadn't translated for the book under my pseudonym. I can't actually remember what word they came up with that worked with Simon. Psycho? Sicko? Something like that.

"I'm so sorry."

I looked at him. Really looked. His dark eyes were open, and I could see the sincerity. I wasn't sure why in the world…Then I remembered.

"Rick…I was out of my mind. Literally. They had me on so many drugs, I had no idea what to think or do. You and Alex, you both got me home when I was pretty damn messed up…"

"And we made fun of you the entire ride home."

I can't help it. I laugh. It surprises him. "Rick, I was wandering around downtown in my underwear in the middle of winter."

He smiles.

I lean forward. "Seriously, forget it. If you two hadn't found me, I'd have had another visit with the cops." I shake my head. "I had quite a few of those, before I got off the meds."

Rick nods. "Okay." I don't think he actually believes there's nothing to forgive, but it's the best I'm likely to get. My mother was the same when she finally understood. My father was gone by then, and my brother still doesn't quite get it.

He rises. "I should go."

I'm not sure I want him to go, but I can't quite think of anything to say. He puts on his jacket and boots, and I rise and stand in the door while he leaves. I hold my hand out into the air and catch a few snowflakes, enjoying their silence.

When I head back inside, the book is still on the table.

❖

"Where are his clothes?"

"Who knows."

The second voice is my brother's, but the first is harder to place. I want to keep my eyes on the statue and the snow. I want to press against it and feel my skin touch the cold stone because then the carver woman is there, and she's louder than everything else. One voice instead of dozens. It's so much better, even if I'm shivering, and my toes are starting to hurt.

"C'mon, Fluke," my brother says, and his hand is on my shoulder. He's not gentle with me, and for a second I think about shaking him off; I'm already losing the voice of the woman who carved the statue, but his grip is too tight, and he pulls me back and down from the stone pedestal.

I lose the carver, and the rest of the world rises up in its usual chorus. I press my hands against my ears, but it doesn't help. The voices aren't from outside.

My brother gives me a shake. I try really hard, and make my hands move away from my ears. I listen as hard as I can to what he's saying, and I try to ignore everything else.

"Where's your pants? Your coat?"

I shake my head.

Alex sighs.

"Dude, he's gotta be freezing." I look at the other guy with Alex, and I can almost recognize him. He's got red hair, and he's taller and bigger than even my brother.

"I know," Alex says. "He has to go in the back seat. He tries to grab the wheel sometimes."

"I'll sit with him."

"Thanks."

My brother's hand is tight on my arm again. As he leads me to the back of his car, I try to say goodbye to the stone carver, but my brother tells me to be quiet and that I'm coming with him.

They never understand who I'm talking to.

❖

I've just caught a few snowflakes when he comes around the corner with more wood.

"You like to do that, don't you?" he asks.

"Snowflakes are very quiet." I smile at him, and I think of his copy of *Psychometry* and how often it looks to have been read. He knows what I mean.

He unloads the lumber onto my porch and wipes his hands across his jeans. His smile is almost lost in his beard. "And I guess they don't last."

I smile back. "They're my favorite. Rain is good, but snow…I don't know. It's better."

"Is it everything? Always?" he asks.

I look at him a long while, and I think we're both wondering if I'm going to answer right up until I speak. "Yes and no. Everything has a voice, but sometimes there's not much to say. It needs to matter to someone, but it's not as simple as that. It's not exactly purposeful, but there's intent in a way." This is the distilled version that I have used on my investigator friends and the rare police I have worked with.

Unlike them, Rick nods. "Like Bailey's ring."

"Yeah. I don't have to listen if I don't want to," I add, because he knew me back when I didn't know how not to hear everything at once.

He waits a moment, and holds out his own hand, catching some snow on his fingers. His hands look rougher than mine.

"About dinner?" I ask.

He turns. One eyebrow creeps up, and I see the smile lines beside his eyes. "Yes?" The deep rumble in his voice makes me shiver again.

"Did we skip the whole coming out to each other thing, or did I miss it?" I can feel my face burning.

"You missed mine," Rick says. "But you told me you liked me quite a while back. I'm just running on the assumption that things haven't changed, because that's a good scenario for me."

"I told you I liked you?" I try to remember, and I'm afraid I know when it was.

He confirms. "You were wearing little blue briefs at the time. It was memorable for me."

I flinch. "The horse statue?"

He laughs. "Was it a horse? I was having a really hard time not staring at you in front of your brother and pretending everything was cool."

"As I recall, it was freezing."

He nods. We stand in a silence that is comfortable.

"Do you like steak?" he asks.

❖

"Can you crank the heat? He's really cold." The red-haired guy beside me in the back seat unzips his jacket and holds it out to me. My teeth are chattering, but I don't want to touch his jacket. I can already hear it humming and whispering. It wants to tell me something.

"It takes a second," Alex says from the driver's seat. Then he sighs. "I need to get him back in the house without my parents seeing him. They'll flip out if they know he snuck out again."

"Here," the guy is saying, and now that the car is moving, it's a bit easier to ignore everything else as the voices drop away behind us.

I look at his coat. "It's too loud."

"Fluke," Alex warns. "Don't be a jackass."

"It's okay," the guy beside me says. His eyes are really dark. I touch his jacket and flinch.

"It's hard to hide in a uniform all the time," I tell him. He looks startled. I put the jacket on slowly, because it turns out that it's the good kind of loud. It feels warm against my skin. "You're not ugly," I tell him.

"What?"

From the front seat, my brother sighs. "Just ignore him."

It takes me some time to get the jacket on, but when I do I tilt my head to listen as hard as I can. "It's like a costume. For an actor." I look at the brown and white bird on the front of the jacket, and I think of the same jacket on my brother. His jacket doesn't talk like this. I look at the guy beside me, and he's watching me intently. He's a big guy, the kind of guy that most of the time I think I should be afraid of, but there's a softness to him that makes me think he'd rather use his size to protect someone.

"We're halfway home," Alex says, turning a corner. I rub my temples a little with my cold fingers and lean back on the seat, closing my eyes. My hands drop. I'm so tired, and it's nice to be warm.

"You're not ugly," I say it again, because the jacket is insisting the opposite, and it's just wrong. "You're strong and you're nice and you don't have to act forever." I open my eyes just a bit and look at the man. "I really like your eyes. You're handsome."

"Okay, Fluke," Alex's voice is rising. "Enough." He's embarrassed. "He doesn't really know everything he's saying. He doesn't mean to sound so faggy."

"It's okay." The voice of the guy beside me is quieter than before.

"It's okay," I say. "I can keep secrets."

I close my eyes again. I'm so tired. The voice in the jacket finally falls quiet. I sleep.

❖

Rick brings the makings of dinner to my cabin—a bottle of wine, the steaks, and baked potatoes with all the trimmings.

"Are there more people coming?" I ask looking at the thick cuts of steak, but he just smiles at me.

"You could use a few good meals."

He cooks on the small stove and grill of my rented cabin with an easy grace that I envy. I shouldn't be surprised. What bear doesn't know his way around a grill? The third time he catches me staring and smiling, he asks what I'm thinking and I say so.

"Woof," he says, and when I laugh, a part of me completely relaxes for the first time in years.

We drink the wine, and eat the meal, and I eventually hand him back his copy of *Psychometry* with Simon's name inscribed inside it.

"This is the only signed copy. You could probably get good money for that online," I joke.

He shakes his head. "It's a keeper."

Outside, it has begun to snow again. Rick asks me about my jobs, and for the first time in my life, I tell someone what I do for a living without euphemism or omission. I tell him what it was like when I touched Hadrian's Wall and heard the voices of Roman soldiers, and that leads to more stories of the places I have been. He *listens*, and I realize how incredible it is to have that luxury. Even though it is cold, we go outside, and I catch a few snowflakes on my hand. Rick scoops up some of the snow and starts to pack it into a snowball, and I give him a wary look.

"Trust me," he says.

He doesn't throw it. He closes his eyes and presses his hands against the snow, shaping it. He turns it over in his hands, and I watch his rough fingers work and feel my skin shiver when I imagine those rough hands touching my skin. Arms like Rick's would make you feel safe, if you were in them.

He doesn't complain about the cold, and he works the snowball back and forth, alternating his hands, twisting and compacting. I watch, not sure of what he's doing.

Finally, he looks at me. He holds it out, and I realize.

I open my hand, and he puts the snowball in my open palm.

It speaks. ·

"I'm going to go get him some pants and shoes and a shirt," Alex says. "I'll bring it back out, and then we can get him dressed and get him inside." He scowls. "You okay to stay with him for second?"

"Sure," Rick says. "Don't worry. It's okay."

Alex shakes his head. "It's not. It's all the fucking time." But he gets out of the car and closes it as quietly as he can, and then heads off down the street toward his house.

Rick looks at Alex's brother. Fluke is still fast asleep, burrowed up in Rick's jacket. *He's cute.* The thought comes faster than he can stop it, but this time the shame doesn't show up on its heels.

"I won't have to act forever, eh?" Rick says to the sleeping kid.

Every morning when he puts on his jacket, Rick thinks of it as a costume, thinks of himself as an actor playing a role. Hearing Fluke say that back to him was pretty intense. Rick swallows.

You're not ugly. You're strong and you're nice and you don't have to act forever.

Rick feels tears spring to his eyes, and he wipes them with his thumb. "Jesus," he says.

I really like your eyes. You're handsome.

Rick leans over and kisses Fluke's forehead. Fluke doesn't wake.

"You're not so bad yourself," he says, then waits for Alex to get back.

❖

The snowball melts.
I touch my forehead.
Rick smiles.

Wants are green.

It took me a long time to understand that, but all the greens, the good and the bad, are rooted in wants of one kind or another.

The palest greens can be sadness, but they are the sadnesses of losses and memory. When they're paper-thin and tear easily around the heart, they're bittersweet fondness for a time they'd like to see again.

When greens tint to blue, they are kinder wants: worry for another, anxiety in the face of hoped-for acceptance. The more they swirl, the more nervous the person is.

Greens can also want escape. When they creep from one to another, clawing and twisting and a sickly shade of rot or mold, they speak of disgust. Best avoided, those.

But be careful of the darkest, sharpest greens. The ones like the final leaves in autumn, holding on to their color despite all the yellows and reds around them, gathered brightest near the eyes, twisting and tightening.

I've seen it more than I'd like to admit, and more than once in my own reflection. I've seen it at parties, at funerals, and weddings. I've even seen that green alongside the satisfied smile of people in power who we are told will protect us.

Jealousy is a dangerous want.

THE FINISH

The last bottle I managed to track down is bleeding drips of condensation onto the white table-cloth in the private dining room. I feel sick, of course. Even the sight of the label—the Byrnes Vineyard dragonfly and frog design, done in gold pointillism on a red diamond— makes me feel queasy. It's a rare red ice wine, meant to be enjoyed after a meal and in small quantity. It's the tenth bottle—no, the eleventh— I've had in two days.

When I uncork the bottle, the scent of it is too much. I stumble to the men's bathroom barely in time, and heave into the sink. I wash my face, not daring to look in the mirror, and then sit down again in the closed restaurant dining room, facing the bottle. I rub my chapped lips, still burning from the last glasses, then pick it up.

I pour, sniff, swallow. As always, I remember the words of a young woman who'd toured the vineyard the first time I'd been present to deliver a tasting of the label. I'd just finished explaining how the mild climate and the rich soil combined in the region, and a perfectly placed frost had garnered the ice wine. "It all tells," I'd said. "The rain, the grape, the soil—it all comes together."

"The aftertaste is like molten strawberries," she'd delighted. I'd explained that in the lexicon of wine, an aftertaste is called a finish. She'd laughed and said, "I'd like to finish the whole bottle."

It's still my favorite customer memory to this day.

To this wretched, wretched day.

I feel the wine so sweet in my throat, and the first hazy glimmers of change appear in the air around me.

"Please," I whisper, to God or Dennis, whichever might answer. Dennis appears, hazy and indistinct, heading toward the kitchen. It seems God isn't listening.

I take another sip, and feel Dennis become real.

❖

Giving summer tours of the vineyard, I often joked that if collecting the January grapes for ice wine sounded like fun, then anyone taking the tour should leave phone numbers. I promised to call if there was a January night frost cold enough to freeze the grapes, likely at around one in the morning.

Unsurprisingly, no one ever took me up on it.

Still, every January frost, if the conditions were right, I found people, usually vineyard workers, their families, or friends, to help.

That was how I met Dennis, who was just another helper of nearly two dozen. Dressed in a scuffed black coat, with a thin scarf and knitted hat covering all but his eyes, I hadn't really done more than glance at him when he'd shown up to work. Terry said he was a friend of a friend of one of the waiters from the vineyard restaurant.

We'd worked all through the night and into the morning, fingers achingly cold, baskets of frozen grapes slowly filling, and passing thermoses of coffee and hot chocolate back and forth that the kitchen refilled every hour or so. It was long work, uncomfortable and miserable. Every year I gathered everyone afterward in the restaurant, and the chef made them all a good hot breakfast on the house. While they ate and warmed up, I stepped into my office and wrote out checks for each of the workers named on the list Terry had made for me. I considered it a point of pride that I worked with everyone else on these frigid nights. Terry had often told me I didn't have to, but I always believed it mattered to the staff that the boss also did the crappy jobs.

"You're rich, buddy," Terry said, shaking his head. "You can pay people to do that shit."

After cutting the checks for the workers, I'd handed them all out but one. Dennis Clarke hadn't come for his money when I'd called out his name. That surprised me. Cold bitter nights and thin gloves working to pick frozen grapes usually left people more than eager to get whatever compensation they could.

"Terry," I said. "I'm missing one. Dennis…" I glanced down at the list. "Clarke."

Terry nodded and went to where the group was rapidly moving off to climb wearily into their vehicles. The plates had been mostly cleared. Terry called out a few times. I went back to my paperwork, rubbing my eyes. It was a decent harvest, and it was going to make some fine ice wine.

"Got him," Terry said, a little while later. "He's deaf. Didn't hear you calling."

"Thanks, Terry," I said. Terry nodded and paused at the doorway to raise his eyebrows. "He's cute."

I shook my head. Terry and I had been friends for a long time, and had even dated for one disastrous year when we were much younger. Now we ran the vineyard together—though Terry handled more of the restaurant side, and I took care of the winery. We were better business partners than we'd ever been lovers. Built like a bulldog and just as tenacious, Terry had a seemingly endless appetite for younger men who tired of him and moved on, generally with pockets full of presents before they left. He was terrible with money. He blew it on expensive toys and expensive boys. I was never sure where he was at, financially, and it had always been like that. It was one of the many reasons we hadn't made it as a couple. That, plus his temper and seemingly endless string of young things on the side.

Taller and, if I allowed myself some pride, in better shape for my age, I hadn't dated nearly as much but still found I could get attention if I wanted to. I didn't hide the grey in my temples like Terry did, and still ran the half-marathon every year. If sometimes the younger men who did hit on me called me "Daddy"? Well. I could live with that.

A moment later, Dennis stepped into my office.

I looked up. Without his hat and scarf, he was indeed handsome, though a little rough around the edges. His dark hair needed a trim. It was just long enough to fall into his eyes, which were a soft green that didn't seem to fit with the rest of his angular features. He had the shadow of a day or two without shaving on his chin.

I handed him the check and thanked him, though if Terry was right, he didn't notice. He was looking down at the check when I spoke. Then he pulled a small well-worn notepad and a pencil from his pocket and flipped it open. He wrote something, then turned it to face me.

Can I get cash? I read.

He was watching my face. I hoped he could read lips. "I don't have cash at hand, but I can have it sent to you later on today once the bank opens. Where are you staying?"

He frowned, then wrote again.

The Y.

It bothered me, I'll admit it. He wasn't a kid, though it's hard for someone on the downward side of their forties not to think of anyone under twenty-five as a kid, I'd learned. But he seemed lean and hungry to me. This wasn't a young man who'd been having a good run of luck. He'd been a good worker, efficient and working hard without break or complaint.

I glanced out my window at the parking lot, then looked back at him.

"Do you have a ride?" I asked.

He shook his head. His lips curled in a slight smirk, and it suited him. That Terry and I were gay was well known in the region. I knew better than this, but I made the offer anyway.

"If you'll wait a few minutes, I can drive you."

He nodded, the smirk growing into what could have been a smile.

I really did take Dennis to the Y. He fell asleep on the drive over, and I stole glances at him. The neck of his shirt was a little frayed, and there was just the tip of an unseen tattoo below the smooth hollow of his throat. When we got to the Y, I tapped his shoulder, waking him, and he rubbed his eyes with one thumb.

I waited for him to look at me.

"I have a spare bedroom," I said. "If you've got nowhere else to crash."

He regarded me for a long moment, then nodded once. He pulled out his notepad.

Gonna get my things. Be right back.

I nodded and waited for him.

❖

He dropped his beaten canvas backpack—not much for anyone to carry their belongings in—at my front door and tugged off his boots without sitting. He shrugged out of his jacket, tossed it over the edge of the chair that sat in the entrance hall, and started to look around before I'd even finished untying my shoes. By the time I'd hung up our coats and followed him into the living room, he was standing at my bookcase, trailing his finger along the spines of the books and stopping every now and then to carelessly pick up a picture or an object d'art from the alternating shelves where I displayed them.

"Big reader?" I asked, before remembering he had his back to me. I felt myself blush when he didn't react. *Deaf,* I reminded myself.

He moved with the arrogant grace of youth. His shirt, faded and short-sleeved, was tight across his shoulders and chest, displaying his lean strength. His jeans rode a little low, exposing the small of his back when he reached for something. There was another tattoo there. When he did turn to look at me, it was with a picture frame in hand and a raised eyebrow.

It was an old shot of me and Terry.

"That's Terry, from the vineyard," I said. "And me. Back when we first bought the place."

He nodded and put the photo back on the shelf. He turned back to me, his amused smirk back in place.

"I'm going to go to bed," I said. "Let me show you to your room."

His lip curled, and he walked toward me. He came closer than was polite. Until that moment, it hadn't occurred to me that what I was doing might not have been safe, but he looked up at me, his eyelids low on his green eyes. I felt some small relief at being taller than him.

His hand cupped my crotch, and what had been a slight stiffness before began to harden under his fingers. He smiled at me again with that crooked smirk and then slowly sank to his knees. As he pulled at my belt and my zipper, I ran one hand through his messy hair.

That he was talented didn't surprise me. His fingers wrapped around my shaft, and his tongue teased my cockhead. He swallowed me, one hand slowly working my pants free, and I tilted my head back and felt the warm wet heat of his attention.

"Wait," I said. "Slow down…"

He'd brought me close to the edge quickly, and I had to take his shoulders and pull him away. He looked up at me, a small frown on his face. Again I remembered he couldn't hear me.

I pulled him back to his feet and tugged his shirt over his head. The tattoo on the center of his chest was a green man, a face of oak leaves, and I traced a finger over it before sliding my arms around him and pulling him against me for a long kiss. His lips parted easily for my tongue, and my hands shifted lower, gripping his strong ass and sliding between his warm skin and his jeans. He made nearly no noise, just gasps and soft breaths against my skin when we parted long enough for me to undo his jeans and for him to step out of them. Then we collided again, our cocks hard and hot against each other. One of my hands gripped his ass tightly, pulling him into me, while the other stroked us both.

His voiceless moans were more felt than heard. I wanted to devour him.

We went to my room, casting off clothes as we moved, kissing and touching with rougher and faster passion. At my bedroom door I finally got out of my shirt, and Dennis rubbed his hands across my chest, obviously surprised to see I was in good shape. I pushed him back onto the bed and crawled after him, licking his throat and neck and pinning his hands above his head while I lay over him. He shifted, making little breathy laughs and gasps while I teased his nipples with my tongue. When I let go of his hands he gripped my ass tightly and pulled me against him, wrapping his legs around my waist with a perfectly clear intention.

I paused long enough for lube and a condom, already so hard for him I could barely stand it. I braced his legs on my shoulders, and never once did his green eyes look away from my face as I pushed my way inside him. He pressed his hands against my chest and squeezed his legs around me, and I fucked him with a need I didn't know I had. He was no stranger to this, and I found myself thrusting into him harder than I'd dared with others. His legs urged me onward, and I tipped over the edge, driving into him deep while I came.

After, he shook his head when I tried to pull out of him, and his legs squeezed tighter. He jerked himself off like that, with me still inside him, and his quiet orgasm was little more than a ragged, throaty exhalation.

I kissed him again and then extricated myself to clean up. I brought a wet towel back and wiped him as well. He pressed against my side and pulled the blanket over us both. His eyes closed.

We slept.

I follow the specter of Dennis into the kitchen, where I watch the sink fill with translucent foamy water. He's washing dishes, and false sunlight is falling in from the window that looks out onto the parking lot. I sip more wine, and his body firms around the edges. I watch him work, see wisps of other kitchen staff out of the corner of my eyes, but it is Dennis that is invoked by this vintage, not they.

"Why?" I croak.

He doesn't turn and doesn't answer, of course.

I see myself arrive in the kitchen, and suddenly I realize which day it is I'm seeing. I want to close my eyes, but I can't. None of these visions have ever had sound. I have watched us walk by the vines. I've seen us fuck by the pool. I've relived each vision as though it were Dennis himself spinning a tale for me, a silent tale from a deaf man. I can't close my eyes.

But I don't want to watch.

We interact, puppets of ourselves in the past. I remember the conversation and flinch when the other me kisses his forehead and then holds up one hand, fingers curled a certain way. Moments later, this wine-conjured image of Dennis kisses me, and the other me leaves, more content than he has ever felt.

"Fool," I growl. "Fucking fool."

At first, he tried to refuse the job I offered, scratching on his notepad that he was on his way out of Niagara. *Lost my job*, he wrote. *Laid off, not fired.*

"Where are you going?" I asked.

He shrugged. We lay in bed, still naked from the night before. When he'd reached out of the bed to get his notepad from his jeans, I'd enjoyed looking at the lines of his back and his lovely ass. The tattoo at the small of his back was a series of moons: a full moon with a waning and waxing crescent on either side.

He scribbled again. *I'm not a hustler.*

Reading it filled me with a kind of aching shame. I nodded.

"I know," I said, and his green eyes read the words on my lips. "And I'm not a sugar-daddy." I thought about Terry, and his penchant for young men just like Dennis. "But there's a spot open at the restaurant—it's just a dishwashing job, but it's a steady thing. I already know you're a hard worker. You can stay here while you get your feet back under you. In the spare bedroom, if you want." I added the last awkwardly, knowing I was blushing.

He looked around the room. I was suddenly aware of how fine my furnishings were.

You invite guys to stay with you all the time? he wrote.

Dennis flashed me that smirk of a smile while I read it.

"No," I said.

He reached over, and ran his hand across my chest, down my stomach, and between my legs. He raised his eyebrows almost comically when he felt how hard I was.

"Yes, well," I said, feeling myself turn all the redder. "You're very handsome. But I'm serious. You can have the spare bedroom."

In answer, Dennis stroked me, and shook his head.

"But—" I gasped as his hand worked my length. "You'll take the job?"

He nodded.

I rolled onto him and kissed him, taking his hands and once again pinning them over his head. I licked at his neck and heard the little gasping noises I'd eventually learn was his laughter. We ground against each other, licking, kissing, nibbling and teasing in a more lackadaisical dance than the night before. We came in turns. I was pleased to tease his load out onto his smooth stomach by burying my face into his lovely ass, his legs on my shoulders, and he returned the favor by taking me into his mouth again, and I watched my own sperm spatter across the green man on his chest.

He looked at me lazily while we caught our breath.

"We need a shower," I said. "And breakfast."

He smiled.

❖

"Reports," Terry said, standing at my door. He had the weekly reports from the restaurant. Ever since he'd nearly run the restaurant into the ground with his fast-and-loose approach to finances, I'd had him keep me up to speed on how the restaurant was doing on a weekly basis. The man knew food and chefs and was amazing at ambience and figuring out what the customers at the restaurant wanted.

He was an idiot with cash.

"Thanks," I said.

He hovered. I looked up at him.

"You always did have a thing for hard-luck cases," he said.

He'd seen me leave with Dennis. I'd been expecting some sort of comment. "Pardon?" I feigned innocence and took a glance at the reports.

Terry laughed. "Don't get me wrong, he's a cute little fucker. Wouldn't mind bending him over the sink myself."

I rolled my eyes. "He needed a job. He worked damn hard when we were picking," I said. "And we're down one dishwasher anyway."

Terry laughed, wide body shaking. "You are such a softie. Just like you to take him in."

I nodded. "He's a nice kid. And I think he'll take the job more seriously than yet another college kid just doing it for some spending cash."

"That's the truth," Terry said. Students were his nightmare, Terry often said. "I'll give him a shot. At least I know he won't talk back." He laughed at his own joke.

"Don't be an ass," I said. "And make sure none of the others give him any crap."

Terry shook his head. "Softie. And don't worry about that. He's a cool customer. I imagine he'll have 'em all eating out of his hand in no time. Just like you." He looked at me. "You seem awfully chipper this morning. Where'd you drop that kid off last night?"

"See you later, Terry," I said, voice firm.

He laughed as he left my office.

❖

We developed a routine that felt fragile and unsettling at first but grew more firm as the days became weeks and the weeks turned into months. Some days I'd make four trips, leaving early to go to work while Dennis often slept in. I had to admit a slight guilt at enjoying having a lover I couldn't wake with my snoring or thumping around in the morning. On my lunch break, I'd come home and pick up Dennis, who'd start at the restaurant a couple of hours later. We'd often eat lunch in my home. Dennis wasn't a half-bad cook, though his range was limited to barbecue and a wide variety of stir fry. After lunch, Dennis worked at the restaurant, and I managed the vineyard and winery throughout the afternoon, and then I'd come home, get myself dinner, and make one last trip around eleven when the restaurant was closed and Dennis had finished his shift. We had different days off, and I often felt a little out of sorts on the weekends, when Dennis worked and I didn't. My house, which had never before seemed lonely, was bothering me if he wasn't home.

In the rare evenings we had together, we'd often just sit on the couch, both of us reading, or watching movies once I figured out how to turn on the bloody closed captioning on my DVD player. Dennis had mimicked my tongue sticking out while I'd worked on the remote, my glasses perched on the end of my nose.

One evening in the early spring, Dennis admitted that reading lips was tiring, so I bought a copy of *ASL for Dummies* and started reading it on the sly. My first attempt to say something to him—I tried to compliment his ass—made him chuckle in his breathy way, and he'd corrected me. He scribbled on a notepad.

Who taught you that?

I showed him the book. He stared at me a long time, then nodded. I couldn't decide if I'd offended him or impressed him in some way, but we began lessons and I learned that signing was far easier than interpreting someone else signing. Still, we made slow progress.

I started training for the next half-marathon, and when I'd come home from running, sweaty and still feeling the high, Dennis would tumble me into the bed, despite my protests of needing a shower, and he'd wrap his legs around me. We'd rut like animals, all swallowed cries and sweat and spit, and I learned that as tender as he could be, Dennis enjoyed sex rough and quick. To my surprise, I learned I liked it myself, and loved to watch his face while I gripped his shoulders and shoved my dick into him with the sole notion of getting us both off, fast.

His breathy cry would always delight me, and when he'd come across his own chest, the pool of his spunk on the tattoo on his chest would always tip me over the edge right after him.

After the vision of myself leaves, this watery version of Dennis looks out the window. I realize with a start that he is waiting to see me get into my car, and shake my head, angry at myself all over again. Dennis is fading. I take another swallow of the wine, and he sharpens.

He shakes his hand, and droplets of water and soap vanish before they can hit the floor. Startled by the movement, I look at him.

He raises his hand to the window, and lowers his middle two fingers. His thumb is out, his index finger and pinky upright.

"What?" I say. I know that sign.

Through the window, I see my car pull away.

The summer months were busy for me, and apart from the half-marathon, what little time I could scrape together for relaxation I spent in my pool. The heat was oppressive, and rain was scarce—I'd been struggling with the growers to make sure the soil was getting enough water from the wells and fighting to maintain the sometimes precarious balances in the earth, and it felt like a daily struggle to make sure everything went smoothly. Watching Dennis swim was a delight, and after one particularly athletic session at the water's edge, I'd been unable to control myself and had hoisted the young man onto the pool's edge and fucked him in the shallow end. He'd shot across his stomach, green eyes never leaving mine while I pounded into him. When I'd come inside him—the only time he closed his eyes was when he felt me come inside him—I leaned over him, chest to chest, our skin sticky with his climax.

He smiled at me as I pulled out of him. His hands moved. *I have to go to work soon.* Our sex had made it too late for him to make the longish walk which he sometimes enjoyed.

I groaned. The last thing in the world I wanted to do was drive back to the vineyard.

"I need to buy you a car," I said, jokingly. He smiled. He couldn't drive. But then, a thought occurred to me.

"What about a really good bike?" I asked. "Can you ride a bike?"

He watched my lips and signed again.

You don't have to buy me anything. It made him uncomfortable.

"I just gave you one of the biggest loads I've ever shot," I said, wagging my eyebrows. "Consider it a reward."

Dennis shook his head and squirmed out from beneath me. I stepped back into the water, surprised. He kept shaking his head and dropped back into the water, making for the ladder despite my useless protests—he wasn't looking at me, but still I was talking, a habit I couldn't seem to break.

"Dennis? Wait!" I bit off the words, finally remembering.

He had his towel wrapped around his waist by the time I caught up to him. When I took his arm, he turned, his eyes aimed low at the deck, frowning.

I'm sorry. What's wrong? I signed.

He looked at me, and there was such hopelessness on his face, I took him by the shoulders, and leaned in close.

"I'm an idiot," I said. "I'm sorry if I insulted you." His eyes watched my lips.

He nodded, barely. He drew his fingertips from his lips into the palm of his open hand. It meant *thank you.*

He went inside to change, and I sat at the edge of the pool and wondered what exactly he was thanking me for. The drives to and from the vineyard were tense. That night his lovemaking was almost frantic. His goal seemed to be to get me off, with no thought to his own pleasure, and I had to slow him down. Eventually, I just wrapped my arms around him, and we held each other. Both of us pretended I couldn't feel the wetness of his eyes against my chest.

❖

"I think I fucked up," I said to Terry, the next day. He was sitting in the restaurant office, piles of paper all over his desk. It made me cringe how disorganized he could be, and I was forever glad that his assistant seemed capable of sorting through his disasters to make sure everything was done on time.

Terry looked up at me from his desk. "The vines?"

I shook my head. "No. I think we've got that covered. They're going to till in some new fertilizer and soil. With a little luck, they also won't destroy all the vines that are growing in the process." I shrugged, and sat down in the other chair. "It's Dennis."

Terry's smile was wide. "Trouble in paradise, Daddy Warbucks?"

I sighed. "It's not like that. He's not like that. He doesn't ask for anything." I shook my head. "In fact, that was my mistake. I offered to buy him a bicycle…I think I insulted him. I made him feel like a hustler or something."

Terry laughed. "Trust you to find the only hot fuck without an agenda." He shook his head. "You're such a lucky asshole."

I stared at him. "Thanks, Terry. You always know just what to say to make me feel better."

He laughed again. "Sorry, buddy. You're the one dickin' the help. If the boy doesn't want anything more than your cock, I say go for it." He grinned. "I'm sure you'll find a way to make it up to him. He's not the sort to stay pissed. Just fuck him good, and he'll come around."

I bristled. "He's not like the boys you hook up with."

"Why? Because he's deaf?" Terry shook his head. "Look. I'm glad you're happy. It's nice to see you happy. Lord knows you work your ass off, and you never do anything fun for yourself. I'm glad you're getting laid. You're lucky. You don't want to know how much cash I dropped on that last piece of trash."

I sighed. "You're such a misanthrope."

"It's why we didn't last," he agreed. "I'm not saying you're not a catch, Jesse. But let's be honest. The kid is hot, he's got that whole 'wounded' thing going on for him with the deaf stuff, and you fall for that crap hook, line, and sinker." He shrugged. "Just have fun. Go places, do shit, get him some decent clothes and shit. He's a boy. He's gonna get tired and move on eventually. Don't sweat it when it happens, just find another. Trust me." He wagged his eyebrows. "There's always another."

I went to go find Dennis in the kitchens, where he was working hard at the sink. He'd gotten a ride in with one of the other workers, and I hadn't seen him since the morning. When I tapped him on the shoulder, he turned, with a dark look on his face that vanished when he saw me. He smiled, looking a little bashful.

Sorry, he signed. Drops of water hit his shirt.

"Forget it," I said, and just like that the knot in my chest was almost gone.

He nodded.

"Movie tonight?" I asked him.

He nodded, then paused. *I'm closing. I might be late*, he signed.

Two staff stayed behind after the restaurant closed to double-count the deposit and lock up the safes. It usually didn't take longer than half an hour. "Do you need me to come pick you up?" I asked.

He shook his head. *I can get a ride, or walk.* He liked to walk in the nice weather.

I leaned in and kissed him, a quick peck on the forehead. He smiled, his crooked smirk firmly in place.

When I saw that smile was for me, some reflex flickered and I lifted my hand and curled in my middle two fingers, spreading my thumb wide.

It was an ASL sign: *I love you.*

He flinched. I felt my face burn. I reached for his shoulder, and he was tense beneath me.

"You don't have to say it back," I said.

He leaned forward and kissed me. The ache in my stomach faded.

"See you tonight," I said.

He nodded.

But I didn't see him again.

The air ripples. The sunlight is gone. I take another swallow, but Dennis fades. He loved me. I close my eyes for a moment, just a moment, to remember that sign through the window—something I never saw. I open my eyes again and turn.

Dennis is in the restaurant. I can see him, watery and pale, through the small window in the swinging doors.

I push through them. Dennis is standing, arms crossed, waiting for something. He checks his watch and frowns.

He's wearing the same shirt. It's the same day, I think. That night. The night he stole the money and left.

My stomach clenches.

The door opens, and someone walks in.

"What?" I say, but of course, neither of them answer.

I take another swallow.

❖

"He cleaned out both the safes," Terry said. "The shop and the restaurant, including the night's dinner earnings."

I rubbed my forehead. "What did the cops say?"

Terry sighed. "It was cash, right? They're not thinking it's likely we'll get it back. They've got people on the lookout for him, but…" He shrugged. "I'm sorry, Jesse. I…I wish it was different."

He looked terrible. I smiled at him. "I'm the one who got taken by the hustler," I said, each word burning in my gut. "Why do you look like shit?"

Terry just shook his head. "If I'd been smarter, I wouldn't have let the kid help with the closing. He wouldn't have known the ins and outs…"

"The safes have to be double-counted every night," I said. "That's how it works. Don't feel bad about it. It was my judgment call, not yours." I smiled, though I wanted to scream. "You get to say 'I told you so' now."

Terry just shook his head, and made for the door. "Will we be okay?" he asked.

I nodded. "There's enough in the bank in the business accounts. It'll suck, don't get me wrong, but it'll be okay. No bonuses this year. And if it really gets bad, I can float the difference from my personal account."

"I'll handle the soil stuff," Terry said. "If you want."

I'd forgotten we were having the soil treated again. Damned dry summer. I smiled at him, genuinely relieved. "Thanks. I'd really just like to go home."

Terry nodded and left.

I put my head down on my desk and cried.

❖

Dennis hadn't taken any of his belongings with him. I'd been at home, so it wasn't something he'd probably felt had been worth the risk. I'd waited for him until nearly midnight before calling the restaurant. When no one had answered, I'd tried the vineyard, but no one picked up there, either. I'd waited another half hour, aware that Dennis had said he might be late, and growing more and more nervous. I'd called Terry, who'd picked up right away and told me he'd call the worker who'd closed the restaurant down with Dennis. Terry called me back and told me that according to the other staff, they'd closed the restaurant and gone their separate ways. Dennis had declined a ride.

Finally, I'd gotten into my car and driven the road between the vineyard and my home. There was really only one way to walk home, and he wasn't on it. I'd driven slowly, feeling sick. What if he'd been hurt? When I got to the restaurant, I saw some of the lights were on and parked the car. If he'd come back, Dennis wouldn't have heard the phone ring when I'd called. I went inside and started looking for him. When I'd gotten to the restaurant's office, and the door to the safe was wide open, I'd stopped, frowning at it for a long while.

I'd called Terry again, and then the police.

It was a lean autumn, but by winter we were doing well, and if we hadn't recovered the loss, exactly, we were breaking even again. We scored a favorable review both for the year's vintage and for the restaurant, and the two went a long way. I worked long hours, not enjoying my quiet home at all.

When the first frost hit in early January, for the first time since I'd owned the vineyard I didn't help with the picking. The grapes might be ideal for an uncommon red ice wine, but I didn't want to see them. I passed the whole event by, letting my staff deal with the process, and barely following up to make sure they were doing things correctly.

Going into the restaurant made me feel sick, and I hadn't stepped into the kitchens in months. By the time the red ice wine was ready to taste, instead of gathering the staff like I'd done for years and opening a few bottles for us all to try, I uncorked the bottle and had a single small glass in my office, after everyone else had gone home.

It was wonderful. Sweet, almost a honey bouquet, and a first-class finish.

"Molten strawberries," I said, but it didn't make me smile. The soil had been worth it. The impact on the wine was obvious.

I picked up the bottle and glass and left my office. I walked through the main building and went into the restaurant, locking the door after myself. I stood among the tables for a while, then walked into the kitchen through the swinging doors.

As soon as I saw the sink, I started shaking with anger. I put the bottle down and threw the glass across the room, hearing it shatter in the huge steel basin where Dennis had worked. It didn't help, and I ended up having to clean up broken glass for five minutes. By the time I was done with that, I felt thoroughly humiliated all over again, and reached for the bottle and drank a swallow of the ice wine like a hobo in an alley. It was an exceptionally good wine.

I pulled out my cell and called Terry.

"The red ice wine is great," I said.

"You okay?" he asked.

"I'm fine. You can go ahead and start shipping it tomorrow."

I went home, the open bottle balanced between my legs, not caring if I was pulled over. Inside my house, I tipped the bottle back again, starting to feel a small buzz. This wasn't the way you were meant to enjoy a red ice wine. It was a dessert wine, something to enjoy on its own merit in small glasses. Maybe with a strong cheese, but certainly not with anything sweet. I poured it into a pinot noir glass, and swallowed more.

By the time I'd finished the large glass, I was buzzing. I refilled the glass and sank onto my couch.

Dennis walked in.

I yelped and sat up, but Dennis wavered and disappeared. I blinked, shaking my head. Tears stung my eyes.

"Oh fuck you," I growled, and swallowed.

He reappeared. I froze, glass at my lips, and watched. Dennis was watery, a blurry vision through which I could see my bookcases. His hair was longer than it should have been, and he was wearing the faded shirt he'd worn the night—

I walked in after him, watery and indistinct.

"Oh Jesus," I breathed. I watched the scene play out silently. I saw myself speak—but there were no words. I saw him pick up the picture of Terry and me, and I watched him walk over, and kneel in front of me.

I swallowed more wine, and the image sharpened.

By the time the bottle was empty, I'd followed myself and Dennis into the bedroom and watched myself make love to the young man for the first time. After, I watched Dennis snuggle into my arms, and the smile on my face when I looked at him cut me to the bone.

"You're an idiot," I slurred at myself. Then I fell over, and passed out.

❖

I came to when my cell rang, late in the following morning. I grabbed it awkwardly.

"'Lo?" My voice was rough, and my head was aching. Not the worst hangover I'd ever had, but still a hangover.

"You sound terrible." It was Terry.

"Ugh," I said.

"You need to take a day?"

"Yeah."

"Okay," Terry said. He paused, like he wanted to say more, but didn't. "Okay."

"Thanks," I said, and rubbed my eyes. At some point I'd crawled into bed. When I rolled to my side, a bottle rolled against me. I looked at it. Remembered.

"Terry, did you send out the red ice wine yet?" My heart was hammering.

"Yeah."

"Get it back."

"What? You said it was fine. I've shipped out quite a few already, and—"

"Get it back," I said. "No one drinks it. Got it?"

"I'll try," Terry said. "Shit. Is there something wrong with it?"

I thought about Dennis and myself, replaying in front of me.

"Yes," I lied. "There's something wrong with it."

❖

Terry and Dennis are arguing in front of me, though I can't hear what Terry is yelling, and for his part Dennis is just shaking his head and pointing at his notepad. I move closer, look at the notepad as Dennis holds it up in Terry's face.

It just says *I won't do it*.

Terry is furious. I've seen him like this before, once or twice, and I wish I could read lips like Dennis to know what Terry is screaming at him. Terry grabs Dennis by the shoulders and physically shakes him. Dennis steps back and writes on his pad again. When he holds it up to Terry, I try to get around to see, but Terry smacks it out of his hand, and it flies off and vanishes.

"Stop it," I yell, but they don't react. The bottle shakes in my hand.

Dennis shoves Terry, hard. Terry punches him, his thick fist landing hard in the middle of Dennis's face. He stumbles back, and his foot catches on something. He goes down, and Terry is on top of him, his hands wrapping around Dennis's neck.

"No," I whine. "No, no, no…"

The images collapse. The bottle is dry. My lover is dead. The last of his memories are gone with the wine.

I don't know how.

I don't know why.

But one of those I can answer.

❖

The police are here when Terry comes in to work. When he sees them, he seems to deflate, and I wonder how long he's been waiting for something like this to happen. I had them dig under the rows of vines from which the red ice wine was born, and when they called out that they had found something, I had closed my eyes, willing the world to slow down and let me not know, just for a moment longer.

Terry had had no time for anything elegant. And through the wine my Dennis spoke to me. Where else could my lover be? It all comes together. The rain, the grapes, the frost. The soil. The soil tells.

The police take Terry's arms. They tell him his rights. He looks at me, and I ask.

"Why?"

"Money," he says. "He was supposed to get access to your bank accounts." He looks at me, a pleading look on his face. "They're going to take my house."

I close my eyes and try to ignore all the sounds as they put Terry into the car and the rest of the business unfolds.

I stand there, eyes closed, and think of Dennis, and Terry, and death. A hustler after all, I think darkly, but it doesn't hold. I remember his hand at the window and swear I can taste molten strawberries on my tongue.

Purples lean on other colors.

Darker purples, especially those that border browns, are born of pain. The deeper the color, the closer to a bruise, the more physical the pain; but when the color flares outward from within, it can be the kind of hurt that has nothing to do with the body.

Pale purple is guilt, a thin, misty color that builds between the eyes and floods down in a wash along the body.

Reddened, purples are desires. Not in the same way a green is a want, but in a more physical sense, with a hope of connection. They're healthy, and watching them reach out between people is like watching a dance, especially when they're the last to know how they feel.

If a purple hums near the surface of the skin but never reaches farther, there's a denial—and if the purple is a bright, clear thing that dances away whenever you catch it, it's fearful.

If it grows thick, if it surrounds someone completely and darkens more and more, it can be terror or defeat.

Those purples darken hospitals and waiting rooms and courts as often as they appear around one person, whether or not they're in a crowd.

There are things people cannot fight alone.

Not all of them are visible to anyone else.

Here Be Dragons

The dragons from my childhood fairy tales used to hide in my closets and under the bed. They were terrifying when I was young, but they were creatures to be beaten. Princes would come, and birds and mice would find a way, and together, love would be triumphant.

Now those dragons are just as invisible and unknowable as they ever were, but they hide among my neurotransmitters, gobbling away names and moments or snatching up entire days in their teeth. They feed on my memories and give me scraps.

❖

Leaving the big house to come to my little sea-foam green room was my idea, and convincing Alan was no minor feat. There's a reason you marry your Prince Charming once you find him, even when you have to wait decades to be allowed. But even the princely types have drawbacks.

For one, they think they can save the day. Every damn time. Stubborn as shit, those princes. They don't ever admit they're in over their heads, not even when they're on the ass end of seventy like we are, and not even when their rescued damsel—that would be me, and I'll thank you not to judge my current state and simply go with me on this one—is falling to pieces in front of them.

Not literal pieces, of course, though between you and me, neither of us has much hair left, and if pieces aren't falling off per se, some of them are drooping in a pretty close facsimile.

"You're fine," Alan had argued when I told him what we would be doing. It was sweet, the way he thought he got a vote on this. We’d always worked as a pair, but sometimes a princess needs to rally her mice, tell the birds to stand guard, and put down her glass slipper with force. This was one of them.

That I was wearing comfort support arches was beside the point.

“I’m not fine. My head is going to be as useless as chenille, darling. And I’m not going to put you in charge of the no-machine, no-hot-water, lay-flat-to-dry shit that is coming down the pipeline.”

“Martin,” he said.

To keep you up to speed, using my full name is my Alan’s way of pulling out the big guns. It used to be Alan’s big guns were his arms, where all the butch boys keep them, and if you ask me, he grew old fine, but I know he feels smaller and weaker than he used to. So now, instead of tossing me over his shoulder—I swear to God this was a thing he used to do and it was *hot*—he uses my full name.

“Mar” means he loves me, and maybe he’d like a snuggle.

“Marty” means he’s feeling maudlin, and he needs a snuggle.

But “Martin”? That means I’m pissing him off.

Unfortunately, he’s my Prince Charming. And I may be old, but I’m no old-school princess. I do love me a Cinderella story, especially the dressmaking scenes with the mice and the birds, but I would fit more with the modern princess types, and I am my own fairy, thank-you-very-much. So he can throw down his “Martin” and frown at me and rub his bald head, but this princess isn’t going to wait around in a glass coffin.

Shit. I’m mixing up my fairy tales, aren’t I?

Oh well. That just goes to show. It’s the whole damn problem, right there.

Back then I was clearer than I am now. The dragons weren’t quite as at home.

“Alan,” I told him. “I’ve already made the arrangements.”

He was mad, of course, but I calmed him down.

Prince Charmings don’t stay mad.

The scraps these new dragons leave behind aren’t the kind I can use, pieces nothing at all like the fabrics I used to turn into clothes that won awards and criticism in equal volume. These scraps are frayed and worn, and I can't conjure a pattern from them when the dragon visits. But I can hold them, and I can touch them, and I can tell they used to be so fine.

I think I was always the sort of person who knew what was fine.

❖

We made love that afternoon while the light faded on a winter day outside the big house. We shared a bath after, in the big bathroom we'd renovated almost entirely around the size of that tub. We dried off, and we had dinner, and we watched two movies together in our Martin Alan brand original silk pajamas and big warm housecoats, eating popcorn from a bowl we passed back and forth.

The first movie was probably some soft romantic nonsense. I don't remember what I picked, but since I picked it, I promise you at some point someone swooned, someone declared, and likely the hero lost his shirt a few times.

What I do remember was Alan's choice was *Cinderella*, and it was when the mice and birds were putting scraps together that the idea came to me.

It was typical, really, that my best idea might come from him.

Prince Charming rode to save the day again.

❖

I'm losing time. Or perhaps time is losing me. The dragons bite and tear chunks of it from me, and I am adrift more and more often.

I think I'm dreaming again, but I'm not entirely sure. I can smell rain, and I can hear the sound of water. The sea? An ocean?

The sea-foam green room, the soft sheets and my special quilt, and the body that lies beneath them I can sometimes barely recognize as my own—the dragon doesn't seem to care to disturb these things.

Those are the places the mice come and hide.

Clever little things, mice.

❖

When Alan found me in the largest walk-in, the clothes laid out before me, he had fear in his face. I'd left him sleeping in our bed. The idea was gnawing at me in a way I knew meant it wouldn't leave me alone until I at least took some action to cement it.

But the panic on his face, giving way to relief now that he'd found me, was a needle to the heart.

"I'm sorry," I said.

He tucked the worry aside, raising his shoulders and smiling at me. He'd always had a killer smile, and he could still dish it out. "Couldn't sleep?"

"New idea," I said.

"Oh." His eyebrows rose. "Do tell."

I raised my hand to the suits and shirts and pants and coats all around me. Most were still in their protective plastic. The vast majority hadn't been worn in years, since the last time I'd taken them to a class I'd taught.

He looked at them in turn. He had a dozen ways to smile, and he used them all by the time he realized what each piece was. These clothes had never been for models. They were things I'd designed solely for us. Vacations or award ceremonies. The suit he wore the night his move to CEO was finalized. The tie he wore the day he got his entry-level job a few decades earlier. There was even a scarf from our trip to Niagara, where we'd gone for a wine-tasting, and the weather had been cold every single day. Byrnes, or Brynes, or something. It had been good wine.

These clothes were us. And I'd made every piece of them.

"I'm going to take them with me," I said.

His worried frown returned. Once he'd calmed down and realized he couldn't argue me out of it, he'd read the pamphlets. He knew the rules of the hospice.

"Marty," he said. "There won't be room."

❖

I'm awake, and I'm myself today. The fragility of that feeling is impossible to get used to. I stood on stages and held statues of glass high and swore in front of crowds who expected finer language. I dressed people in costumes meant to make them think about things they didn't want to think. Starvation. Disease. Hatred.

Love.

Oh, how it pissed them off when I designed clothes for *love*.

I smile and turn my head. Alan is sitting in the chair again, asleep, the book on his lap now forgotten. Today I know him, and he is not someone the dragon tells me is a stranger. My Alan, who suffered my wins and my losses with equal calm. Who, from the first few designs and the first hints of success, never let me forget what was most important. Alan, who took my talent and his know-how and turned us into a giant. We couldn't marry back then, but we locked our names together anyway and we were a label. Martin Alan meant style.

It also meant "Fuck You" to all the people who'd sneered at the fags playing dress-up. I hope it still does.

I just watch him for a while, thinking it's more important than ever to find some way to remember what is him. *Labels. Companies. Triumphs. Kisses. Prince Charmings. Popcorn.* Behind Alan the sun is coming up, but the blinds here make even the brightest day soft around the edges, like clouds parting after a storm. My dream returns to me again.

Beaches.

I pull on my quilt, and I trace a square of deep blue.

❖

Once I explained, we both pretended neither of us had tears in our eyes, and Alan went to make tea. By the time he brought back a pot and cups and a folding table to set them on far enough from where I was spreading out the clothes, he'd recovered.

Princes are like that. We princesses get to be weepy and wail to our mice and our birds about how *unfair* it all is. Princes are too busy slaying the dragons.

Well. The ones you can slay, anyway.

"Phoebe," I said, once I'd selected the pieces I wanted to work with.

He nodded to show me he heard me, but his eyebrow rose too. He didn't understand.

"She was in the last class I taught. Trans woman. Opening up a store of her own, in Ottawa, I think. Whatever is left…" I gesture to all the other pieces around me. "Send them to her. She's got guts."

"I will." His voice was a bit maudlin, and I thought maybe I'd nudged him too far into planning, so I looked at the clothes again.

"Do you remember this day?" I said, holding up a deep blue shirt. It might very well have been the first thing I ever made for him, though with my dragons, I wasn't sure. It was the first thing I remembered, though. Maybe that was good enough.

I certainly remembered taking his measurements in my tiny apartment the week earlier. He'd flexed, and then we'd found much more interesting ways to measure him.

"The beach," Alan said, with a wink. "We were lucky."

I nodded, reaching for the next item, a tie. Lucky. Right. I wanted the clothes in order, and I'm playing the game of "do you remember" as much for the project as for the joy. I'd made a note and looked at the shirt once more with a smile. It could have been a perfect day, really. It wasn't, but it had come damn close.

"That was after," Alan said, pointing at the tie. "My first industry job interview."

"And it required a morning blow job for good luck, as I recall?"

"It's a well-known tradition," Alan deadpanned. He eyed the tie. "Is there enough?"

"Absolutely." I made a note on the pad.

We took a break when the sun came up for breakfast. We stopped again at lunch and braved a walk while the sun was out. It was cold, and we bundled up, watching where we stepped. It would have been just my luck to fall on the ice and bust a hip now that I'd put together an actual plan, but no. With Alan beside me, his arm in mine, our little walk through our neighborhood was safe and pleasant.

When we get back to the big house, we finished our trip through the clothes, and I started undoing the seams and cutting cloth.

I'm a modern princess. I didn't need the mice or birds.

Not quite then, anyway.

❖

A storm…

My finger traces the blue square. It's the first square on the blanket, and for a moment, I grasp that as *important*. It feels soft and worn down. Loved.

A storm…There was…

For some reason, I think of my needles and thread. And mice and birds, perhaps. It's strange to think of mice and birds. I usually think of Alan, or of parties, or of those awful dragons. I can feel them, even today, a good day.

My finger traces the square of deep blue cloth.

I try to thread a mental needle. A mouse dodges the teeth of a dragon to help me.

❖

The quilt wasn't finished by the time we moved me in to the little sea-foam green room, but Alan ensured the squares were packed and protected, and I was quite happy to have a project. Alongside the therapy sessions and Alan's visits, it filled time in a way that seemed to anger the dragons, and between you and me, I've always come down on the side of pissing off dragons.

It also reminded me of another quilt, and in a way I feel like I'm in exceptional company. We princesses might never defeat all the dragons, but the important thing is the dragons never win. They come into our blood, and our bones, and our minds, but they never get us. We continue. We *exist*. We're remembered.

So, day by day, I added squares. It took longer than it should have, but I spread it over my bed when it was done. It hung over both sides and the bottom. A lot of blues—Alan always looked smashing in blue—but square after square of memory for me to see.

The day after I finished it, Alan came to visit at his usual time, and I lay there waiting for him under the blanket. His smile was brilliant.

"This bitch can still stitch," I said.

He laughed and joined me under the blanket, and we went square by square.

At one point, he chuckled again.

"What?" I asked.

"It's a stitch in time," he said.

I groaned. "This is why I always named the product lines. You are far too corny and prone to puns." But I kissed him, and he kissed me back, and it's possible we broke a few rules about visitors that afternoon.

❖

I close my eyes. I thread the needle. The mouse darts away from the deep blue square.

When I open my eyes, the beach is cool, the sand is still wet from the downpour and covers our bare feet. We walk with our fingers laced together, each carrying our soaked shoes in our free hand. It hasn't been a beautiful day, but it is wonderful despite—or because of—the unexpected. We have kissed in the rain and listened to thunder, raising our faces to the sky and laughing while a storm fell all around us. The shore is empty where we are, and the clouds above still seem angry, but despite the wet, this is a moment I will always treasure.

Except.

I remember just in time, and when I let go of Alan's hand, he is surprised but doesn't say anything. He shakes some of the water out of his curly dark hair, and a moment later we round the rocks midway down the beach and he sees the group of men who have just arrived, out of sight from where we walked hand in hand just seconds ago. They are all as big as Alan, they outnumber us, and seem far less happy about the rain.

The men look at us, notice how drenched we are, and then they look away, disinterested to even comment on the rain we've all no doubt been caught by. They are just as wet. They see two men walking, but *only* two men walking. What sense they might have of our spirit has found no confirmation, and I feel a loosening in my chest. They make no comments, no hurled insults, no threats. Nothing to ruin this moment the way it was ruined the first time.

The first time?

I frown, digging my toes into the wet sand. *What does that mean?* I feel like I am holding on to something more important than I can ever really know, but it wiggles out of my grasp like a mouse breaking free or a bird taking flight.

I shiver, and for some reason I am now thinking of a little sea-foam green room. I shiver again.

No. Not yet.

We are out of sight of the men now, coming around the pier. Alan's free hand reclaims mine, and he squeezes. The sea-foam green room recedes.

"You okay?" he says with a smile. He is young and handsome, and I think I might just love him for the first time ever.

I squeeze back. I lead him under the pier and his eyebrows rise to the edge of the wet curls of his hair. I press him against one of the large concrete pillars and kiss him again. I kiss him how I've never kissed him before, how I'd always wanted to kiss him on that very first day at the beach.

How I would have kissed him on that day before it was ruined by the hatred of strangers, I think, and the world sways as I close my eyes.

❖

I open my eyes to find myself in the sea-foam green room.

"Remember the beach?" I ask.

Alan startles awake on the chair. The curls of hair are long gone, but his eyebrows still rise when I surprise him. "Sorry?" he says, rubbing his eyes.

"Remember the beach?" I ask him again.

"By the pier? In the storm?" He smiles and nods. "Our first trip to Fuca." The lines around his eyes have grown deeper over the years, but they are good lines. Laugh lines. Oh, how we have laughed. But not always, not all days, and he deserves that. Alan deserves every good thing.

I have to know.

"That group of men," I say, and I wait, hesitant. The dragons, after all.

He has to pause and think, but he nods. "That's right. There were some people there, weren't there? Rough-looking bunch. But you saw them and you pulled me under the pier." He's smiling again now. "And as I recall, once we were under the pier, you became a very wicked man." He winks at me.

That's not what happened, I almost say, but the truth is I have scraps of memory instead of bolts, and the pattern on that original cloth was meaner and crueler and torn after our lovely walk on the beach in the rain. My finger moves on the square of deep blue fabric.

It feels wet to the touch.

That day was a good day. This new memory of that day is better. I smile back at Alan. I even wink.

He stretches, rises, and asks me if I'd like a cup of coffee. I tell him I would, and he leans forward and kisses me four times—right eyelid, left eyelid, forehead and lips. He leaves for the cafeteria, and I shift, uncomfortable in the bed. My favorite nurse, Lisa, whose name seems somehow immune to the appetite of dragons, comes. And when she pulls off the quilt and the sheet, she gives me a strange look from behind her glasses.

"How did you get all that sand in your bed?"

My feet are covered in the stuff. I play dumber than I am, feigning a worse day than I'm having, and she quickly forgives me. Surely this is among the least of the transgressions on her rounds this morning.

She is efficient, quick, and pleasant, and I try to be the same. By the time I'm resettled in the bed, the sheets and quilt restored, Alan still hasn't made it back. Lisa is just that good.

I close my eyes, and my hand moves to the next square. Silkier. The material came from a tie, I think. The dragons are angry. It's possible they know they're being used, somehow. I smile to myself. I can almost feel the threads of memory and time between my fingers, and my hands itch for a needle to sew with.

Tiny feet guide my fingers. Whiskers and bird feathers tickle my hand.

I'll still have to go. The dragons will still have me.

But my Prince Charming's life will be dressed so fine before they do.

Yellow is happiness.

It can blaze like joy, filling a room and spilling out like a sun, or it can be a single beam showing the way back to another. When aimed from one person to another, it's a kind of pride.

The palest of yellows, washing out from within and driving away other colors the way a dawn chases off the dark, is relief.

Yellow often streaks the other colors. It can brighten all the other shades and nearly always softens them. It is bright and warm and caring, and—my favorite—contagious.

People who light the way for others are almost always overflowing with these kinds of yellow. And when the yellow reaches a peak near their forehead and glows almost golden-bright, it becomes something more.

I've seen it in priests, and a sculptor, and a girl speaking out against the rules that constrained her. I've seen it at protests and rallies, and once at a wake. That golden crown goes beyond that shared joy.

Some people share their happiness.

Others inspire you to seek out your own.

STRUCK

I'm going to fix your life!"

Chris balanced a dozen copies of the latest teen hardcover in his left arm. The customer who'd spoken had just walked right by his boss Laurali, who was at the cash registers leafing through a magazine. Why customers avoided obviously free staff to go ask questions of the employee with his hands full was one of the mysteries of working at Book It.

"Is that the title?" Chris asked.

"What?"

"I'm going to fix your life," Chris repeated. The books were getting heavier by the moment. It was probably all the angst.

"No," the customer said. "I am."

"Pardon?" Chris tried not to stare at him.

The customer was trim and blond and had eyes an impossible shade of blue. Chris could see his contacts. He was very tanned, sporting a skin-tight blue shirt the same shade, as well as a deep frown.

"Oh!" the customer said suddenly. "You think I'm looking for a book!" He laughed, as if he'd just gotten the joke.

This is *a bookstore*, Chris wanted to say. Instead, aware that Laurali was now looking at him with her "disappointed" stare burning a hole in the back of his head, he said, "How may I help you?"

"No, no," the blond repeated, chuckling now. His teeth were so bleached, they dazzled. "I'm here to help *you*, uh…" His eyes glanced down to Chris's name tag. "Chris."

Was he being scouted? For a brief instant, Chris allowed himself the fantasy. This blond was going to swoop in, hire him to be the manager at a beautiful gallery somewhere incredibly warm all year round—it would have to be, given the blond's tan—and…and…Uh. Maybe a beach?

Oh my God. I've lost the ability to even fantasize about a better life.

"Okay," Chris said, coming back to reality. More likely the blond was about to offer him a personal connection to Jesus Christ. If Jesus Christ would take the damned teen books out of his arms, Chris would consider it.

"I'm Lightning Todd," the blond said.

"Okay," Chris said, wary. Maybe this was a joke? Lightning Todd? *Oh God. He's a stripogram. I'm going to get fired.*

Lightning Todd frowned again. "Don't you know who I am?"

"Lightning Todd?" Chris said gamely. The back of his head had to be smoking by now. He could hear Laurali sighing theatrically at the cash desk.

The blond nodded. "The one and only. So, here's the thing. I've tuned in on you, which, as you know, is totally awesome."

"Totally." Chris shifted the books from his left arm to his right. Tolstoy didn't weigh this much. Shouldn't classics weigh more than teenage hormones? "Listen, I'm really flattered, but I'm at work right now." He offered his best smile.

"What?" Lightning Todd frowned again. It didn't seem to take much to confuse the guy. "Oh! Oh!" His eyes widened. "Oh my God, no! Ew! I'm not hitting on you. You're *old*!"

Chris clenched his teeth. "I'm thirty-six."

"Really?" Lightning Todd peered at him. "Whoa. I wouldn't have said more than thirty-two. Well done."

"Thank you." Chris felt his face reddening. "Listen, I need to get these dealt with." He lifted the hardcovers slightly. "So if there's nothing I can help you with…"

Lightning Todd shook his head. "You're not open to it right now. But listen, after the coffee issue and the zipper thing, I'll come back, and we'll chat again, okay…" Lightning Todd paused and glanced at Chris's name tag again. "Chris?"

"Sure," Chris said. *The coffee issue and the zipper thing?*

Lightning Todd nodded and walked past him. Chris could have

sworn he heard the blond mutter "Thirty-six!" under his breath with something like disgust. When Chris got to the cash registers, Laurali was scowling at him.

"Friend of yours?" she asked. Chris reminded himself she was only a temporary problem. Laurali was covering Tracey's maternity leave. Tracey was the greatest boss Chris had ever had. Laurali, Chris was sure, had been sent by his own personal devil to make his life as miserable as possible. She had the worst sense of "business casual" Chris had ever encountered. Today's blouse was leopard print, and she wore faux glasses that didn't have a prescription because "people equate glasses with management."

"No," Chris said, putting down the books. His arms felt light and rubbery. "Customer."

"He couldn't have been a customer," Laurali said. Her voice was singsong upbeat. That meant trouble.

"He wasn't a friend," Chris repeated. Laurali hated it when the staff had friends drop by. Unless they were hers.

"But if he was a customer, you didn't convert him from a browser to a buyer," Laurali said, looking over her glasses and down her nose at him. She held up a finger. "Remember the mantra: *Conversion is King!* You may be only an assistant manager, but if you don't model the behavior, how will the rest of the staff buy in to it?"

"We're the only two people on shift," Chris said. *And you've been reading that gossip magazine all morning.*

Laurali shook her head. "This is the attitude problem I was talking about at our last rap session."

"I need to go put these on the display," Chris responded before he said something else he'd regret.

Or enjoy.

He grabbed the books and turned sharply, slamming into the customer who'd appeared with ninja stealth behind him. The coffee the woman was carrying went all down Chris's front, covering his vest, shirt, and half the hardcovers.

"I'm so sorry," Laurali said. She sounded positively cheerful. "He's such a klutz."

❖

The roof of the mall had manicured green spaces, plant boxes, and even some trees. It was Chris's favorite place to take his break, especially now that autumn was bringing a lovely coolness to the air. It was serene up here. Calming. He could even see the river.

"Just four more months. I only have to make it four more months. If I killed her, I'd have to go to jail," he said aloud, peeling his orange. "So that's out."

"I'll pretend I didn't hear that."

Chris jumped. One of the security guards—the best security guard, in Chris's opinion—was smiling at him. He had hooked his hands into the front of his vest, which made his biceps strain the fabric of the grey shirt he wore underneath. His name was Liam. Chris had once placed an order for him for some science fiction books. Liam had a great smile that tilted a little on the left side. Also, he was tall and had no wedding ring. It was really enjoyable to watch him come and go through the mall. Especially go.

The uniform pants were really snug in the behind.

Chris had noticed Liam took his breaks on the rooftop garden a few months before and had been all the more vigilant to use the green space himself ever since. Which had a downside, apparently.

"How long have you been standing there?" Chris asked. He felt his cheeks burning.

"Long enough to learn that you're planning to murder your boss because she's a hypocritical harpy. And passive aggressive." Liam's eyes flicked down. "What happened to your shirt?"

"I bumped into a customer, and she spilled coffee all over me. You realize now that you've heard my plotting, you know too much, right?"

Liam laughed. "I'm pretty sure I could take you."

Yes, please. Chris's tongue glued itself to the top of his mouth. "Gluh."

"What?" Liam asked. He had the most expressive brown eyes. Right now they were expressing amusement. Or maybe pity.

Chris came back down to earth. "Nothing, sorry. I promise not to kill anyone today."

"Or in four months?"

Chris sighed. "In four months, my real boss comes back from maternity leave, and Laurali will be a bad memory."

"Think you can make it that long?"

"I'll try. Murder is so messy. And you know my plans." Chris smiled. He loved Liam's slightly crooked grin.

"Well, if you can't wait, at least wait until I'm off today," Liam said. "I have an important dinner tonight."

"Sounds like fun," Chris said. He wondered if he could maybe sound more moronic if he really, really tried. This was the most they'd ever talked. He could feel his IQ dropping the longer he spoke.

"We're having a big anniversary dinner. My folks are in town."

We. He must have a girlfriend. He and his girlfriend are celebrating their anniversary, and even his parents are coming. She is such a lucky woman. I hate her.

Chris nodded. "Cool." *Cool? That's all you can say?*

Liam nodded.

Chris nodded back. He was pretty sure it couldn't possibly get more awkward.

"Uh." Liam sounded apologetic. "Your fly is open."

I want to die. Chris reached down and zipped up. "Thanks." He wondered if Laurali had noticed, and if she had, how long she'd enjoyed knowing he looked foolish.

Liam walked back to the doors. Chris rubbed his eyes. This was turning into a truly bad day. His phone chirped. He had five minutes to get back to the store before he'd be late from his break. The last thing he needed was to give Laurali any more ammunition. She'd hated him from the first day Tracey had left on her maternity leave.

He tossed the half-peeled orange into the garbage can beside the door. Liam had a girlfriend, and they were having an anniversary. Well, it was an unrequited crush anyway. Besides, between the coffee issue and the zipper thing, all hope would have been lost anyway.

Something about that nibbled at the back of Chris's thoughts for the rest of his shift.

❖

"See?"

Chris counted to five, put his smile in place, and turned around. It was Lightning Todd again, though this time his contacts and his T-shirt were both a deep green.

"Hi," Chris said. He had a cart full of books to shelve, and Laurali had been on the warpath about their lagging conversion numbers after she'd gotten a call from the regional manager about the store's flagging sales. If Chris heard "Conversion is King!" one more time, he was going to vomit. Not that Laurali had been actively talking to customers herself or anything.

Lightning Todd spread his hands wide. "Well?"

"I'm sorry?" Chris frowned.

"The coffee?" Lightning Todd rubbed his left hand across his chest. Then he pointed his right index finger at his crotch, bouncing his arm up and down. "The zipper?"

Chris stared. It looked like Lightning Todd was doing some sort of erotic dance. Or maybe masturbating.

"Chris!" Laurali's voice was loud in the nearly empty store. "No friends. We've talked about this."

Lightning Todd turned and glared at her. "I'll just be, like, a minute. Don't freak out." Laurali's eyes bugged out behind her glasses. Lightning Todd turned back to Chris, and in a whisper louder than his already boisterous voice, he added, "What a colossal bitch."

That's it, Chris thought. *I'm fired.* "What do you want?"

"The coffee and the zipper. Called it, right?" The blond looked inordinately pleased with himself.

Chris blinked. He had, hadn't he? "How…?" He shook his head. When had he lost control of this conversation? "Listen, I don't get the joke, but I'm at work. If I can help you find something, I will, but otherwise—"

"No, you don't get it." The blond shook his head. "I go where I'm needed. Ever since That Day." He said the two words with feeling. Chris had no idea what he was talking about, and it apparently showed. "Didn't you check out my website?"

"You have a website?"

Lightning Todd sighed. "Listen. Here's the sitch. You need me. I only tune in on people who need me. And you need me bad, Chris." He nodded briskly.

"I thought I was too old for you."

"What?" The blond frowned. "Oh! Ha. You're funny. But listen. Before you quit and never come back, you totally have to kiss the guy who won't wear pink."

"Kiss the…Before I quit?" Chris said. Given his situation, that was rather unlikely.

"Because of the *Titanic*."

"Because of the *Titanic*." Chris leaned forward. "Are you high? Do you need me to call someone for you?"

"Chris!" Laurali called again. She was using her singsong voice.

"Ugh." Lightning Todd rolled his eyes. "She's horrible. Her vibes are, like, sticky and smell like purple. Anyway, the sixes and ones will make everything better once you're stuck for a way to go home."

"Chris, I need you to finish the shelving." Laurali had come out from behind the counter for the first time all day. She gave Lightning Todd a tight smile and looked over the top of her glasses at him. "I'm afraid you'll have to go. It's company policy not to allow friends to interfere with our employees while they work."

"You know," Lightning Todd said to her, "if you just got over the whole cheated with a gay guy thing your husband did, you'd be open to some bliss and stuff."

Laurali went white. "Get out."

Lightning Todd shrugged. "I'll see you Friday night at Bittersweets?" It took Chris a moment to realize Lightning Todd was speaking to him.

"I close the store Friday night."

"You might be free," Lightning Todd said and shook his head. He made two finger guns and said, "Todd has spoken. You've been struck." Then he trotted away, waving.

Laurali stared at Chris. Her neck was turning red.

"I…" Chris cleared his throat.

"Shelve the cart," Laurali snapped.

Chris got back to work.

❖

"I didn't take you for the techno sort."

Chris glanced up at Liam from the bench on the rooftop garden. Liam was doing the undercover thing today, though it was easy enough to tell he had the vest on under his hoodie. He was wearing a pink cap, though, which surprised Chris and made him think of Lightning Todd's words. Obviously, Liam was a guy who would wear pink. No kissing him.

Also: girlfriend, he reminded himself.

"I'm not," Chris said. He held up his phone. "It's a website."

Liam sat beside him on the bench and looked at the screen.

"Lightning Rod?"

"Lightning Todd," Chris said.

"Is that a stripper?"

"See!" Chris felt vindicated. "That's what I thought."

Liam's eyebrows rose. They were good eyebrows, even if he did look a little dorky in a pink ball cap.

"He's a psychic, apparently," Chris said.

Liam laughed.

Chris shrugged. "He got hit by lightning a few years back. Ever since, he says he can…" Chris looked at the little screen. "Tune in to the vibes of the universe and help people find their bliss." Chris winced. "He used the contraction for 'they are' instead of the possessive."

"Sounds completely legit." Liam smirked.

Chris thumbed off the phone. The pounding bass stopped. For a second, he thought about telling Liam about the coffee and zipper thing, but he felt a little stupid for considering Lightning Todd's advice. Quitting because of the *Titanic*? He shook his head.

"So how was the anniversary dinner? Did she love it?"

Liam seemed surprised. "Yeah. It was nice."

Chris smiled. His phone chirped. He groaned. "That's my five-minute warning."

"Time to go back to the hypocritical harpy?"

"You have a good memory. I shouldn't have plotted murder in front of you." Chris gave Liam's shoulder a shove. Now that Liam was completely unavailable, he was much less daunting to talk to.

Liam laughed. "I should get back to looking for shoplifters."

"And I have an entire cart of romance novels to shelve. Our lives overflow with excitement," Chris said. He got up and the two walked back into the mall together.

"What else would you do?" Liam asked. "If you weren't married to romance novels."

Chris looked at him. It wasn't a question he was often asked. But it didn't need any thought. "I'd work at a museum. The National Art Gallery, if I could. I have most of an art history degree."

"Most?"

They stepped onto the escalators. "I had to drop out third year. My father died."

Liam flinched. "I'm sorry."

"It's okay. He had a heart attack and hadn't put a will together or anything. My parents were living check to check. My mother ended up bankrupt. I got the job at the bookstore part-time to help pay for university, but it ended up becoming a permanent gig after that so I could help keep her afloat." He smiled. "I do like the job."

They were at the bottom of the escalator.

"Except for the harpy."

"Except." He was a little surprised Liam had asked, and more surprised he'd answered honestly. It was easier to be candid when you weren't trying to impress someone.

"What about you?" Chris asked.

"And give up all this?" Liam raised his arms.

Chris laughed. He was running out of break time. He turned to go.

"Photographer," Liam said. "Black and white."

Chris smiled. "So we're both art lovers."

Liam smiled. Chris headed back to the store. He turned a few paces away. "Kudos for having the guts to sport the hat, by the way."

"What?" Liam asked.

"Very Don Johnson," Chris said and gave him a thumbs-up before he turned around and went back to Book It.

❖

"The *Titanic* had to be sunk, you know."

Chris froze. He'd been walking by the transportation section with an armload of Curious George, and the customer had reached out and taken his shoulder. He was an older man with bushy grey eyebrows and a bit of a manic smile.

Chris stepped back, but the man's grip stayed firm. "We have a couple of books on the *Titanic* right there." He gestured. He felt a little tremble in his stomach. *The* Titanic.

"None of them are right." The man didn't let go.

"I'm sorry?" Chris asked. He twisted a little bit, and the man finally removed his hand.

"There were too many real people on board. That's why they had to sink the *Titanic*."

Do not engage. Be polite. Move on. Chris smiled. "I'm afraid that's all we have. They might have more selection at one of our other locations."

"If you squint just right, you can tell who's real and who isn't." The man reeked of mouthwash. Chris felt bad for him. His clothes were a bit heavy for the season and none too clean. He wondered if he was homeless. "Too many real people wanted to ride the *Titanic*. Made themselves a target. They don't want the real people to live, you see."

"I see," Chris said. He glanced up at the front, but Laurali was talking to Jason, the only other staff member in the store. She seemed to be giving him crap about something. Of course.

The man squinted at him. "You're real."

This wasn't comforting, given what Chris had learned about real people thus far.

"I'm afraid that's all we have," Chris said.

The man took both books from the shelf and started walking to the front of the store. Chris hesitated. He was pretty sure the man wasn't heading to the registers. A moment later, it became obvious. He jogged up to the man.

"Did you want me to put those at the register for you?" he asked, raising his voice a little. Laurali, however, didn't stop her ranting. Chris heard the word "conversion" and tried not to groan.

The man's eyebrows rose high on his forehead.

"You're real!" he said.

"I've heard that," Chris said. He reached for the books. "I can put these on hold for you, if you'd like."

The man bellowed at him, an inarticulate noise louder than Chris would have given his slim frame credit for producing. Then he threw the books on the floor and ran from the store.

"Okay," Chris said, shaken.

"What was that?" Laurali's voice was back to that grating singsong. Chris knelt and picked up the two books. One was ripped.

"He was a little confused. He was going to walk out without paying, so I offered to put the books on hold, and he kind of lost it."

"You're not supposed to confront thieves," Laurali said.

"I thought we were supposed to offer them extra help so they know they've been spotted," Jason said. Chris could have hugged him on the spot.

"Not if they're dangerous or determined. Then you're supposed to let the manager know and have security called." Laurali shook her head. "I'm disappointed, Chris. That could have been handled better."

"I tried to get your attention," Chris said. "You didn't look at the floor even once."

Laurali bristled. "I'll call security now and see if they can apprehend him."

"No, don't," Chris said. "He was just confused. I think he might have been homeless."

"Then he shouldn't be in the mall at all," Laurali said. "They need to ban him." She picked up the phone. "What did he look like?"

"I don't really remember," Chris said.

Laurali put the phone down and looked at him over the top of her glasses.

❖

"You're writing me up for insubordination." Chris tried not to grind his teeth.

Laurali shook her head sadly. "Chris, you're really struggling. I'm not sure why you have such a problem with policy and professionalism…"

Count to five. Just count to five.

"But it can't go on like this." Laurali sighed. "I know you had a different relationship with Tracey, but I expect a level of propriety."

"Propriety?"

"Yes. The way you undermined me in front of Jason, and your friend who kept making those obscene gestures…It's not okay."

One. Two. Three. Three and a half.

"We have customers who find your lifestyle upsetting."

"Lifestyle?" Chris's voice grew even.

Laurali crossed her arms. "This is what I'm talking about. You're defensive. You're aggressive. Frankly, I find you hostile."

"I find you lazy," Chris said. "And you're a hypocritical, passive-aggressive bitch. You possess half the humanity found in a clogged drainpipe. With less style."

Laurali's eyes widened. Her lips narrowed. She took a breath. "Chris," she started.

Chris held up his hand. "Don't ruin this with words. I quit."

He left her in the back room, walked up to the front of the store, and passed Jason at the cash desk.

"I just quit," he said. "I told her she was a bitch. Sorry about the rest of your afternoon."

"You're my hero," Jason said.

Chris kept walking. He made it all the way to the bus station before he realized his bus pass was in his jacket, which was in the back room of Book It.

❖

"Thought I might find you here."

Chris sat with his back against one of the trees on the rooftop garden. He frowned at Liam. "Pardon?"

Liam was doing his undercover thing again. No ball cap, though. "We got a call from your boss. She wanted to make sure you left the premises."

Chris sighed. "Fantastic. My bus pass is still in the store. I was waiting here until she left for the day, and then I was going to ask my coworker…my *former* coworker…to get it for me."

"You okay?" Liam sat down on the grass beside him.

"I really needed that job. My mother…" He sighed. "Well."

"I get it. I'm close to my parents, too, obviously." Liam gave Chris's shoulder a squeeze.

Chris wasn't so sure what was obvious about it, but the sentiment was nice.

"I guess I should go get my bus pass and head out. Ugh. I'd hoped never to see her again." Chris rubbed his eyes. "I kind of told her she was a complete bitch. And had no style."

"Harsh." Liam's lips were twitching.

"I may have also intimated she was without a soul," Chris said.

"I'll walk you. That way she can't pitch a fit."

"Thanks."

They rode the escalator in silence, and when he arrived at the store, Laurali held up one hand before he even crossed the threshold.

"You're not allowed in here. I've filled in the paperwork, and you'll be served with a trespass notice as soon as home office approves it."

"Super," Chris said. "I just need my bus pass, and then I'll happily never see you again." Chris looked for Jason and saw him at the back of the store with a customer. "If you'll get it for me, I'll leave and never look back, you miserable harpy."

Liam took his shoulder and squeezed. Chris took the hint and tried to calm down.

"I mailed your belongings already," Laurali said. Her voice was triumphant.

"Pardon?" Chris said.

"As per policy, I packed up your belongings and took them to the post office. Now, please escort him out of the mall." Laurali looked over her glasses at Liam.

"Do you want to go?" Liam asked. Chris took a moment to enjoy the look of frustration that crossed Laurali's face.

"Gladly," Chris said and turned around. Once Book It was out of sight, Chris sighed. "Is it okay if we swing by the lotto booth before I'm banned from the mall so I can buy some bus tickets?"

"Of course," Liam said. "You're not banned from the mall. She can't do that."

"You'll forgive me if I never come back," Chris said.

"That'd be disappointing."

Chris glanced at him, surprised by the comment. It was sweet. Which was probably why his girlfriend loved him so much. Liam looked slightly uncomfortable, and Chris forced himself to smile. No point in being morose. They walked to the lotto booth and got in line.

Liam chuckled.

Chris glanced at him. "What?"

"Miserable harpy." His lips twitched. "Sorry. I know it's not funny."

"I feel kind of bad about it."

Liam look surprised.

"It's an unfair comparison. Harpies aren't so bad."

Liam laughed. Chris liked his laugh. Ahead of them, a woman was apparently buying three years' worth of lottery tickets. The poor clerk had pulled out all three trays from the plastic cover that ran across the countertop. Chris took a deep breath. He was amazed at how much better he felt, even if he had just quit his job. Book It had been awful since the day Tracey had left, and he'd just not allowed himself to think about it. Because of his mother.

That was going to depress him again, so he decided to change the subject. He smiled at Liam. "No cap today?"

Liam scowled. "No. Thanks for giving me the heads up."

The woman in front of them stepped aside, a few dozen pieces of paper in hand, and Chris stepped up. The clerk said, "I just need to put these away."

Chris nodded. "Take your time." The clerk gave Chris a grateful smile. Chris turned back to Liam. "What do you mean? What heads up?"

Liam shook his head. "The rest of the guys were playing a trick on me."

"I don't get it."

"What can I help you with?" the clerk asked.

"I just need a sheet of bus tickets, please." Chris smiled at the clerk.

"Seven-eighty," the clerk said, turning around to open a drawer behind him.

Chris dug into his pockets and then closed his eyes. "Oh, crap."

"What's wrong?" Liam asked.

"My wallet was in my coat. Which Laurali just mailed to me." He fished through his pockets and came up with a five-dollar bill and a bunch of coins. He put them on the counter and started sorting them on top of the clear plastic holders covering the lottery tickets.

"Sorry," Chris said. "Go on."

"They know I'm color-blind. The pink cap was their idea of a joke. Make the gay guy wear pink. I thought it was grey."

"Oh," Chris said. He pushed a stack of dimes and two quarters to the side. That was six dollars. Then he stopped. "Wait. What?"

Liam shrugged. "They're kind of jerks. Not all of them, but…" He shrugged.

"Your anniversary was with your boyfriend, not your girlfriend," Chris said.

"I don't have a boyfriend," Liam said. "Why would I flirt with you if I had a boyfriend?"

"You've been flirting with me?"

Liam was turning red. "Well…yeah."

"But you had an anniversary dinner."

"My parents' anniversary. I told you that."

"No, you didn't."

"Sure I did." He paused. "Didn't I?"

"No."

"But you asked me how my mother liked it," Liam said.

"No, I asked you how your girlfriend liked it."

"I don't have a girlfriend."

"Yeah, I got that part now."

Someone cleared their throat. Chris turned. A woman was standing behind him. As were three other people behind her. All of them were watching.

"Go ahead," Chris said and stepped aside. The clerk moved to help her. Chris took Liam's arm. It felt strong. His hand shook.

"You've been flirting with me?" Chris said.

"Well, you started it," Liam said. "Up in the garden."

Chris was grinning. "Because I thought you were straight."

"You flirt with straight guys?" Liam raised an eyebrow.

"No." Chris laughed. "I just…I'd relaxed…I figured you weren't available, and that…Wow." He looked at the guard again. "Thank God for pink hats."

"I don't wear pink," Liam said.

"Lightning Todd," Chris said.

"The psychic stripper?"

"I have to kiss you before I go," Chris said. The moment the words were out of his mouth, he wanted to take them back. Liam was grinning and Chris felt his skin burning. Had he really just said that?

"I can live with that," Liam said.

"Don't mind us," one of the customers said behind them. Chris closed his eyes, mortified, but a second later, he felt Liam’s fingers on his chin. He opened his eyes and saw Liam leaning forward. They kissed. Liam’s chin was a little rough with stubble, but Chris didn’t mind a bit.

“Suddenly I’m not having a bad day at all,” Chris said.

The clerk and the two remaining customers gave them a small round of applause. Liam looked past him and blushed.

“You need your tickets?” the clerk asked.

“Yeah,” Chris said. He turned back to the counter and resumed counting his coins, his fingertips shaking a little.

“Do you have enough?” Liam asked. He put his hand back on Chris’s shoulder. It felt very good there.

“I think so.” Chris moved aside a coin and looked through the clear plastic at the lottery ticket beneath where he’d been counting.

The numbers caught his eye: 1. 6. 11. 16. 61. 66.

“Ones and sixes,” he said. It was a scratch-and-win, and one of those tickets where the grand payout was cash every week for the rest of your life. “Ones and sixes when I’m stuck for a way home.”

“What?” Liam asked.

“Can I get that ticket, too?” Chris said, pointing. The clerk nodded and pulled out the tray.

“That’ll be twelve-eighty.”

Chris looked at his pile of change, then at Liam. “If I told you I had a good feeling about this, would you go halvesies with me?”

Liam smiled and pulled out his wallet.

❖

At the mall exit, they kissed again. Chris grinned. “Friday night, what are you doing?”

“I work here until five, but after that, I’m all yours,” Liam said.

“Ever been to Bittersweets?”

“The coffee place? Yeah.”

“It’s a date,” Chris said. “Six?”

“You got it.” He sighed. “I should go back.” He rubbed his chin. “It really sucks I won’t see you until Friday night.”

“Two days is a long time to wait,” Chris said. “How about tonight I make you dinner. I suddenly have some free time on my hands.”

Liam winced. "I'm sorry about your job. Are you okay?"

"I feel good about it. Let me give you my number. I live near Bronson and Somerset."

They exchanged numbers, tapping them into their phones. Then Liam rolled back on his heels. "I should go back."

"I know."

"You gonna scratch that on the bus?" Liam asked.

Chris was clutching the lottery ticket. He shook his head.

"Nope. Half is yours, remember? How about I keep it for dessert?"

Liam laughed. "Sure thing. I'll see you later." He went inside.

Chris got on the bus and looked out the window as the mall disappeared behind him. He found himself smiling. When someone flounced into the seat beside him, he glanced over.

"So, can I call it, or what?"

Lightning Todd's shirt and eyes were a dark brown today.

"You can call it." Chris smiled. He looked down at the lottery ticket in his hand. *I hope.* "Sixes and ones."

Lightning Todd saw the ticket and grinned. "Awesome. So can I get a testimonial for my website?"

"Only if you let me fix the typos."

"What? Oh. Sure." He wrinkled his nose. "I never take the bus. Does it always smell like this?"

Chris grinned. "Quite often."

"Gross."

They rode in silence for a while.

"What was it like?" Chris asked. "Getting hit by lightning, I mean."

Lightning Todd looked at him. "Did you kiss the guy before you left the mall?"

"Yeah. I did."

The blond grinned and aimed a finger gun at him.

"Ah," Chris said.

"Okay, I can't take it. It totally smells purple in here. I'm gone." Lightning Todd got up and pulled the string. He paused, holding the bar while the bus slowed down. "I'll see you Friday," he said. "For the testimonial."

"Bittersweets," Chris agreed.

Lightning Todd smiled. "Awesome. Oh, you're gonna love your new place."

Chris blinked. "My new place?"

The blond was already moving down the steps, the door opening in front of him. "Together. With the guy who hates pink."

Then he was gone. The bus pulled away from the stop, and Chris watched Lightning Todd walk away. Then the blond stopped in front of a young couple with a stroller and said something to them, but Chris couldn't see how they reacted.

Good luck. Chris aimed a finger gun out the window and fired at them. Then he looked at the ticket and wondered how soon he could register for classes at the university.

When the colors dim, and absences fade the edges, there might be time left to do something, to have something be mended.

Every color, every pattern fading or vanishing in a different way can help you decide what to say, and what to do. Regrets are born in those palest moments.

Blues can be loves undeclared; yellows can be memories and stories as yet unshared.

Make the time. You will never regret final moments if you go into them knowing what they are, and treasure them for what they offer.

There's a gift in loss and in knowing the loss is approaching. Time to say, time to do, time to prepare—though I've never quite mastered that last part.

There are two important things to remember when the colors fade, though.

Almost never will there be anything left you can possibly do to stop it.

And when there isn't, it wasn't your fault.

HEART

I met Jeremiah Carey at a bar. Now, before you think I'm a typical raver freak, club kid, or something even less savory, I didn't want to be there. Every now and then, Tony, my ex, shows up on my doorstep, demands I be social, and drags me out somewhere loud and bright and obnoxious.

Thus, the bar.

Some DJ from Toronto had Tony's attention, and the music was pulsing so loudly I figured half the glasses behind the bar would be chipped by last call. I didn't recognize the music, which meant I wasn't likely to endure the night for very long.

Tony didn't take long to get to the center of the dance floor and show off. He's good at that. In fact, his ability to capture a room was one of the things that first attracted me to him. That, and he just sort of grabs life by the neck and hangs on for the ride. He's a good guy, but he's also self-absorbed and has the attention span of a goldfish.

Thus, the ex.

Still, shirtless, sweaty Tony doing the groove on a speaker sparked memory lane, and I couldn't help but smile from my vantage point at the bar, where I was perched on a stool, nursing a Canadian after enjoying dancing to the first—and only—song I'd recognized all night.

The DJ stopped the music and started "shouting out" to guests and sponsors, so I wouldn't have heard the voice beside me.

"He's good," he said.

I nodded, not looking over at him, still watching Tony, who'd leaned in close to talk with a blond guy in a blue tank top. "He loves music. Loves to dance," I said. Tony saw me watching and blew me a kiss. Blue Tank Top turned to scope out potential competition.

"Mary Higgins Clark," the guy beside me said.

I turned and looked at him for the first time, blinking. "What?"

He was a little guy, though he looked about my age, really slim. He wore a red T-shirt and a pair of plain jeans and had very fair skin that matched with his sandy hair and soft grey eyes, giving him this aw-shucks look that was sort of refreshing, in a country-bumpkin way. He smelled like soap. No cologne, just soap.

"Mary Higgins Clark," he repeated. "She wrote a novel called *Loves Music, Loves to Dance*. It wasn't bad."

"You read a lot?" I asked, speaking louder as the next song began thumping from the DJ booth.

"Occupational hazard." He grinned. "I work in a used bookstore down in the Village." He turned his back to watch Tony dance some more, now nearly chest-to-chest with Blue Tank Top, and then sighed, flashing me a slightly gamy grin. "I don't suppose he's a big reader?"

I laughed. "Nope. Tony never understood why I could spend a whole night reading instead of heading to some rave or something." I had to lean in close to his ear for him to hear me.

The guy turned his grey eyes back to me, and he seemed a little surprised. I'm over six feet tall and a solid one-ninety, and I hit the gym every workday, given it's what I do for a living. I get mistaken for a dumb jock a lot. Other than having brown hair, unlike Archie's buddy, there's a reason my nickname is Moose.

Okay, two reasons, but I won't brag.

Either way, when someone is surprised I have a library, and it's not all back issues of *Men's Health*, I don't take it personally.

Much.

"Who's your favorite author?" he said, warming to the subject. It was the strangest conversation I've ever yelled back and forth in a busy bar.

"Lately? Christopher Moore," I said, and a delighted smile crossed his face. Suddenly his eyes weren't grey at all, they were blue.

"I loved *Lamb*! Have you read that one?"

I nodded and put my beer down. "Aiden." I offered a hand.

"Jeremiah," he shouted, and took it. "But call me Miah."

It was the first time I've ever stayed at a bar longer than Tony.

❖

When he finds me sitting outside the hospital, Tony takes my hand, something he has never done in public, even when we were dating.

"Moose, I'm so sorry." He's wearing a tight black T-shirt and the lucky necklace he got in the Village. He's been at a bar. His hair is messed up from a night out, when I interrupted him with my call.

"Tony, I just…I need to be alone for a minute, okay?"

Tony squeezes my hand and rises. "I'll be right inside, okay?" He sounds a little hurt, but like he's okay with it. I'm not even looking at him.

When Tony leaves, I first see the flickering yellow-white at the other end of the hospital parking lot. I stand and start toward my dead lover, trailing angry, impotent fire behind me.

It's a pity nothing burns.

❖

The first time he spent the night, Miah walked around my bedroom, his eyes lighting on everything. He walked slowly, the way he did everything, deliberately touching nothing but noting the photos, observing my plants, and stopping at the pictures I had hung over my bed. He liked the one of the lightning bolt striking the ocean.

"Wow," he said, voice hushed. "That's powerful." Then he turned to the bookcase in the bedroom, which made my bookcase tally rise to four so far on his tour of my apartment. He grinned. "More books."

I smiled. "Not just a dumb jock, eh?"

"I dunno," he said. "You're a trainer at the Y. For all I know, the books are for show. Maybe you use them as weights." He smiled up at me.

I watched him from my bedroom doorway. Since that first conversation three weeks ago, I'd been entranced. His beautiful sometimes-grey, sometimes-blue eyes devoured the world. He wasn't aggressive, or even hyper, like Tony, but the way he *watched*…it was insatiable. His body was sedate, but his *eyes*…

He glanced at me when I didn't reply. "What are you thinking about?" It was one of his more common questions, I'd learned.

"Kissing you," I said truthfully.

"That's straight out of the *Big Book of Boyfriend Things to Say*." He blushed. "Where are you hiding your copy?"

"Are we boyfriends?" I said.

Miah stopped and sat awkwardly on the bed. Perched on the edge, he looked around the room and fixed on a pair of my socks on the floor.

"Are you okay?" I asked, and sat beside him.

"There's something I have to tell you," Miah said, and his eyes were very grey.

❖

Afterward, he slept with his cheek on my chest, and I did something I hadn't done since my grandmother died. I tried to touch that source of the thing she said made me special. I let the font rise inside me, the hot, liquid-gold sensation filling my pores. It was harder than when I was a child, but so much more seemed to be inside me that for a moment I was ashamed.

All that gift, I could nearly hear my grandmother say, *and you keep it for yourself*.

And then all I could hear was the rush of it in my ears, painful, a thundering heartbeat.

Heartbeats…

Miah had taken off his shirt slowly, shyly, and showed me the long scar where they had cut him open and fixed the worst of his faulty heart. He told me how he took a pill every morning, and how it was probably enough to keep him going for as long as anyone usually goes. He told me that although he loved music, unlike Tony, he sure couldn't dance. He kept himself sedate for a reason, I realized. He tired easily and moved so gently. It was frightening to think of a heart as something so fragile.

Then, very quietly, he'd added a request.

"So, being as it's already sort of cracked, try not to break it, okay?"

I kissed him. I wanted to wrap him up in my arms and make him warm all over.

So I did.

But now, with the gold fire filling me so close to my skin I was crying from the heat of it, I could see the life in him. It flickered every now and then, his cracked heart skipping a beat.

Gently, I curled up against him, slowly rolled him onto his back, and straightened his head on the pillow. I kissed him again and let a little of the fire pass between my lips. In his sleep, he stirred a little, but didn't wake.

The flickers died down. His frail glow grew steadier for a while.

I smiled, kissed his forehead, and went to sleep holding him against me, rubbing my thumb slowly up and down the scar that bisected his chest.

You're a good boy, I heard my grandmother say.

Or maybe it was just a dream.

❖

At the end of the parking lot, the echo of Miah is gazing at me with eyes more golden than grey. The memory of him looks at me with a vaguely pained expression, and then he reaches up and touches his own chest.

I nod, and my vision blurs with tears.

Miah's echo puts his arms down and looks around. It's a cold night, but he's wearing a plain red T-shirt and blue jeans, exactly as the day I met him, except now I can see the parked cars right through him, and somewhere near his calves, he fades into flickering bits of pale yellow light.

He opens his mouth, but then a confused and frustrated look covers his face. He cannot speak, or can't remember speech, or doesn't have enough life in him to do it.

I draw my font up and exhale a fiery stream. It settles into him, and his edges tighten, his eyes grow brighter, and he smiles.

"What are you thinking about?" Miah's echo asks me. Like warm breath on a winter's night, clouds form at his words, but they are gold and yellow and orange.

"Kissing you," I say truthfully, and the tears come.

❖

"We need another bookcase." Miah grinned from where he was sitting on the floor, putting his paperbacks in between mine on the bottom shelf. He turned to look at me as I came in from the cold. He had all his books unpacked now, his entire library piled up alphabetically by author all across the apartment floor.

"Then we need another wall, too. You've been at that all day?" I asked, tugging off my jacket.

Miah lay down on his back, putting his hands behind his head. "Reading is to the mind what exercise is to the body." Then, in segue, "How was work?"

"Clever." I smiled and crouched down beside him. I kissed his forehead, and he reached up and took the back of my head, dragging me down for a lip-lock. I sat down, and he shuffled and put his head in my lap, looking sleepy and pale.

I brought a sliver of the font to heat my vision, and saw he was pale in more ways than one.

"Are you feeling okay?" I asked.

He glanced up at me and smiled wryly. His eyes were impish blue. "You're as bad as Ian."

I raised an eyebrow in mock jealousy and was a little disturbed to find I really was jealous. "Who?"

"Ian. He runs the bookstore. Haven't you met him yet?" He seemed surprised at that, and I realized I'd never really gone to his bookstore, beyond picking him up after work. I decided I needed to visit soon, especially when this Ian was working.

"No," I said. "And if he cares when you look tired, I like him already."

"I'm always tired," Miah said, without heat.

I stole another kiss. "So long as that's all he cares about."

Miah laughed. "He's a nice guy, and he has a boyfriend of his very own." He reached up and touched my chin. "He's really sharp, though. Like you, he takes one look at me and says," Miah's voice dropped a little, "'Miah, you need a break. Did you take your pill this morning?'"

I smiled, mostly at the news of Ian's happy relationship. "*Did* you take your pill this morning?"

He nodded. "I've been feeling so good lately I'm tempted to skip, but I take them anyway."

"Don't skip them, okay?" I was a little scared.

"Cross my heart." He did so with his finger as he winked. I took it in my hand and kissed the fingertip.

"Clever," I said again.

He frowned. "I really do feel better. It's…strange."

I took a deep breath. "There's something I should tell you."

❖

The echo of Miah reaches toward me, and his flickering fingertips touch my lips. They have pressure, presence, and he blinks in surprise.

"I'm sorry," I say, crying still. "I'm so sorry."

He pulls his fingers back and touches his chest. "Nothing," he says. Already his voice is less distinct.

❖

I was staring at the ceiling when he spoke, not yet sleeping.

"How did you…I mean, when did it start?"

I turned on my side, moving the covers and sheets, and I took his shoulder to turn him toward me. In the darkness, his eyes shone slightly in the faint glow from the streetlights through the bedroom window. He smelled like soap.

"My Nan told me I could do it. She could tell it was in me."

"Just like that?" he said.

I thought back to it. One afternoon, playing at her house, before my grandfather was sick, my grandmother had taken me aside.

"She asked me if I saw lights inside people," I smiled at the memory, "and taught me how to look for it. She said I was different from her, that I saw suns where she saw oceans, but that font poured out of us pretty much the same."

"Font?" Miah snuggled under my chin, and I wrapped my arms around him.

"She called it her font, like a fountain. To her, every life was like this wonderful, cool river, and she—" My voice caught, and I had to stop for a second.

Miah shifted on my chest. "What happened to her?"

"My grandfather had a stroke when I was eleven," I said. "She did something, with her font. He got better, really quickly, but I could tell it wasn't good for her. Her own fire—you have to understand, I was watching everyone at that point, figuring out what I could see, what I could do—it got so low, so unsteady." I sighed. "It was awful. It was like he got better a little bit and she got worse a whole lot, day by day."

I gripped him tighter for a moment.

"Then, when he started to talk again, and could walk, she went to sleep one night and didn't wake up. The doctor said it was an embolism, but I think it was just the side effect of emptying herself out into him."

Miah went quiet. He kissed my chest.

"So I stopped," I said, a little defensively. "I mean, I saw what happened if you gave too much, and I didn't want to die."

Miah kissed my chest again. "I think you're wonderful," he said. "But I don't want you to hurt yourself over me. The pills are good. I know how to live like this, I really do. I'm used to it."

I kissed him on the forehead.

Miah lifted onto his elbow. "I'm serious. I don't want you to do it anymore."

"I'm not doing what she did," I said. "It really is like a spring. It fills up again a little every day. I'm just giving you the extra, the stuff I get back just from sitting in the sun for a while."

"But—"

"No." I shook my head. "Miah, please. I'm not hurting myself. There's a lot inside me, enough to share with other people. It's what—"

I broke off, and heard my Nan's voice.

You, me, we are springs for other people. We're here to give them a little extra. Our font is to be shared, not kept, or all that extra life? It just seeps away. Don't waste it.

"It's what I'm supposed to do," I said, feeling guilty. Maybe even ashamed.

He shifted and kissed me, full on the lips, slow and lingering.

"What's it like?" he said. "What do people look like to you?"

I smiled into the darkness and lit the fire behind my eyes. It was getting easier with practice, though it still felt like stretching an old muscle. Miah's outline, a soft golden aura with that guttering dark place over his heart, burst into being in front of me.

"It's like seeing souls." I smiled. "And yours is the handsomest."

He laughed. "More from the *Big Book of Boyfriend Things to Say*. You're just trying to get me to put out."

I let my hands wander. "Is it working?"

❖

When it happened, I finally got to meet Ian. He was in the emergency room, standing to one side. The name tag clipped to the pocket of his black polo shirt was the only reason I knew who he was. He had mismatched eyes, one green, one blue, and that's all I seemed to be able to focus on when I looked at him.

"What happened?" I said.

"He just fell down," Ian said, stepping back from me. That was when I realized I'd almost yelled my question, and that I was angry. "He was stacking some books, and then he sort of slid down the wall." Ian shook his head and swiped at his eyes with the back of one hand. "He started laughing, at first, he…he said he had a head rush. And then…" Ian shivered.

"Where is he?" I asked. Ian blinked at me, and I left him, went to the desk, and found the nurse. I gave Miah's name. She asked who I was. I lied.

I was already calling the font to the surface of my skin.

❖

"Miah," I say. *This is not really him. He is gone. This is what remains of my lover.*

Echo is too cold a word, and I can hear my grandmother's voice again in my head: *People don't always go right away, baby.*

Miah's eyes, as golden as sunlight, close. He is still touching his chest, but it's easier to see through him now. The faintest smile touches his lips, and he opens his eyes and tries to speak. But the words don't come.

Sometimes they need a little help in moving along, something they gotta say or do first, and I give 'em a bit of my font to keep going.

The font fades fast without a cup.

Sometimes you can see them for a bit after they die, before they go on. My grandmother's eyes were hard. *But only a bit, baby.*

Miah should be going. He is—*was*, damn it!—a beautiful, wonderful, special man and he should already be gone. I have stoked him with my own font, and I do not know if it was the right thing to do.

But I have done it.

I open my mouth, and kiss my dead lover, and flame pours into what is left of his soul.

❖

Wires were in his room, and a little tube under his nose with two nubs aimed at his nostrils. He looked like he was merely sleeping, his eyes shadowed deeply, his lips a terrible color I told myself wasn't blue. Machines blipped, and a nurse was writing something on a clipboard. I stepped inside, and she frowned at me.

"I'm sorry, he can't have visitors right now." I looked at her, and she softened. "Are you family?"

I'd just finished this dance at the front desk, and I wasn't about to try it again. I hated lying, saying Miah was my brother, when we looked nothing alike, when we had different last names, when I was obviously lying.

"He's my—" My voice was hoarse, and I cleared my throat, thinking that at any minute I was going to lose it completely. His skin was so pale. "He's mine," I said.

The nurse got it, and she touched my arm as she passed me. "You can't stay for very long, okay? He should sleep if there's any chance he's going to—" She stopped and swallowed. "He should sleep."

I nodded. I think I thanked her. As the door closed, I let the fire boil inside me, the font rise until it felt like it would sear my tongue.

Grandad is getting better, Nan. I can tell.

To my own eyes, brimming with gold, the room swam with yellow light.

Yes, he is.

I brought the flames to my lips.

Are you okay, Nan?

I pulled the only chair over and sat beside him. I took Miah's hand and leaned over his exhausted face to kiss him.

I'm just tired, Aiden.

Pale grey eyes opened.

"No," he said.

❖

Miah slips his arms around my waist and puts his head on my chest.

"I'm so sorry," I repeat, tears striking my face now. "I should have..."

Miah pulls back and looks at me, golden eyes shining. "It doesn't hurt," he says, wisps of gold flickering from the edges of his lips. He slides one hand up onto my chest, taps a heartbeat with his fingers, and then lets his hand fall.

"I'm not tired," he says, and he holds out his free hand. I take it in my own, and he smiles up at me. I am nearly blubbering now. My chest is shaking with each breath, and my tears hurt my eyes. And my heart...

"Can we dance?" Miah asks, voice nearly a whisper now. I can see through him again.

We dance in the parking lot, and I close my eyes. He presses against my chest, and I spin him. We step and turn and rock back and forth gently, without music. He grows lighter in my arms, and for a while, my tears gather in his hair. I can even smell his soap.

My heart.

There is wetness on my arm, and when I open my eyes, he is gone. Another tear falls off the end of my nose. I take a long, shaky breath, alone in the cool night.

And my heart keeps beating.

Sometimes, the most important color isn't.

There can be absences, or patterns, or holes in the shapes and movement.

The body doesn't always speak loud enough or is willfully ignored, causing gaps.

Staccato blinks are often illnesses or pains that come and go. Around the hands or the feet, they're most often the joints and the bones, and most commonly found among the oldest of us. Arthritis. Bursitis. Pains born of life that interrupt but don't bring purple.

A pain that habit has erased—still present, yes. Still painful, yes. But endured and pushed aside, forgotten as much as possible.

Whole palettes can be pushed aside that way. Forced away. Lost and erased and denied, until all color bleeds from what might have been seen.

I've never seen good come from that denial.

I've often seen loss.

If you find those spaces between the color, the spaces behind the pain, and you figure them out, the colors can come back.

There can be joys again.

Negative Space

Almost done.

Each stroke of André's pencil steadied his hand. He felt calmer now. He always did once he started working, started *doing* rather than being.

The face unfolding on his sketchpad was average. Just some random guy. The subject wasn't someone you'd call handsome. His lips were a bit too thin and his chin a bit too weak for that. But not ugly, either. Nice enough eyes, which André knew were on the greener side of hazel despite the shades of grey he was drawing with.

Not for the first time, he wondered if he should try sketching with color.

He worked the piece for another twenty minutes, from the first, lightest lines to the final strokes that completed the face. A hint of crow's feet. A small scar on the weak chin. Beside the close-up of the face, he had also sketched a full-figure drawing of the man, taking a few moments to add emphasis on the winter boots and the jacket.

He finished. A man's face. A close-up of a ring. A full-figure drawing of his outfit.

You could see a lot in two minutes and thirty-eight seconds.

Leaning back on the bench, he closed his eyes and tilted his head up to the sun. The warmth on his face and the bright red afterimage burning on the inside of his eyelids helped. He tried to think of it as the sun helping him step outside his own body and destroy the bad.

Of course, it wasn't. And it didn't destroy anything.

He opened his eyes and looked at the drawing again.

This person, on the other hand.

He glanced at the apartment building opposite the small park. This had been the closest place he could find privacy after touring the apartment. He could never have lived there, but he'd been watching, knowing it would eventually get listed. It was a prime spot for students. Apartments often weren't easy to get to, which was a mixed blessing, and he was never sure how long he'd have to wait for a showing. At least that meant he was in control. Forewarned. He'd never have accidentally walked into apartment 4A.

The first time it had happened, he had been on a street corner, and it had taken him completely by surprise.

He didn't walk near that corner anymore.

He took a moment to write the address on the drawing, then pulled out an envelope from his messenger bag.

Tearing a picture from his sketchbook was the closest he felt to strong.

André regarded the model, trying to shift his gaze to the negative space around her. This wasn't the first time the teacher had asked them to approach their work from a new angle, but it was the first time he was struggling to do so. He leaned away from his easel and tried to regroup, charcoal in hand.

Look beyond the body, the teacher had said.

How could someone like him *ever* do that?

"You're getting there," Jill said, walking her slow circle around the outside of their easels. She gestured with one finger to the center of his drawing. "That space there, the triangle formed by her arm, elbow, and side. That's where you're getting it. It's easier to see a negative space closed in. Apply that perspective everywhere else."

Closed in. Well, that he had practice with. André nodded. When Jill moved on to the next easel, she murmured appreciation to the woman beside him and rested her hand on the woman's shoulder for a moment while they spoke. Back when the class had first started, Jill—"Not Ms. Binder, not ma'am, just Jill"—had touched his shoulder the same way when she paused to praise his eye for detail, and he'd flinched.

She was a wonderful art instructor and a quick study. She hadn't touched him since.

André closed his eyes, even though he knew that was part of the problem. His method had always been to look, see, remember, and recreate. Even before. But he couldn't figure out how to look at negative space.

He blew out a breath and opened his eyes. The curve of the model's neck, the reach of her hand across her thigh, the angle of her knees… He turned back to his easel and worked again, trying to keep his gaze on the things that *weren't*, rather than what *was*.

By the end of the class, he felt marginally better about the result. Jill nodded to him and smiled in a reassuring way that said she knew full well this was his least favorite class to date.

"Sometimes it's just as important to see the around the subject," she said.

He understood what she meant in theory. Any composition was more than representation.

"It's definitely not coming to me naturally," he said. His voice was rough, and he cleared his throat. He realized this was the first time he'd spoken to anyone all day.

"Me neither."

Jill turned to the man who'd spoken. André hadn't paid much notice to him before. The man had joined the course midway and, like André, had more of a gift for representation than for the more abstract or theoretical approaches to art Jill was having them explore these last few classes. He couldn't remember the man's name, something Chinese or Vietnamese.

"You're both doing fine," Jill said. "Flexing a new muscle always hurts at first."

The fellow certainly had muscle to flex, André thought. He couldn't help but wonder if their teacher had made that particular metaphor on purpose, trying to connect to the wide-shouldered man beside him.

She waved and moved on. André pulled his drawing off the easel and debated the merit of keeping it for a few moments before he rolled it up to slide it into his tube. He'd decide later if it was worthwhile.

"The only thing I think I flexed was my butt. These stools are torture."

André looked up and saw the other man smiling at him. He stretched his arms over his head and left no doubt how much serious time in the gym he spent. He had thick muscle on his chest, his shoulders, and his arms.

He also had a single dimple, and a friendly, open voice.

André forced a smile in return.

"The stools are not great." Polite, but not warm. André had mastered that in the last couple of months. Like anything else, it took practice.

"You're really good."

André regarded the man again. Taller than André, he wore a stylish pair of glasses with clear frames that drew attention to his brown eyes. Nice cheekbones, too. He'd already gathered his supplies, and now he was standing near André's easel. André felt cornered, but he shook it off. Late afternoon sunlight streamed in through the windows, and both Jill and the model were still in the room, as were multiple students taking their time packing up.

He wasn't in danger, no matter how strong the guy was.

"Not at negative space I'm not," André said.

Another smile, another flash of the dimple. He was handsome without being intimidating, and he had a matching confidence. "Between you and me, I'm not so sure negative space is the next big thing."

"I hope not." André turned away again, giving his hands a quick wipe on a handkerchief. He tucked away his case of pencils and charcoal. When he was done, he picked up his messenger bag and saw the big man was still standing there.

"So is this a hobby for you, or do you draw professionally?" he asked.

"I'm in freelance graphic design," André said. "But most of what I do is with a computer, not a pencil." He shifted uncomfortably, but the man didn't seem at all put off by his awkwardness.

"Would you like to get a coffee?" He asked the question with just enough of a smile to restore the dimple.

André had to work hard not to take a step away. He tightened his hand around the strap over his shoulder and swallowed, finding his voice.

"Another time?" he said. His voice was rough again. "I'm in a bit of a rush right now. There's something I do after class. Somewhere I have to be, I mean."

The man met his gaze and held it. André felt caught again, like he would not be able to move until this man released him. He trembled.

"Sure," the man said, and gave him a little bob of the head. "Next time, then?"

André let out a breath. "Maybe."

He fled.

❖

André parked his car and rested his forehead against the wheel. Maybe this was a mistake. After 4A, maybe he should allow himself a break. Before 4A, there had been the town houses along Chesterton. Before Chesterton, there'd been the gas station near Fifth. Before that…

He couldn't remember.

Maybe it will stop happening.

He breathed in, held it, and breathed out. Letting go of the steering wheel, he sat upright again and repeated the deep breath. In. Hold. Out. The sensation of something scrabbling for purchase inside his rib cage eased with each measured breath. He reached over to the passenger seat and grabbed his bag, then climbed out of the car, locking the door behind him.

He'd need to walk a bit down the pathway and then head off the trail. He tugged out his phone and pulled up the photo he'd downloaded from the news website. The trees could have been any trees, but the bend in the river, with the large rock visible near the far end of the curve, was a bit more distinctive.

He started walking.

It took André longer than he'd thought it might, and he was on the edge of giving up when he finally saw the stone breaking the surface of the water. It was more visible now, in summer, than it was in the picture. Spring meltwater must have been in play. He got as close to the water's edge as he dared, and he waited.

Nothing.

Damn.

It had been a gamble, and he'd known that. He looked back toward the path, trying to decide. He still had a good hour of light left, but he didn't know which way to go. He caught a glimpse of movement and swallowed.

A stray piece of faded yellow crime scene tape was wrapped around a branch and fluttered in the breeze.

He looked back at the water, considering. Farther up the current, he supposed, would be the logical thing to consider, but how far? And where? And really, he had no guarantee that where the body had been thrown into the water was where the woman had…

André closed his eyes. That scratching feeling was back. Like rats inside his chest, terrified and trapped and trying to find their way out. Circling in the dark, scraping at him from beneath his skin, frantic…

"Breathe." He said the word out loud. It came out strangled.

In. Hold. Out.

In. Hold. Out.

After a few minutes, he unclenched his fists.

Okay. This hadn't worked. That was okay.

Lord knew he wasn't going to run out of opportunities.

Maybe it will stop happening.

Maybe that was it. Maybe it already had.

❖

"You okay?"

André had tried not to react beyond a polite smile when the burly man in the clear-framed glasses had chosen the easel next to him, but now the eyes behind those glasses were full of concern.

"I didn't sleep very well," André said. He shrugged. "I was working on something pretty late into the night."

A mailed-off portrait. Another address. Two minutes and thirty-eight seconds waking him up with seemingly infinite resistance to even a second sleeping pill.

The man seemed to be about to say something else, but then Jill started discussing the virtues of a value study, and André turned his attention to her. When the model took up her position, André threw himself wholeheartedly into the project of the evening, steadfastly avoiding so much as glancing to the left for the rest of the class.

Building on negative space, the image André ended up with surprised him. The value study that resulted showed a woman in repose, yes, but it robbed her of most of the defining features of her face, and even her body seemed more suggested than represented. This was not the model in front of him but any woman who might have been here, or might ever have been her.

As Jill circled the easels, André realized his hand was shaking. He put down his charcoal. It clattered. He felt more than saw the man beside him looking his way.

Any woman. All women. Not a woman at all.

Faceless and reduced to nothing but shapes of light and dark. A form.

Like a body.

André was going to be sick, he was sure of it.

He slid off his stool and mumbled something to Jill as he made a break for the small bathroom at the far end of the classroom. He closed the door and poured cold water into the sink, splashing it onto his face.

The cold shock helped.

So did conscious breathing, though it took longer than usual. He wiped his face, ignoring the smudges under his eyes in the mirror, and then he stepped back. If he disregarded how pale he was, he didn't look completely unhinged. So that was something.

He shook his head. Maybe he needed to stop. Maybe…

He sighed and went back out into the studio. Most of the students were already packed up, a few had left, and the teacher was waiting for him.

As was the guy in the clear-framed glasses.

"This is wonderful," she said.

"Thank you."

"Are you feeling okay?"

"Not really."

She reached out, almost patting his arm, hesitating only at the last moment. "Go get some rest," she said instead, smiling at him.

"Thanks," he said.

She left, and he started undoing the picture from the easel, trying hard not to look at it.

"I'm guessing you'd rather not get that coffee?"

André turned to the man beside him. He'd pulled out his wallet, and André felt a little bad. Had he led the man on? If so, it hadn't been his intention. He couldn't remember the last time he'd felt like making a connection with someone, and he knew that should bother him more than it did.

He couldn't quite grasp why the man would want to have coffee with him. André knew that on his best day, he could achieve cute. This guy was hot.

"I'm sorry," André said.

The man looked around the room. The teacher was with the model at the front of the class, and the two or three other students were out of earshot.

"I'm going to have to insist," the man said.

When André frowned, the man opened his wallet and lifted it so André could see the badge.

"Are you going to arrest me?"

They were sitting in Bittersweets. Two cups of coffee sat untouched between them. The man—no, the *cop*—had brought him here. Just like he'd offered, they'd gone for coffee. But André felt like he was already wearing handcuffs. He clenched his fists under the table, waiting.

Instead of answering, the man reached into his bag and pulled out a newspaper. When he put it down in front of André, André glanced at the headline.

Arrest Made in Apartment Slaying.

So. 4A. André started to rub his wrists against his jeans.

"How?" the man asked. His voice wasn't rough or even angry. In fact, he just sounded curious.

"Police work, I assume," André said. His voice wavered.

The man shook his head. "Don't. I've been trying to track you down for half a year. Please don't insult my intelligence."

André looked at him. He did look intelligent. Maybe it was the glasses.

"Does it matter?" André asked.

"This is the fourth," the cop said, tapping the paper.

André swallowed. "I know."

"Don't you wonder why there's only four so far, given how many *tips* have been sent in?"

André bit his lip. He did wonder. He hadn't exactly kept track, but he was sure he'd sent at least a dozen packages to the police. Different stations, from different mailboxes, all across the city. Maybe even two dozen by now. He uncurled his fingers, pressing his palms onto his thighs. He didn't want to touch anything. Fingerprints or DNA or whatever. He'd seen enough television to worry about how much of it was true. Was this man—this *cop*—trying to trick him somehow?

"Proof," the man said.

André blinked. "What?"

"Proof," he repeated. "With these four, we had enough proof."

"Oh," André said.

They sat in silence. André watched him pick up his coffee and take a sip.

"You have no background in police work or forensics."

André shook his head. He didn't. There was no point lying.

The cop blew out a breath. "Give me something here."

"Look, Officer…uh…" André said, and then he frowned. He still had no memory of what this man's name was.

"Detective," he said. "Detective Nguyen. But Bao will do."

André took a deep breath. Held it. Released. "Bao. Okay. I'm not doing anything illegal, am I?"

The detective's laugh was a small surprise. "That depends on how you're managing to sketch murder suspects and mail them to us."

"I think you know they're not *suspects*," André said.

"See," Bao leaned forward, pointing at André across the table, "that's the part that's got me so nervous." He saw André flinch, and he lowered his hand. "Sorry."

André shook his head. "It's okay. It's not you."

"I know about your case," Bao said.

"Okay." The rats began to scratch.

"No arrests, right?"

André managed a weak nod.

"What you're doing or however you're doing it, it's such a risk," Bao said. "This case?" He tapped the newspaper. "Her mother wept when we told her we caught that son of a bitch. And we caught that son of a bitch because of an *anonymous tip* that made us look at someone we'd dismissed a whole lot closer." He lowered his voice. "Do you have any idea what would happen if people found out the investigation was based on someone mailing in a random drawing?"

André was shaking. "No."

"It might get him off. Despite the other evidence. Despite the DNA. Despite…" Bao took another long look at him. "Despite *anything*. That's why only four. We've only had four we can prove." His voice softened. "So far."

André stared down at his coffee. He felt sick. He was barely keeping himself from bolting from the table. His heart was pounding.

Breathe. Hold. Out.

"You weren't in the city when this happened," Bao said, tapping the paper again.

André looked up. He hadn't actually known that, but it made sense when he thought about it. Over the winter, he'd gone to stay with friends in Montreal. He'd needed the recovery time.

"How are you drawing these?" Bao asked. "Is it some kind of leak? I can't find anything or anyone connecting all the cases, and you have nothing to do with them either, as far as I can tell. I used to be a sketch artist myself. I could tell they were all done by the same artist, and I could tell the skill was improving. I tracked you through sketch pads, pencils, apartment viewing records and some damned good luck with a security camera. I've seen you at the gas station. You just stood there a couple of minutes and left."

André couldn't stop himself from reaching out to the cup of coffee in front of him. He wrapped both hands around it and tried to lift it, but he was shaking so hard it nearly spilled. He put it back down on the table and closed his eyes.

Warm hands wrapped around his. He jerked, surprised, opening his eyes and seeing Bao touching him.

"You can tell me," Bao said. His hands were rough, but somehow that was comforting.

André blinked hard. He didn't want to cry. "I need to move," he said. "I need to be moving. Can we walk?"

The cop let go of his hands, but it was a gentle withdraw. "Okay."

André rose, and Bao followed.

"Where are we going?" Bao asked.

"You'll think I'm crazy."

Bao shrugged.

André exhaled. "Cooper, near Bronson."

He could actively see rough-handed Bao fade and Detective Nguyen come to the fore. He furrowed his brow, a single line dividing his eyebrows, and André imagined him rolling through a mental list of unsolved crimes. Finally, he nodded at André. "Okay."

They walked. It wasn't too far from the Village, and once they were on Cooper, André slowed, looking up at the numbers on the buildings as he tried to figure out which way to go.

"It was this way," Bao said, gesturing. "Between those two buildings."

André swallowed hard and walked ahead. Bao followed.

André could feel it at the mouth of the alley between the two buildings. A heaviness tugging at him. Like lying in a bathtub full of water and pulling the plug, but instead of the water being pulled down the drain, it would be *him*. Not just his thoughts, but his worries. Not just the things that made him smile, but the things that woke him up at night and left him curled up in a ball, rocking back and forth, struggling to remember how to breathe.

He was so damn grateful for the relief.

❖

The man had been pulled into the alley by two others, a hand over his mouth. André felt the arm around his neck, the grip of hands on his arms, and the pressure in his chest from wanting to breathe out gasps of air.

A bloom of hot pain dug into the small of his back. Even as part of André felt the agony, another part ignored it. He could sidestep what was happening to not-him and *look*. He could see, even in the dark of that night. He sensed what was behind this not-him despite the hand covering not-his face and the arm around not-his throat. He just *could*.

So he did.

The man behind was unkempt. Dirty hair that was long and in need of a cut. He hadn't shaved in a day or two. He was murmuring, but André didn't listen, looking for something he could use. He didn't see any obvious scars, though the man did have a particularly narrow nose. An earring that was just a simple stud.

Look. Find. Remember. Recreate.

There.

On the man's neck, low, and mostly covered by the V of his T-shirt, the top of a tattoo. As the three men grappled, André saw the tattoo clearly, despite the shirt, despite the impossible angle, despite it being night in a dark alley.

Heat was pouring down not-his body, fanning out across not-his back, down not-his legs. A knife had been driven deep.

André looked at the man. Memorized the face. Memorized the tattoo.

❖

Bao had a hand on his shoulder. "André?"

André nodded. He didn't trust himself to speak. Not yet.

The detective was frowning, looking into the alley and then back at him. He raised an eyebrow.

"I was dead for two minutes and thirty-eight seconds," André said.

"Pardon?" Bao said, frowning.

André shook his head. "Not just now. I meant when…" He swallowed.

"I read your file," Bao said.

Right. He'd said that. "I don't remember much," André said. "They sort of just came at me. I guess they saw me come out of Chances." He left it at that. The gay bar was well known.

Bao nodded.

"When the paramedics got there…" André stopped. He was clenching his fists again, and never mind rats, his chest filled with wolves and snakes and bigger creatures with claws and teeth and he couldn't catch his breath. He closed his eyes.

"AED. You were one of the lucky ones," Bao said. "They resuscitated you."

"Right." *Lucky.* André laughed. "After two minutes and thirty-eight seconds. You know how I know?"

"How?"

"Because that's how long I get to see." André pointed into the alley. "I get to see the two minutes and thirty-eight seconds that lead up to when they die."

Bao stared.

"Every week. After class. I've been going somewhere, somewhere where someone was found, to see if I can see. And you know the best part?" André said. "The best part is for two minutes and thirty-eight seconds I'm *them*. I'm not me."

The line returned between the detective's eyebrows.

"It helps," André said. "It helps you, and it helps me. Please. Just let it be."

He turned and walked away.

Detective Nguyen didn't stop him.

Detective Bao Nguyen wasn't in class the next week. Or the week after. André visited two more sites, but only the second pulled him out of himself. The first had been another body found out in the woods. He was pretty sure he knew what that meant.

No one had died there. It was just where the body ended up.

But at the second place, he sketched what he saw and mailed it in.

He went online, looking for more places. He added them to the ongoing list. Some were from as much as two decades earlier, but he had less luck the farther back he went. Were the reports wrong, he wondered, or was that piece of trite advice actually true: did everything fade in time?

He watched the papers. Four became five. And by the time the classes were winding down, five became six.

The rats scurried all through the last class. He felt raw inside. Chewed from within. He hadn't finished his list, not by any means, but from the first day he'd started the drawing class, trying to increase his skills with pencil and charcoal as much as he could, he'd been on a kind of mental deadline.

He didn't have to. Not really. He didn't have to do *any* of it.

But what if it stopped happening? What if…What if one of these times, he stood where the last beats of a heart had played out and *nothing happened*?

What if one of these times, he felt so much of the not-him that the him-him, the real-him, went with them?

He thanked Jill. She asked him to consider taking a follow-up class to this one, and he told her he would think about it. She seemed pleased. He gathered his tube, his messenger bag, and his coat, and was almost unsurprised to find Bao waiting for him outside.

"Last class," Bao said. He wasn't wearing his glasses. He wasn't wearing a uniform, either. The black sweater suited him.

André nodded. Breathe in. Hold. Out.

"Got somewhere you need to be?"

André bit his lip. It was raw and cracked.

"If you'd like," Bao said, "I'll drive."

❖

He hadn't come this far downtown since it happened. Seeing Chances, even in the fading afternoon light, made him want to retch. Maybe this was a mistake. Who knew if it would even work? After all, he wasn't like the others. He wasn't dead now.

But he *was*.

Bao hadn't asked where they were going, and André hadn't been surprised when Bao had pulled off the highway at Nicholas. However the detective had known, he'd known. It must have been obvious to him in some way. André supposed that was what Bao did for a living. He read people. Understood them.

Caught them.

The closer they got to the parking lot, the harder it was to breathe. No amount of conscious control was going to work, André thought. Not this time. If he felt the weight, there was no escaping himself. No blissful moments of being someone else, even as they struggled and fought and died. No being not-him because the person who'd died here, who'd been *beaten to death* here…

Is me.

The car had stopped moving.

"I'll come with you."

André looked at Bao. It hadn't sounded like a suggestion.

"Thanks."

They got out of the car, and André walked slowly across the parking lot. It was nearly full, which made sense at this time of day. He walked slowly to the far corner, where it would have been dark at night and it would only be through luck someone might notice someone else lying there, motionless.

Bleeding.

Dead.

Strong fingers took his hand. André fought the urge to flinch and instead found himself squeezing back. He turned and saw Bao watching him.

"You let me know if being here triggers any memories for you. I know you don't remember much, but sometimes revisiting the scene of the crime can bring back fresh memories," he said. Each word was spoken carefully, as though he wanted André to weigh each and every one of them for hidden meaning. "If you remember anything useful," Bao said, "we will nail those bastards to the wall."

André swallowed. "Okay," he said. Then, because he couldn't stop himself, he said, "You believe me."

"You're not the first...*person* I've met," Bao said.

André didn't know what to say to that, but somehow it made him feel better.

He could feel the pull, even from here.

He took a step, and Bao came with him. He was grateful for the feel of the man's hand in his. The pull grew stronger, and he knew where to go without even having to remember. The feeling guided him. And even as it pulled him in, he could feel it was different. Everything had come from this spot, everything he'd been able to do since that night.

It would end after this. He knew that. He wanted to feel bad about it, but he just felt tired. And ready.

So. Time to stop escaping. Time to stop looking at the pain of others and trying to convince himself how lucky he was.

Two minutes and thirty-eight seconds.

Time enough to learn how to be himself again.

Some colors linger long after the people are gone. I've caught twists of muted mint sadness lingering in graveyards, playgrounds flickering with bright sunny yellows, and churches alight with gold despite their empty pews and not a single lit candle.

I tend to avoid hospitals.

There's a statue of Galahad in front of Parliament that is incandescent with love and sadness both. It was raised in honor of a man who tried to save the life of a woman in an accident, and though he failed, it has always struck me as a reminder.

Trying matters.

So while I've never decided if places learn feelings or if people simply leave themselves behind whether they intend to or not, I always pause to watch. I try to understand.

It seems important, somehow, to listen to these places that know how to speak.

After all, I'm one of the few who can listen.

Elsewhen

It's late on a Thursday night, and I'm watching Parliament burn down again. The heat is intense, the smoke makes my eyes water, and I have to struggle not to cough.

I can't get close enough. I'd like to figure out which wayward soul is stuck, what need or wrong has kept this echo repeating all these years. But the same quirk that lets me see these ghostly reenactments makes it too real for my flesh. I have enough scars from other souls. I don't want to burn.

I long ago stopped being angry about it. Like anything else, sometimes it is beautiful, sometimes not. Sometimes I have to ask questions of a spirit to learn who they were, and return when they echo again with the right answers. I love helping children. So often they just want to know their parents lived good lives. Sometimes I cannot learn anything, and so I lie and hope to find the right words to help them to their next place. A lie for a good cause. The angry are harder. And some wrongs I cannot right. Those continue to echo without solution, a tug on the back of my mind that I know will never go away.

Watching the old Parliament buildings burn is like that. Ghostly men in thick jackets spray water into the smoke. It was February when they caught fire. No one knows what sparked it. Many perished. In the flames and smoke of the past, someone needs help, but I can't figure out how to do it. These kinds of haunting make me wish there was someone to go home to. Someone to whom I could tell these stories of the dead. Someone who isn't my dog, as wonderful as she is.

"Sorry I'm late. There was a dead woman at the market who kept me later than I thought. How about pasta for dinner?"

Not likely.

I turn my back to the heat, frustrated that I am no closer to solving this problem. Ottawa's downtown—the real downtown, not the icy echo of the night Parliament burned down in 1916—spreads out before me. The early spring breeze is cool, and by the time I reach the War Memorial, the only heat I can feel is from the sun sinking low amongst the buildings behind me.

I'm about to start walking home when the air around the federal Conference Centre ripples. I feel the tug, and I turn before I can help myself. The bridge over the canal starts to shimmer like the air over hot concrete. The flags lose their color. The entirety of the Nicholas Expressway warps and blurs. Everything shifts slightly out of focus, and I feel my hands clench into fists as I hold on to the now.

Tracks appear, snaking up to the Conference Centre.

It used to be a train station, but it's been closed since the centennial. I vaguely remember a tour guide telling me the Conference Centre was once a major hub of the massive railways that ran through Ottawa. The Grand Trunk, I suddenly recall.

I cross the street, squinting to make sure I still catch view of the living world. It would be easy to see the echoes of past streetcars and miss the reality of an SUV on my literal and figurative cross-over to the other side. I hear the beat of an engine on a railroad. The Conference Centre is already shedding its current facade and returning to the station it once was. Pillars stained with grey smoke stretch out above me. Archways and spherical lamps form out of the whitish mists of the past. My feet touch the opposite pavement, and a train coalesces farther down the translucent tracks that have completely replaced the traffic on Nicholas. It grows louder and more solid as it approaches, passing through buildings and lamps and flagpoles as though they weren't there.

A train is pulling into the Grand Trunk station, which has been closed since 1966.

This is new.

❖

I find a real bench and sit. With three deep breaths, I rise with only half of who I am, feeling the tenuous shiver run through my body. The now fades into the barest of shadows, and all around me, the echo of an older Ottawa sharpens.

I walk into the station as the train hisses and whistles its arrival. I can't help but look around. The Conference Centre isn't open to the public. It's beautiful. Wooden benches with glass shaded lamps are arranged in rows across from the tracks, and the pillars reach the ceiling in flared arcs that form arches and curves of carved stone. All around me, echoes of the dead are walking. The train is the sharpest image, holds the most color, and I direct my attention to it. The third cab is nearly shining, so I move toward it.

I shouldn't do this. It's one thing to stand at the edge of an echo and find out what went wrong, or to call to a spirit and speak with it. It's enough to try to help a soul realize it is time to move on. It's another thing entirely to walk into the false past. But I've been seeing Parliament burn down for weeks. The desire to help is a constant itch. I'm tired of watching.

The train stops, and shifting shapes that are more or less people drift from the cabs. It's easy to skim the crowd when they are barely a part of this echo, so it doesn't take me long to see him. He stands at the opening of the car. He keeps one hand on the threshold while he faces out into the station. I think he would be scanning the crowd for someone were it not for the cloth running across his eyes. His uniform is plain—simple khaki, simple buttons, two front pockets—his pants clean and pressed even after a train ride. His boots are shined. He has short fair hair and is so clean shaven I think he might not need to shave often at all.

I watch, torn. He doesn't move. Soon, I think, the train will move on. Soon, whatever or whoever he is waiting for will not have appeared, and the echo will move on until it replays again. And again.

I start walking through the crowd of half-remembered people. I'm at the bottom of the steps before long, and I reach out with one hand, not quite sure that even this vibrant echo can be real enough to support me.

I take the bar and tug myself up onto the train. The soldier's head tilts toward me, and I hesitate a moment before I touch his shoulder. Speaking to an echo casts me in the role they need the most, and they see who they want to see, but his eyes are bandaged. I steel myself.

"Julian?" he asks. His voice is uncertain. "Is that you?"

The coincidence is shocking. I shiver. Whoever this dead soldier waited for shared my name. I clear my throat and say, "Yes." It is refreshing to play a part without lying from the first breath.

❖

With a hand tracing the walls of the car, he leads me farther into the train. It's old fashioned, with narrow wooden doorways and curtained windows. Close behind him, I can smell the faintest trace of talcum powder. He isn't tall, coming only to my chin, and the cloth wraps around the back of his head, where it is clipped with a single silver pin. We reach the third door from the steps. He opens it, steps through, and sits on one of the two benches that face each other.

I come in after him and close the door.

The train whistle blows. I sit. Moments later, there's a lurch as the train begins to move. My stomach clenches.

"I didn't know if you'd come," he says, finally.

This is dangerous. I have to play a part, but I don't know my role. We're inside a train that isn't, moving across tracks that aren't, and I'm sitting across from someone who shouldn't be, but is.

"I had to," I say. Oddly, it feels true.

His lips quirk. It's handsome and natural. I get the feeling that before, he was someone who often smiled, and the habit isn't one he's having luck breaking.

"Julian," he says, and again the coincidence of names makes me shiver. "I…" He swallows. He's sitting so still on the bench seat. He breathes out.

I wait. I don't know my lines.

"You pity me," he says.

"No," I reply, and it comes out quickly and firmly because it is the truth. I have scars myself, and I have never wanted pity.

Another quirk of his lips. "I suppose it does mean I won't have to see that ugly mug of yours."

I laugh. I like this dead man. The train picks up speed, turns a corner. We rock to the left. The view out the window is indistinct and colorless. The unfinished business is not about out there.

"Remember the blackout?" he asks. I know enough history to know how cities turned off their lights to avoid giving bombers targets.

But there's a specificity to his tone that tells me he means a particular blackout.

A particular night.

"Yes," I say. There it is: my first lie.

He nods. "All night in the dark. You and me. The noise..." He swallows. "You remember how you said it was easy to talk in the dark because you didn't have to look me in the eyes? The dark is for truth-telling, you said." He offers another almost-smile, and with one slender hand, he touches the cloth across his eyes. "Well, here's a truth. It'll always be dark for me now, and I love you." He breathes. "I love you, Julian."

Oh God.

I'm frozen. I can't think or speak. I don't know what to do. Some reflex makes me reach out and take his hand. He squeezes.

"I know it's harder for you," he says. "I have money. My father's money, but it will be mine. I'll never lack. And I know you have Lindsay and Laurel and Audrey to look after, and the farm, but..." He squeezes my hand. "I could...We could...Somehow..." Each aborted sentence makes his hand shake a little more.

I move from my bench to kneel in front of him, and I put my other hand to his cheek. He stops talking and I kiss him. His free hand takes the back of my neck.

The kiss breaks.

"The door," he says.

We break apart long enough for me to find the latch and snap it shut. I draw the curtains over the small glass window above the handle. I press my forehead against the wood that isn't there and feel the sway of the train that doesn't exist. Then I turn and take his shoulders in my hands and kiss him again.

❖

He doesn't let me remove the bandage, pulling my hands away when I touch it, but everything else is soon shed beneath us, between the benches. His body is lean, with sinewy muscle and fair skin and a strength belied by his frame. He is quick with his fingers and mouth, tugging my clothes off and kissing my throat and chest, pausing to call me a "hairy beast," and then my nipple. His fingertips find my scars:

shoulder, forearm, the left side of my stomach, and he kisses each place without comment.

I go for his neck, which is soft, and his thighs, which are hard. When I take him into my mouth, he makes a noise somewhere between a gasp and a whimper, and I tease his length with my tongue.

I can taste him.

Before long, his hands are tight in my hair, and he is breathing in short bursts.

"Julian…Wait…" he gasps.

I release him and slide awkwardly along his body, crammed between the two benches, finding his mouth for another kiss. We grind, his hardness against mine, and his touch, his mouth, and his soft swallowed cries have me so hard I can barely breathe.

We move, the rocking of the train a delicious counterpoint, sweat building as we rub against each other and tease each other further and further. He twists in my grasp until I am lying on top of him and he is on his stomach beneath me.

"Please," he says.

"I don't want to hurt you."

"You won't."

I try everything I can think of to make that true. My tongue, my finger, so much saliva and sweat, but when I enter him, I'm sure it hurts him. He breathes sharply, and I hesitate, arms straining.

"Please," he says again.

I push into him, and he surrenders to it. We shift into a new rhythm, each clack of the track beneath us another thrust opposite to my own. We breathe, then gasp, then move to more base noises before a release that leaves us both collapsed on the floor of the compartment.

"I love you," he says again.

This time, he doesn't fight my fingers when I remove the cloth around his eyes. They are ruined. Scarred, burned and sightless. I kiss one, then the other.

"I love you," I say.

The train shimmers. I feel a sob in the depth of my chest.

"I love you," I say again.

I mean it.

Between the start of his smile and the touch of his hand to my cheek, the world comes apart. I am sitting on a bench in front of the

Conference Centre that was once the Grand Trunk station, and a brown-eyed police officer is shaking my shoulder and asking me if I need a hand.

I tell him of my "seizures." He's patient and assumes my tears are born of embarrassment. He tells me not to worry, that he doesn't think anyone else noticed. I don't bother to contradict him. He lets me leave after I convince him I am fine.

I go home.

❖

Julian is not an incredibly common name. With time, finding a Julian with relatives named Lindsay, Laurel, and Audrey doesn't prove impossible. Speaking to him does. Julian Mitchell has been in a long-term care facility for a number of years, no longer brought out in a wheelchair even for Remembrance Day, since he cannot speak and doesn't react to voices anymore. He has a nose that was obviously broken more than once, and in pictures I find online of his younger self, I can nevertheless see a rugged, if somewhat brutish, handsomeness to him.

The train pulls into Grand Trunk two weeks later. And again the week after that. Sometimes I watch, sometimes I climb aboard again. The same police officer finds me there twice more, and I switch to a different bench along the canal after that, when his kindness starts to make me think of pity. For nearly four months this is the routine. I tell the fair-haired soldier I love him, and sometimes for as long as two weeks, his echo abates. But it always returns. I wonder what I'm missing, but a part of me isn't sure I want to know.

I haven't even tried to learn the soldier's name.

When Julian Mitchell's death notice appears in the paper, I almost miss it, but my eye is drawn to my name. I wait at the Conference Centre for four nights for the train to appear. When I step into the Grand Trunk station this time, I look through the crowd carefully.

Julian Mitchell is there. Young, strong and afraid. His uniform is the mirror of the young soldier's on the train. I move to his side.

"Laurel will marry well, and the farm won't need you," I say.

Julian turns, surprised at my voice. "What?" he says. "Who are you?"

The train has stopped. Indistinct passengers are disembarking.

"It doesn't matter," I say. I wonder who he sees.

There is some fear in his eyes, but more than that there is a kind of recognition. I think about his time. How hard it must have been.

The passengers have all stepped out of the train. The soldier appears at the opening of the car. I hear Julian's shallow gasp.

"His eyes," he says.

"Yes," I say. Then, unable to help myself, I ask. "What's his name?"

Julian's jaw tightens. He looks at me again. "Stephen."

"Stephen," I repeat it. "For the rest of your life, you'll wish you got on that train with him."

"What can I do?" Julian says. His voice is low, pitched for privacy from people who can no longer hear us talk. "His father can take care of him. I can't."

Stephen stands there still. I want to go to him. I look at Julian again.

"Close your eyes."

"What?"

"Just do it!" This is louder than I intend, and he flinches. But he closes his eyes.

"It's dark," I say, and touch his shoulder. "So tell the truth. Do you want to go get on that train?"

There is a long pause. I look at this strong young man, who spent the rest of his life on a small farm, even after his sister's husband took it over. Julian Mitchell never married. According to the obituary, Julian Mitchell was a brother, an uncle, and a veteran. No one's beloved.

"Yes," he says, and opens his eyes.

I watch him walk to the train. He climbs aboard and touches Stephen's shoulder. I watch their lips move, unable to hear them. They walk deeper into the train.

I wait for the whistle. Then I wait until the train leaves. I wait until the walls of Grand Trunk fade into clouds of nothing. I wait until I cannot even see the ground at my feet. When there is nothing but white mist as far as the eye can see, I let go and come back to myself on the bench by the canal.

I'm crying. I won't see the train again, I know. Nor Stephen. The train will take them to a place and time that never was. They'll be happy, I tell myself, not caring that I don't know any of this for sure. A lie for a good cause.

I shift, and I realize that someone has draped a heavy jacket over my shoulders. Beside me, sitting quietly, the same brown-eyed police officer looks out over the water. He's not in uniform. When he hears me move, he looks at me.

"Thought you might like some company," he says.

I nod.

"My father had seizures," he says. "Bad ones. Not like yours. Cracked his skull once."

I clear my throat. "It's not a seizure exactly."

"Oh?" He looks at me. He has kind eyes, but there's no pity in them.

"I'm Julian," I say, and offer a hand.

He takes it. "Dave." Our handshake lingers just a little. He smiles.

I pause. "Did you know there used to be a train station here?"

He shakes his head.

I start to tell him.

I sit here and I wonder if it will ever be enough.

I can speak of blues and oranges, greens and purples. I can teach about reds and yellows and the spaces between, and I know it doesn't compare to the first real glimpse.

So I'll say this.

Those colors aren't just colors. They're people. It's not just joy, it's someone's joy. It's never just pain or loss, it's someone in pain, someone losing. And to be a witness to joy and pain and loss is to take some of it, whether or not that was ever intended.

Whole days will surround you with yellow. There will be golden hours, too. You will fly on red wings, and you will wrap yourself in purple and wait to heal. There are so many colors, so many ways the colors layer and move and braid themselves around a person's heart. All of them matter.

The people matter more.

So when I tell you to find the blue, I mean the people who conjure it. You shouldn't walk through all the dark—but you will, and you can— if you deny yourself the light after.

You'll never have to doubt we love you.

I'll promise you that, even though I don't have to.

I know you can already see it.

Here & Now

Ian woke up from his nap with a start. He'd been dreaming about the ocean, he thought vaguely, but then the dream slipped from his mind with the second ring of the phone. In case it was Robert, he let it go to voice mail. When the screen lit up with a notice, he scooped up the phone. There was a message.

But it wasn't from Robert.

"We're all booked, same train, same time. We'll meet you in Vancouver. I really didn't think we'd manage on such short notice, but Fairouz and I will be there." Dawn's voice was enthusiastic. "This'll be great."

He put the phone down.

Yeah. *Fantastic.*

Ian tapped the tickets against the table, where they'd been ever since he'd come back to his apartment. Two tickets, two weeks, a and cabin in B.C.

Intended for two.

He sighed. He should call Dawn and tell her to cancel. He should try selling the tickets, since he hadn't bought cancellation insurance.

The irony of his not having done so wasn't lost on him. Behold, the guy who can see the future sometimes.

Emphasis on *sometimes.*

He picked up his phone again and dialed her.

❖

Ian hadn't been sitting long, but he was already nervous. He wasn't sure where it was coming from. He fiddled with a fork and rolled his eyes, annoyed at himself.

Maybe five minutes later, she arrived.

As soon as he looked up at the opening restaurant door, his nerves vanished. In high school, Dawn Solati had been slender and angular and had worn her hair in a bob. The bob was gone, replaced by delicate waves that flowed artfully down one shoulder. And slender was now curvy. Dawn might have always had a draw to her, but once she saw him and smiled and started crossing the room, she drew all eyes.

"If you say, 'Dawn, you look just the same,' I will kill you," she said.

He rose, and they hugged. She squeezed him tight, and he returned the gesture. He hadn't expected the ache in his chest, and his eyes grew a little wet.

Dawn. This was *Dawn.*

She pulled away and swiped at her own eyes as she took her seat.

"I was going to go for something in a 'Holy shit!' actually," Ian said. He sat, grinning at her. "You look incredible."

Dawn flipped her hair over one shoulder in a practiced move, then winked. "Thank you. You look good yourself. I like the goatee."

"It's my evil doppelganger look."

"*Star Trek*, right?" she said.

He nodded.

"Ten years," she said.

He blew out a breath. "Really? I was trying to figure that out on my way here."

"Just think, soon we'll probably get invitations to our twentieth high school reunion."

Ian laughed. "Hard pass."

"Let's get some wine so we can toast that sentiment."

Over the salads, whatever awkwardness he'd worried about was gone. Ian found himself relaxed into a friendship paused ten years earlier. Finally, after the first dishes had been taken away and he saw her staring at him again, he couldn't help himself. He asked.

"What is it?"

"How are you? Really?"

Ian smiled. "Honestly? I'm okay."

"It's just…" Dawn said.

"Just?"

"Okay, so part of my job is to work with lawyers and PIs," Dawn said. "Have you ever googled yourself?"

"I wouldn't want to go blind."

She smiled. "Well, I won't lie. I looked into you. There are many Christian Simons, but only one with a secondhand bookshop and such an interesting reputation with certain police."

Did she mean Bao? He wondered, but he wasn't going to ask her to clarify this time.

Dawn put her glass down. "Sorry."

Ian shook his head. "It's okay. It's just…I don't do that anymore. It got to be…" He swallowed. "Well. I don't do that anymore."

She regarded her wine. "That's fair. If it helps, it wasn't a bad reputation."

Huh. Ian swallowed. "It does."

There was a wash of lovely blues across the distance between them, and Ian looked up to see she'd picked up her glass again.

"To taking out the trash and never thinking about it again," she said.

He raised his glass. "Didn't we already toast high school?"

She laughed.

❖

Ian undid his tie, pulled it off, and hung it up, then stood in the master bedroom, looking into the closet where Robert's shirts hung in an ordered row—Gucci, Armani, even some original Martin Alan—all color coded, and all hung on matching wooden hangers. His own, smaller collection without fashion names looked jumbled and out of place beside it, though Robert had insisted he at least get the same hangers.

"Ian?" Robert was at the door.

The numb paralysis fled. Ian shook his head. He undid the buttons on his black shirt. "I hate funerals."

Robert came in and wrapped both arms around him. Ian closed his eyes, ignoring the colors blooming around them.

"I really wish I could have gone," Robert said.

He easily ignored the way the auras flickered around his boyfriend when he lied. White lies—which were anything but—were a social necessity. Most of the time, Ian managed not to pay attention when they happened.

Today, though, he closed his eyes tighter. He found he couldn't quite do it.

"I do, too," he said, surprising himself with the admission, which he knew Robert would hear as a criticism. Still, he leaned back into Robert's chest and found comfort there.

"You said it yourself, though," Robert said. "It wasn't a surprise."

It was true. Miah had had a bad heart. But knowing *why* the colors were pale around his coworker and being okay with the way it took him were two different things. Miah was younger than Ian.

Not was. *Had been.*

No, he didn't have it in him right now.

"I don't really want to talk about it. Is that okay?"

"Of course," Robert said. He kissed the back of Ian's neck.

❖

The entrées arrived, and Dawn looked at Ian frankly. "Okay. Time to spill. Love life?"

"Robert. So far out of my league, but somehow it happened. He's got the romance novel cover thing going on for him, too. Tall, dark, handsome. Great legs." Ian leaned forward. "An accountant, if you can believe that."

"Well, you always did like math," Dawn said. "How long have you guys been together?"

"Six months," Ian said. He grinned. "In gay years, that's close to retirement, though I still have my apartment over Second Page. It's just too convenient, and my bookshelves wouldn't fit in his apartment anyway." He picked up his fork. "You?"

"Fairouz and I are going on four years, which is lesbian for ten minutes, but also forever."

Ian choked. Dawn bit down on some cannelloni and waited, a smile on her face, while he coughed his way through the missed swallow.

"That was mean," he said. "You waited till I was chewing."

Dawn's smile had more than a little bit of triumph to it. "Maybe."

"Dawn the lesbian, eh?" Ian laughed. "We were ahead of our time. We would have made quite the modern Prom King and Queen."

"I'm bi," Dawn said. "But I think you rocked your tux. No one would have voted for us anyway."

"Fair enough. I wish I'd known," Ian said. "Back then."

She nodded. "Me, too. But it takes some of us longer. Not all of us are psychic."

"Touché. Though don't sell yourself short. You did help write the manual."

"I did, didn't I?"

"I still have it."

"That journal?"

He nodded. "Yeah. Can't remember the last time I added to it, but I've still got it."

"That's really nice." She leaned back in her chair. "I didn't keep very much from back then."

"Me neither," Ian said. "It's one of maybe four things."

They ate in silence for a few moments.

"He's not, by the way," she said.

"Sorry?"

"Robert. Out of your league." She regarded him, and in that moment Ian would have believed she'd lied and he wasn't the only one in the room able to see things. "He's not."

"I was just kidding." He shrugged it off. He was pretty sure she didn't buy it, but she let it drop.

"So. Got a picture of this amazing Fairouz?" he asked.

Dawn pulled out her phone. The woman was stunning. She had black hair that curled around her cheeks, a sly smile, and eyes so dark a brown it was difficult to see the pupil, even in the close-up.

"Wow," Ian said.

"Tell me about it."

❖

"Let's go on a trip."

Robert looked up from a spreadsheet and blinked at him. "A trip?"

"A vacation. A real one," Ian said.

Robert leaned back in his chair. A flickering greenish surprise danced around him. "You don't like crowds. Or airports. And you don't drive."

"I know, but I was thinking of a train trip. A big one. I never take time off, and neither do you. And if we take the train, you don't have to do any driving, either."

"And your store?" Robert said.

"Riley can handle it," Ian said. "He's not in school right now." He was surprised Robert had asked. The bookstore wasn't often on Robert's mind, unless it ate into their alone time. He didn't mean to, but he saw the grey in Robert's aura before he could ignore it.

Ambivalence. Okay, well, that wasn't opposition, at least.

"Where did this come from?" Robert said.

"Aiden came by the store today," Ian said. A pale red annoyance streaked through Robert's aura, and Ian felt his own irritation rise in response. "He was picking up some things. He's sort of…*lost*." Ian hadn't met Aiden much before Miah had died, but he usually had such an amazing golden radiance around him, something Ian had long associated with inspiration and a kind of vibrant joie de vivre. On Aiden it had been dialed up to the nth.

But today it had been barely there.

"Ah," Robert said, as though somehow this explained everything.

Ian tried again. "It was something he said. Aiden, I mean. He said, 'We should have done more things together.'"

Robert softened at that, and Ian snuck another glance. Royal blues gathered. Kindness. Patience.

"A train trip, huh?"

❖

They ordered dessert and leaned back, as comfortable now as if the last ten years hadn't gone by with only Christmas cards, texts, emails, and broken promises to make time to see each other face-to-face at some point. As though the last five years hadn't gone by with barely even that.

"What were you like as a child?" Dawn asked. "We only met when…well, then. In high school."

Her aura flashed with nervous greens. This, Ian realized, was the whole point of dinner.

"You mean before…" He waved a hand in front of his eyes.

She nodded.

"Honestly? I was a pretty boring kid, I think. My sister was always the one who needed time and attention. I liked to read and draw, of course. I was quiet," Ian said. "Why?"

Dawn took a deep breath. "Fairouz and I want to have a baby."

He smiled, about to congratulate her, but the nervousness in her aura flared out so brightly and so directly at him that he was taken aback. Why would it make her nervous to tell him…

What she meant clicked.

Dawn laughed at the look on his face.

"Oh." He managed the word with no small amount of willpower.

The waitress arrived with their desserts. Ian looked down at his apple crumble, and his hand shook when he picked up his spoon.

She was still looking at him.

"Will you consider it?" Dawn said.

"I…" He put his spoon back down. "*Why?*"

Dawn frowned.

"Sorry," Ian said. "Not why do you want to have a kid, why do you want…" He swallowed. "Why *me*?"

Dawn took a single bite of her crème brûlée, cracking the skin with the side of her spoon. "I can't have children," she said. "I think you knew that."

He nodded.

"So when Fairouz and I decided, we looked at a lot of options. The reality is we'll never have a child that is partly her and partly me." She shrugged. "That's okay. Years ago, before there was even a Fairouz, when I was dating a man and we were serious, it was something I had to make peace with."

"Was that Thomas?" Ian said, trying to remember who Dawn had been with when they'd last really spoken.

"Yes, Tom. We're still good friends. He's married now."

"That's nice. Sorry," Ian said. "Go on."

"Well, when Fairouz and I started talking about babies, the *who* came up. The idea of a stranger just didn't sit well."

Ian waited.

"There are very few men in my life who I trust to be kind, caring, compassionate, and selfless, and who I trust enough to know this could work," Dawn said. "And when it came down to it, the list really only had one name on it."

His eyes were filling up. He blinked and finally spooned up some apple crumble.

"I'm not asking for an answer now," Dawn said. "But I hope you'll consider it."

Her words were echoing. Kind, caring, compassionate, and selfless? Was that even true anymore? He thought about Miah, and so many other moments in his life where he'd seen something, and he hadn't done enough. He thought about Bao, who had transferred to Ottawa nine months ago to be a part of the Hate and Bias Crime Unit, and how he hadn't so much as replied to an email.

He'd been afraid of what Bao might ask. When Bao had stopped reaching out to him, the relief had barely outweighed the guilt.

But Ian never wanted to see a police building again. Or a hospital. Or a cemetery. Or…

"Your ice cream is melting," Dawn said. "Finish your dessert. Like I said. No rush, and no pressure."

Ian forced a smile.

❖

"Dawn is coming to Ottawa," Ian said, hanging up his jacket.

"Sorry?" Robert was still in his running shorts and shirt. They clung to him. Ian was reminded once again of how nice Robert's legs were, but the general foul mood ruined the effect. Robert must have had a long day at work if he was only getting back from his run now. He was flushed and breathless.

"Uh-oh," Ian said. "Bad day at the office?"

He earned a rueful—and accusatory—smile. "Are you doing that *thing* you do?"

Ian held up both hands, patting the air. "Nope. Just deduction. You're usually showered before I make it home."

"Only because your store takes too much of your time."

Whoa. Okay. Grumpy Robert was definitely in the house. "Go have a shower," Ian said. "I'll start dinner."

That seemed to help. Protestations aside, Ian could see Robert's aura was dark, and it roiled around him. It was hard *not* to see when

Robert was frustrated or annoyed. Which was often, lately. They really did need to get away.

"So, what's at dawn?" Robert said, passing him.

"No, Dawn is a who. She was a high school friend. One of the only ones I kept in touch with. Well, for a while. I don't think I've seen her in a decade, and we haven't really spoken in a few years."

"Oh. Nice," Robert said, and then he was in the bedroom.

"Yeah," Ian said to himself. "It is."

He went to start a dinner. Maybe a stir fry. Robert loved a good stir fry, and if Ian could break his mood, maybe they could finally pick a time for that train trip. Ian checked the cupboard and pulled out a bottle of ice wine, putting it in the fridge. It was a Byrnes, a rare red and expensive, but Ian thought it might just be the thing to sweeten Robert's mood.

❖

"I've overwhelmed you," Dawn said.

They sipped coffee, now the only customers in the restaurant.

Ian smiled. "A bit."

"Can I ask you something else?"

Ian made a show of bracing himself against the edge of the table. "Okay."

"Relax." She laughed. "It's the name thing. Ian. I knew you preferred it, but I saw you did an actual, legal name change?"

"You really do your homework."

"It's an occupational hazard."

"Well," Ian said. "It was two things. After my family flipped over the gay thing and cut me out I was filling in a form, and I just sort of noticed the last three letters of Christian were Ian. I was here in Ottawa, about to start university, completely alone, broke, and terrified, and I guess I realized I was leaving everything behind. Seeing that Ian felt like finding myself inside myself. A fresh start, I guess."

She nodded. "And the other?"

"It didn't seem right to keep the Christ in my name, what with all the sodomy I was planning."

She burst out laughing, and after a second, he joined in. By the time they recovered, she was wiping her eyes with a corner of a napkin.

Her smile made the last of the tension he was feeling melt away, and he realized just how much he'd missed her.

"Robert and I are taking a train trip across the country," he said. "In a couple of months. I know it's short notice, but…If you two came, we could all meet."

Dawn's aura became so brightly yellow, it made him blink.

"You'll consider it," she said.

"I will," he said.

❖

Robert stepped through the door with his briefcase, and Ian held out the tickets.

"Ta-da!" Ian grinned. "You and me, train trip, the entire country. All aboard." They'd already packed, of course. Robert had a weird thing about packing for vacations by putting their clothes in individually sealed plastic bags, and even though they had another two weeks, they'd been ready to go since the weekend.

And now the tickets had finally arrived in the mail. They already had downloaded bar codes on their phones, but this felt like something to celebrate, too.

Robert smiled, stepped forward, and kissed Ian on the cheek.

And just like that it ended.

At the touch of his lips, the sight of Robert in front of him shattered. Too fast to stop it from coming, Ian saw someone *else* at the door. Greeting Robert. Kissing Robert. Then dropping to their knees. And then again, a different day. And another day. And another.

He blinked, forcing the parade of visits to end, and he pulled away.

Robert's face went guarded. The colors around him coalesced into something tense and grey and barely moving. Prepared.

"You're sleeping with the bartender from Chances," Ian said. It annoyed him on a visceral level that he couldn't remember the man's name. "Not Clive. The other one. The new one. The *young* one."

"Josh," Robert said. He put his briefcase down. "Yes." Wisps of yellow. Relief. And, worse, tiny fluffs of a beautiful, pale blue. Love.

"Did you think I wouldn't *know*?" Ian said. Robert had been a skeptic at first, but even he'd changed his mind. Or was he faking?

But Robert was shaking his head. "No."

"So you knew I'd know. Eventually." Each word was coming out a hair slower than the last. "You were just waiting for me to pick up on it."

Robert nodded, then finally had the grace to look down.

Ian swallowed.

"At least," Robert said, then cleared his throat to begin again. "At least you still have your apartment."

Ian stared. That was it, then.

"I'll come back for my things when you're at work tomorrow," he said.

"Okay."

Ian left.

❖

He paced, the phone to his ear, trying to come up with the right words. Were there any? *Hey, so, Dawn, turns out my guy is a cheating ass, and maybe this isn't the best time to hand over some sperm, so sorry about the short notice and all, but...*

He blew out a sigh, listening to the ringing on the other end of the line, and turned, catching his reflection in the long mirror on the back of his bedroom door.

Fractures skimmed across the world in front of him. For just a second, the position almost made him think his mirror was breaking.

Distantly, he heard a message tell him Dawn couldn't come to the phone right now.

Ian hung up, slipping the phone back into his pocket.

Shards spun away in front of him, and as the vision cleared, Ian could see a figure facing him in the mirror. It took effort to focus, a muscle he knew he'd let atrophy over the months with Robert. If he was honest with himself, even longer before. But he pushed with that spot behind his eyes, and the last of the pieces obstructing the view broke away.

It was a young kid, maybe sixteen or so, with his mouth hanging open.

Ian saw the eyes, then. Right eye green. Left eye blue.

Both eyes were exhausted. A little broken, too.

Oh God, Ian thought.

They stared at each other. Ian couldn't help smiling. *Just look at him. He's so young.* And the way he was looking at Ian was intense. Careful, but curious. Sharp, too. This kid might be a little surprised, but he wasn't about to be beat down by some random glimpse of a stranger in a mirror.

Hell, he'd already handled worse.

Ian held one hand and pointed at the kid. Then he flashed an okay symbol.

The kid on the other side of the mirror—on the other side of *when*—frowned.

He repeated the gesture, and the kid's expression remained blank. Ian felt his eyebrow rise. Surely he'd been smarter than this. With every fiber of his being, he willed the kid to understand.

You? You're okay. In fact, you're amazing. You're strong. You're about to walk away from everyone and everything and it is going to be so much better. And you know what? Dawn's right. Robert doesn't deserve you, Ian Simon. He beamed with pride.

He saw the moment the kid got it, and some part of him even remembered this happening some twenty years ago, but it was a slippery thought full of impossible angles and hard to hold on to.

He smiled again, and between blinks, the vision ended. The reflection returned to his current self, who was older, who had a goatee, who maybe needed to get a haircut.

He pulled out his phone. This time, when it went to message, he didn't hang up.

"Hey, Dawn, it's me. That's great news. I'll see you at the station. It's just going to be me, but don't worry about that. I'll explain when I see you. I'm really looking forward to it."

He hung up and glanced at the mirror once more, but it was just himself, with a curious little smile that looked like it belonged on the face of someone much more confident and capable.

Frankly, it looked good there.

He lifted his phone again, tapping out a text.

Sorry I've not been in touch. I'm an ass. Lunch in the Village sometime this week?

The reply from Bao came less than a minute later.

Absolutely. Then, after a moment, another text. *You're okay?*

Yes. Funny you ask, though. Someone just reminded me I can be.

I owe that person a drink. I'll touch base with which day, need to make sure I can step out. Let you know in the morning?

It's a date, Ian typed, then hesitated, not sure if he should send the text. He hit Send before he could overthink it.

I'd like that.

❖

It took nearly an hour digging through his office in the Second Page before he found the plastic tub. He'd stayed after closing and was cross-legged on the floor among the other boxes he'd glanced at and dismissed during his search for this one.

Popping the lid, he took a deep breath. It smelled very much like the old paper it was. Books, mostly. The container was full of some of his favorites, and some things he'd never parted with despite having no use for, including a particularly worn red-covered Bible.

He piled the items carefully, pulling each one out and looking at it for a second or two, placing it in some memory or other, before reaching back into the box for the one thing he was really looking for.

And there it was.

A single spiral-bound notebook.

He stood up, stretched until his neck popped, and went into the store proper. At the desk, he tossed the notebook on the counter and flicked the kettle on. When he turned back around, a little girl was standing at the counter, holding up a copy of a large journal he recognized. They had prints from FunkArt on the cover, and the gallery owner, Michel, worked with the artists to get them printed. Ian sold them from his small display of journals and notebooks, happy to give back to the Village that had done so well by him.

Given he'd been closed for over an hour, though, he wasn't sure how this little girl had gotten in, unless she'd picked the lock.

"How—?" he started to ask, but then he saw the gossamer fractures in the air all around her. It was daylight where she stood, on the other side of a when. She held up the journal, a big smile on her face.

Oh. He'd barely felt it happen, and it was only now the pressure behind his eyes was noticeable. Then he saw the little green frogs on her dress and the white sandals with daisies, and he realized it was *her*. A bit older this time, but definitely her.

He'd seen her before. Many times. Different places. His grandmother's grave. His apartment. Outside the hospital. In the Village.

She brandished the journal like it was a small shield, and he saw now it was a little bit battered and scuffed. On the cover, in black marker, someone with very familiar handwriting had written "Shamini's Book."

He waved despite knowing it was just a vision, wondering how long it would be until she was here in person.

But then the little girl *waved back*. He could almost hear her laughter.

He had just enough time to blink in shock before she vanished.

She saw me.

The kettle clicked behind him.

Ian swallowed, pouring himself a cup of tea and waiting for it to steep. He turned around again slowly, wondering if the image of the little girl might return, but it didn't. The slight headache was settling in now, but it wasn't much to worry about. The peppermint tea would likely take the edge off.

He flipped open the spiral-bound notebook. Colors and emotions were scrawled all over most of the pages, as well as notations to himself that might have made sense to him at one time but now meant nothing at all.

It was a mess. As haphazard and confusing as it had been when it had all started. Still, as he turned pages, a note here and there would make him smile.

Yellow is happiness? Dawn running.

Brown = boredom.

Bao jealous (green at the eyes).

Mr. Pike.

Ian sipped his tea and looked at every page. Finally, when he got to the end and closed the book, he looked up and saw the display of journals. The design the little girl had was one of Justin Cochrane's abstracts.

Ian went and got one of the journals, unwrapped the plastic, and reached into the cup of markers by the cash.

Genetics was a funny thing. He thought of the picture of Fairouz Dawn had shown him. The little girl—Shamini—would have the same dark eyes, the same dark hair, but without the curls. Other than a lightening of her skin, and even then not much, she wouldn't resemble Ian much at all. She wouldn't inherit his mismatched eyes.

But.

She'd waved back.

She'd *seen* him.

And more than that? She'd *recognized* him.

She might not get his eyes, but his daughter was sure going to get his sight.

Ian uncapped the marker and wrote "Shamini's Book" on the cover. It was a good name. He liked it. He wondered who'd come up with it. Then he picked up another pen and opened the book to the first page.

He took a sip of tea, pausing. Where could he even start?

Of course.

Love isn't red. That's probably the first thing to know.

About the Author

’Nathan Burgoine grew up a reader and studied literature in university while making a living as a bookseller. His first published short story was “Heart” in the collection *Fool for Love: New Gay Fiction*. Since then, he has had dozens of short stories published, including Bold Strokes titles *Men of the Mean Streets*, *Boys of Summer*, and *Night Shadows* as well as *This Is How You Die* (the second Machine of Death anthology). He has also released two gay romance novellas, *In Memoriam* and *Handmade Holidays*. ’Nathan’s nonfiction pieces have appeared in *Equality: What Do You Think about When You Think of Equality*, *A Family By Any Other Name*, *I Like It Like That*, and *5x5 Literary Magazine*.

’Nathan’s first novel, *Light*, was a finalist for a Lambda Literary Award.

A cat lover, ’Nathan managed to fall in love with and marry Daniel, who is a confirmed dog person. Their ongoing “cat or dog” détente ended with the rescue of a husky named Coach. They live in Ottawa, Canada, where they bake more than they should, go snow-shoeing less often than they should, and play board games like the geeky nerds they are.

Books Available From Bold Strokes Books

Of Echoes Born by 'Nathan Burgoine. A collection of queer fantasy short stories set in Canada from Lambda Literary Award finalist 'Nathan Burgoine. (978-1-63555-096-2)

The Lurid Sea by Tom Cardamone. Cursed to spend eternity on his knees, Nerites is having the time of his life. (978-1-62639-911-2)

Sinister Justice by Steve Pickens. When a vigilante targets citizens of Jake Finnigan's hometown, Jake and his partner Sam fall under suspicion themselves as they investigate the murders. (978-1-63555-094-8)

Club Arcana: Operation Janus by Jon Wilson. Wizards, demons, Elder Gods: Who knew the universe was so crowded, and that they'd all be out to get Angus McAslan? (978-1-62639-969-3)

Triad Soul by 'Nathan Burgoine. Luc, Anders, and Curtis—vampire, demon, and wizard—must use their powers of blood, soul, and magic to defeat a murderer determined to turn their city into a battlefield. (978-1-62639-863-4)

Gatecrasher by Stephen Graham King. Aided by a high-tech thief, the Maverick Heart crew race against time to prevent a cadre of savage corporate mercenaries from seizing control of a revolutionary wormhole technology. (978-1-62639-936-5)

Wicked Frat Boy Ways by Todd Gregory. Beta Kappa brothers Brandon Benson and Phil Connor play an increasingly dangerous game of love, seduction, and emotional manipulation. (978-1-62639-671-5)

Death Goes Overboard by David S. Pederson. Heath Barrington and Alan Keyes are two sides of a steamy love triangle as they encounter gangsters, con men, murder, and more aboard an old lake steamer. (978-1-62639-907-5)

A Careful Heart by Ralph Josiah Bardsley. Be careful what you wish for…love changes everything. (978-1-62639-887-0)

Worms of Sin by Lyle Blake Smythers. A haunted mental asylum turned drug treatment facility exposes supernatural detective Finn M'Coul to an outbreak of murderous insanity, a strange parasite, and ghosts that seek sex with the living. (978-1-62639-823-8)

Tartarus by Eric Andrews-Katz. When Echidna, Mother of all Monsters, escapes from Tartarus and into the modern world, only an Olympian has the power to oppose her. (978-1-62639-746-0)

Rank by Richard Compson Sater. Rank means nothing to the heart, but the Air Force isn't as impartial. Every airman learns that rank has its privileges. What about love? (978-1-62639-845-0)

The Grim Reaper's Calling Card by Donald Webb. When Katsuro Tanaka begins investigating the disappearance of a young nurse, he discovers more missing persons, and they all have one thing in common: The Grim Reaper Tarot Card. (978-1-62639-748-4)

Smoldering Desires by C.E. Knipes. Evan McGarrity has found the man of his dreams in Sebastian Tantalos. When an old boyfriend from Sebastian's past enters the picture, Evan must fight for the man he loves. (978-1-62639-714-9)

Tallulah Bankhead Slept Here by Sam Lollar. A coming of age/ coming out story, set in El Paso of 1967, that tells of Aaron's adventures with movie stars, cool cars, and topless bars. (978-1-62639-710-1)

Death Came Calling by Donald Webb. When private investigator Katsuro Tanaka is hired to look into the death of a high-profile lawyer, he becomes embroiled in a case of murder and mayhem. (978-1-60282-979-4)

The City of Seven Gods by Andrew J. Peters. In an ancient city of aerie temples, a young priest and a barbarian mercenary struggle to refashion their lives after their worlds are torn apart by betrayal. (978-1-62639-775-0)

Lysistrata Cove by Dena Hankins. Jack and Eve navigate the maelstrom of their darkest desires and find love by transgressing gender, dominance, submission, and the law on the crystal blue Caribbean Sea. (978-1-62639-821-4)

Garden District Gothic by Greg Herren. Scotty Bradley has to solve a notorious thirty-year-old unsolved murder that has terrible repercussions in the present. (978-1-62639-667-8)

The Man on Top of the World by Vanessa Clark. Jonathan Maxwell falling in love with Izzy Rich, the world's hottest glam rock superstar, is not only unpredictable but complicated when a bold teenage fan-girl changes everything. (978-1-62639-699-9)

The Orchard of Flesh by Christian Baines. With two hotheaded men under his roof including his werewolf lover, a vampire tries to solve an increasingly lethal mystery while keeping Sydney's supernatural factions from the brink of war. (978-1-62639-649-4)

Funny Bone by Daniel W. Kelly. Sometimes sex feels so good you just gotta giggle! (978-1-62639-683-8)

The Thassos Confabulation by Sam Sommer. With the inheritance of a great deal of money, David and Chris also inherit a nondescript brown paper parcel and a strange and perplexing letter that sends David on a quest to understand its meaning. (978-1-62639-665-4)

The Photographer's Truth by Ralph Josiah Bardsley. Silicon Valley tech geek Ian Baines gets more than he bargained for on an unexpected journey of self-discovery through the lustrous nightlife of Paris. (978-1-62639-637-1)

Crimson Souls by William Holden. A scorned shadow demon brings a centuries-old vendetta to a bloody end as he assembles the last of the descendants of Harvard's Secret Court. (978-1-62639-628-9)